Longtails

Book One

The Storms
Of Spring

By

Jaysen Headley

Longtails: The Storms of Spring

A Novel By Jaysen Headley

Cover Art by Dexter Allagahrei

Senior Editor: Carl Ka-Ho Li

Assistant Editor: Amy Chang

© 2018 Jaysen Headley Writes

ISBN: 978-0-9908283-1-0

Ebook ISBN: 978-0-9908283-3-4

This Book is Printed in the United States of America

10 9 8 7 6 5 4 3 2 1

First Edition

FOR JESSIE, STEFAN AND MICKEY.

TWO HUMANS AND A DOG WHO REMIND ME
EVERYDAY THAT DREAMS COME TRUE AND MAGIC IS
REAL.

CONTENTS

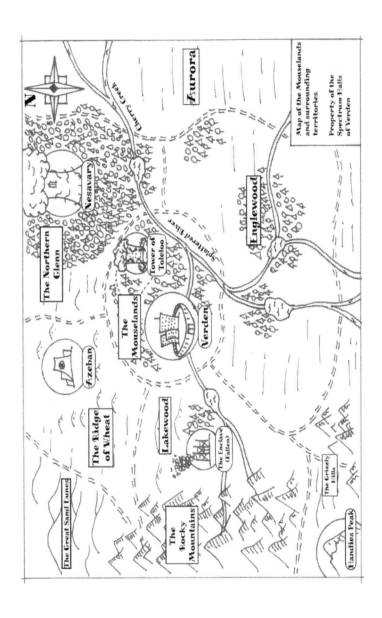

The Future.

Humanity is Extinct.

Ruins of human civilization lay as the bedrock of a new world order governed by animals of all shapes and sizes.

Biological warfare and radiation during World War 4 have had surprising effects on the creatures of the world. Some for the better. Some for the worse. Raccoons scour the countryside for motorbike parts. Squirrels have taken to the sky aboard flying ships. Danger lurks around every corner.

A large population of mice, small as they are, has migrated to the city of Verden. There, they created a thriving society protected by a magic-casting, sword-wielding team of intrepid soldiers, adventurers and explorers—the Longtails.

This is their story.

CHAPTER ONE

The Not So Special Mouse

Del Hatherhorne was anything but a hero. In fact, he was the epitome of a nobody as far as mice were concerned. His short, coarse fur was the color of brown commonly referred to as *mouse-brow*n. Typical. His whiskers were of perfectly average length. Forgettable. His tail was not too long—nor too short, and his belly was rounded in a way that suggested he didn't get much exercise but also didn't gorge himself on treats. Ordinary. Even his age was average. He was six seasons old, making him no longer a youthful mouse, but also not elderly. But it wasn't just an amalgamation of his height, weight, age or appearance which made Del so unfathomably unmentionable.

Most mice grew up knowing exactly what they wanted to do with their lives. His brother Jerrik, for example, knew that he was meant to build a farm where he could raise a family and help provide food to the Mouselands. As soon as he was of age, approximately two seasons old, he marched south with his seeds and his books. He built a thriving farm atop a *Descimator Mk III*, a human army tank. Ever since he was a pup, Jerrik researched seeds, soil and weather patterns. The day he managed to save each and every one of the various plants their mother had tried in vain to grow, his parents knew that he was going to make something of himself. Jerrik had smiled wide, whiskers bristling, delighted to be working at the farm every day until their family was not just getting by but thriving. Del's mother shed a tear of pride, and his father proclaimed his son all grown up.

Del's sister, Cassie, the oldest child, had known she would grow up to be a scholar, organizing and preserving tomes in the libraries of the Spectrum Halls, where young magically inclined mice were sent to train and study. Named for the 'spectrum' of colors which delineated different classes of magical mice (Scarlets, Violets, Coals, etc.), it was a place full of wisdom from ages long past. Hundreds of mice worked day and night to preserve the information of the old world in the books which were housed there, collecting dust by the day.

The first time Cassie visited the Halls, she knew that she was meant to be one of the purveyors of knowledge. The elder mouse who ran the library had practically had to pull her away, kicking and screaming, from one of the books on ancient Egyptian mythology as Cassie had insisted that the book ought to be in a different section of the library than it was. (She was, of course, right about this fact. Ancient Egyptian Mythology had no place in a section marked "Chinese Military Tactics.")

The elder had held her by her scruff and loudly proclaimed to the astonished patrons gathered in the library, "Please claim this mouse pup if she is yours. She's leaving paw prints on the books." In a strange sense of irony, Cassie was now up for the elder scholar's job at the library in the next year or so.

Del was the middle child to Rosak and Melen Hatherhorne, and unlike his siblings, he did not have a calling or a purpose. He had never made his mother cry—at least, not out of pride, anyway. His father had never proclaimed him to be all grown up. But what he lacked in useful skills and life-sustaining abilities, he more than made up for in obsessions, all of which he was an expert in, and all of which his mother called "incredible wastes of time and brain space."

Unlike most other mice, Del did not care for the outdoors. Things were always too unpredictable out in the world, and dirtier than he liked. He preferred to stay inside and tend to his hobbies, of which there were plenty. In fact, the one thing Del was quite skilled at was obsessing over the culture of a world long gone, chronicled by shut-ins like himself.

He was captivated by humanity, that dead species which haunted every corner of the world they'd left behind. In particular, he was infatuated with the sub-culture which, if he understood correctly, was known as 'Geek.' Other terms included 'Nerd' and 'Dork.' These fantasy-reading, super-hero-worshipping, board-game-playing, anime-watching monoliths of old were his people.

Del adored everything 'Geek' he could get his paws on. movies, books, games, artwork. But his favorite things to collect, by far, were ancient tomes crafted on thin paper, illustrated with beautifully painted pictures. He not only loved these artistic creations known as 'comic books,' he craved them.

His sister, when they'd still lived together, had scoffed at these relics filled with flimsy paper and more pictures than words. "They're the artistic equivalent of garbage," she'd said with her nose held high in the air, as if smelling something unsavory. She simply didn't understand them, that was all.

It was as if the creators of these books had spoken a language that had been all but forgotten until Del came along. He loved reading about heroes fighting villains across sprawling splash pages; knights battling monsters through panels that cascaded down the page like waterfalls; and samurai vanquishing yokai, oftentimes in black and white images, with hundreds of lines delineating fast-paced action. He simply couldn't get enough of the stories held within the pages of these comic books, and like any addiction, once he finished one book, he simply had to have another.

It was because of this addiction to consuming and collecting comic books that his parents had finally asked him to leave the nest—forcefully so. "If you're going to continue to bring home rubbish like this, then you're going to have to find a *new* place to store them," said his mother one evening, holding a copy of *Green Lantern #48,* by a corner between her two fingers, like it was a filthy rag. (It was the issue where Kyle Rayner was introduced. Many men had held the mantle of 'The Green Lantern,' but Kyle was Del's favorite. He liked that the man had once been an artist, which seemed to say to Del that greatness could indeed come from anywhere.) "And while you're at it, you can store yourself there as well," his mother added, her way of not-so-subtly saying *give up or get out.* Del got out.

He came to live in an abandoned apartment room in the northern part of the great mouse city of Verden. His new home was on the third floor of a complex, located at the corner of 14th Street and Larimer—according to their corresponding rusted green street signs at least. While not all mice lived in the city, protected by a massive wooden wall around its perimeter, most did. Safety was a big part of the reason for this, but the fact that every mouse family could have a whole human-sized apartment to themselves didn't hurt either. The humans had conveniently built their housing upwards instead of outwards, making plenty of room for any and all mice to live comfortably alongside their fellow kind.

He'd fallen in love with the vacant studio apartment the moment he'd laid eyes on it. Shelves adorning pale blue walls were filled floor to ceiling with everything from manga (Japanese comics which read right to left), to comics (mostly published by *DC* but with a spattering of *Marvel, Image and Darkhorse*), to video games (a wide assortment with role-playing games and puzzlers making up the bulk of it), and even old movies (names like Spielberg, Lucas and Ridley Scott were embossed along the spines of the shimmering boxes.) There was a large window overlooking the street below, though most of it had been covered by green vines which snaked up the exterior brick wall. More books were stored in molded boxes under the bed, which Del had chewed through in a fit of true mousiness in order to discover the hidden treasures within. And even more books were piled high in the bathtub, located through a door at the south side of the single room.

All of these books, movies, comics and board games (stashed in a closet in tall towers which leaned precariously to one side) had compelled Del to take the apartment instantly. He'd used his entire savings of chez—mouse money in the form of small bronze coins—to buy the apartment outright from the city's treasury, which handled all matters of mouse real estate.

Del never really worked for the money he earned. It was simply a by-product of his need to collect all things 'Nerd.' While rummaging through nearby trash heaps and buildings, too run-down to be lived in, for geeky items to add to his collection, he'd come upon odds and ends like gears and tools and such. He often sold these at the market, a sprawling street filled with mouse merchants. Until his parents had forced him out, he'd just been saving the chez he'd earned from his sales. Those savings were what had allowed him to buy a home, pre-stocked with items he would have otherwise had to dig, search and hunt for. For all the disdain his parents held for his hobby, it was what served as a lifeline in his time of need.

Del didn't know much about humans. Not really. To him, they were a fallen race from long ago—not as long gone as dinosaurs but gone nonetheless. All he knew about them was what he found in books and movies. And if you asked him, humans might have been powerful once, but they had also been overly dramatic and emotional. Still, he couldn't help but love their stories.

From Spider-Man's troubled youth to Kenshin's search for redemption, to Batman's vengeance for his parents' death, Del was hard-pressed to ever take his furry face away from the pages of a book. But at night, he would finally take a break from reading, only to use an old fuel generator to power up the computer. He'd set himself up on the desk, which was one of the only other pieces of furniture in the apartment besides a bed, a small couch and a chair. The computer was loaded with ROMs of old games that he quite enjoyed. He would run, jump and climb as the bird/bear team called Banjo-Kazooie, then switch over to hide behind large crates while infiltrating military bases as Solid Snake. He only allowed himself an hour at most on the computer each night, in hopes that he wouldn't burn out the generator that was starting to sputter and cough with age. But he relished every minute of it. His life was filled with stories, other people's to be sure, but stories nonetheless. When exhaustion finally overcame him, he would curl up under the moth-eaten navy-blue comforter atop the twin size bed in the center of the room and fall into a deep restful sleep.

Every so often, he considered striking out on his own to create his own adventure, like the ones he read about. But at the end of the day, he knew that it was far too dangerous outside the walls of his home, let alone outside the walls of the city, where most adventures were had.

The furthest he ever traveled was to the market, laid out in an alleyway between two large skyscrapers bordering Lawrence and Arapahoe Streets. It provided good shelter from the sun, which in the summer months could cause a mouse's tail to burn to a deep red hue. And it was only a few short blocks away from his home. Del's ideal adventure was one where you could leave and be home within the hour.

He would browse different stalls, selling any scrap he'd found on his expeditions, and purchase food—grain, grapes and corn—as well as whatever fizzy drink Marbel Beaks was selling. The old shopkeeper had a knack for finding all sorts of odd beverages, preserved from the old world. "They don't start to go sour until you open 'em up," he'd say to Del with a crooked smile and a lazy eye which never could stay focused on Del's face. Sometimes these drinks filled Del with energy, so he could read his books all night. Other days, they made him woozy and unable to walk in a straight line. Either way, the 'surprise' was what made trying the beverages fun. And this beverage taste testing was the extent of Del's appetite for risk-taking.

It wasn't all business at the market though. Del also enjoyed overhearing stories of the brave members of the Longtails, a mouse-made military force commanded by the Council of Five. The Council was the ruling body of the Mouselands that decided all things in the way of mouse livelihood. From magic-wielding members of the Spectrum Halls, who fought off an infestation of horned beetles; to brave fighters and sharp-shots defending the Mouselands from foxes and roaming raccoons just past the borders of mouse territories; Del found these stories almost as exciting as those involving Harry, Ron and Hermione as they fought to stop the rising evil of Voldemort alongside their rising piles of Potions homework.

Though the Mouselands were spread out over miles of land, the epicenter was within Verden's high walls. Mice with special talents had taken over large buildings, turning

11

them into guilds or halls—hubs where mice with similar talents could train and master their craft. Perhaps you were a fledgling fighter needing a place to train with a sword or axe—one of the many fighter's guilds would suit you just fine. Or maybe you were a mouse with fine culinary tastes, in search of like-minded mice to share recipes with—you'd be right at home at the Fork, a building with a permanently darkened neon sign reading *Benihana* above its doorway. If a mouse had a skill, chances were that he could find a place to hone it in Verden.

The Canticle, a place where mice specializing in the healing arts were sent to perfect their skills, could be found in The Field, which had once been used by humans to play a game that Del had seen in some of his books, called baseball. In the center of the enormous field was a shrine to the great mouse Ganafeila, who many mice believed had been the founder of the city and of the Longtails. It was said that a spirit had spoken to her and told her to send out her best warriors to seek a new home for the mice. In olden days, it was believed that mice with the longest tails were destined to live the longest, luckiest lives. In actuality, mice with big tails were typically just bigger in general, making them tougher and hardier. Their tail size was irrelevant.

Ganafeila had thus created a band of five mice, those with the longest tails among her followers, and sent them out to find a new home for her followers. This was the very first 'band' of Longtails, which was what teams of Longtails were still referred to. The five brave mice had marched south and founded Verden, creating the very first Council of Five: themselves.

Other magically-inclined mice, the Scarlets, Violets and Coals for example, took up residence in a large center in the southwest part of the city. The building had enormous passageways and gigantic rooms filled with nothing at all. The most captivating thing about the building was its exterior. Standing just outside its large glass windows was the sculpture of a gigantic blue bear, which stood forever frozen as it peered into the second story hallways.

Just west of this, across the Splattered River, were several buildings which stood next to each other, making up the multiple small guilds for melee fighters: the Eagle's Guild, which trained mice adept with long-ranged bow weapons, not actual eagles; the Blade's Guild, which specialized in mice who were trained in swords and daggers; and the Woodcutter's Guild, made up of fighters who wielded axes of varying sizes, just to name a few.

But Del knew that the best stories came from beyond Verden and the Mouselands surrounding it. There were lands governed and inhabited by all manner of other animals. To the north, tall clusters of trees created a dense forest. While many animals called it home, the mighty Allegiance of Blue Jays was the main governing force. The Allegiance resided in a massive tree at the center of the forest, known as Nesavary, and they kept the peace for the birds, excommunicating any flocks who weren't willing to follow the laws put into place.

To the west could be found a quaint, wooded area, still populated by many old homes and broken-down cars. The long-vacated suburb was overgrown with endless blades of grass and weeds which snaked their way into any crack or crevice they could find. This green land was known as Lakewood. North of this was a land of golden fields of wheat and barley, watched over by the Democracy of Raccoons, in a territory known as the Ridge of Wheat. Further west were the Rocky Mountains which stretched high into the sky, obscuring the horizon with their massive forms. Their snowy peaks could be seen no matter where in the city you were standing. No mouse dared to venture there. It was much too cold and far too dangerous.

South of the Mouselands, plants didn't grow quite as well, and smoke seemed to permanently permeate the air. Streets were cluttered with rusted cars, left behind by humans who had fled with only what they could carry. Large homes, once symbols of a family's wealth, now lay crushed by time and the elements. Engelwood, as the area was called, was home to animals like skunks and weasels, porcupines and opossums, all fighting over every little bit of land and possession they could get their greedy paws on.

Further south still was the region known as the Highlands. Larger animals roamed there—elk and deer. There had even been claims of bear sightings, though most of these giant creatures had been wiped out when one of the last human reactors had exploded, destroying all the land around it. Nowadays, grizzlies were mostly used for scary stories to frighten baby mice into doing their chores: "Finish cleaning the dishes, or a bear will come and take you in the night!"

To the east was prairie land as far as the eye could see: Aurora, the 'cursed land.' Much of the fields were flat, untamed and scorched black by the human war from so many years ago. Some mice believed that radiation had warped the creatures here to a point of being more monster than animal. The Longtails had once been sent into the prairies on recon missions, but few had returned. For the safety of mouse-kind, Aurora had been abandoned by the mice.

Del had no intention of seeing *any* of these wild places. He rarely chose to leave his home, and for those times when he *had* to, he made short work of it. Days like today, he was content to stay inside from dusk until dawn, barely even knowing the weather outside his own window, let alone the business of beasts which roamed the outer territories.

A light pattering of rain was falling outside, which meant it was a good day to stay in and read. Then again, *any* day was a good day to stay in and read, if you asked Del. He had been saving a dark graphic novel series called *Locke and Key* for a day just like this one. It was written by an author he adored named Joe Hill, and it chronicled the story of a family of humans who moved into a house which was full of horrors, all revolving around several mysterious keys which each unlocked a magical secret within the house. Del was just as interested in the stories he read as he was in seeing what the world had looked like before the last great war before the humans went extinct.

After sleeping in past the time that a respectable mouse would wake up, he ate a quick breakfast/lunch, if that's what you could call several peanuts, a strawberry and a slice of pumpkin from his brother's farm. He preferred to take his meals at the end of the twin-sized bed, sitting them on a wooden cutting board which he had hefted there through great effort. When he was finished, he leaped down to the hardwood floor of the apartment using the bed's comforter which hung over the bed and onto the floor, to break his fall. It was like landing atop a fluffy cloud.

Del had always assumed that the human who had amassed the collection in the apartment was just as much of a shut-in as he was. A Nerd. A Geek. Del wore these titles like badges of honor. While most mice were proud of their work or their families, Del was proud of the things that made him seem more like the apartment's previous human occupant. He was proud to have read every issue of *Ultimate Spider-Man*. He was proud to have beaten every *Final Fantasy* video game. He was proud to know that Han shot first.

Del scurried across the floor and up the nearby black bookshelf to the third shelf up where sat all seven volumes of *Locke and Key*. He used a combination of paws and buck teeth to pull the first volume from the shelf. He would never have done this with other mice around, as it was considered uncouth to use a mouse's teeth in such a way. The thin book fell to the floor with a thud. He then raced back down to the floor and grabbed the book by one corner, maneuvering it into a small cart he had made from the wheels of a toy truck and a small wooden plank.

Del had the mind of a puzzle solver and was good at discovering uses for thing that may have otherwise been useless. He imagined this was why he was so good at games like *The Legend of Zelda* and *Metroid,* which were loaded with puzzles and mysteries just waiting to be cracked. He pushed the cart around the bed, placing it just below the window, where he had built a pulley system to act as a small elevator. He moved the book from the cart to the lift, then ran up the brick wall and used a crank—built of pencils, a can lid and glue—to steadily lift the book up to the deep windowsill. There he could read while peering out at the rain-soaked world beyond—not that he really ever looked outside once he was engrossed in a good book.

He pulled the book onto the sill and over to a large plush pillow in the shape of a panda. He grabbed a match from a stack near the corner of the sill and lit a round red candle, which already had long strands of wax pouring down its sides. He crushed the flaming tip of the match down on the sill, putting out the fire. *Safety first*. He then jumped onto the panda pillow, nestled himself into it, and propped open the book.

"Just our luck it would rain," came a female voice from down on the street outside. Her voice was audible but muffled by the window.

Del's large ears twitched with surprise. A smaller-eared animal might not have even heard the voice over the rain. The street he lived on, though within the city limits, was especially overgrown with plant-life. Moss and vine-like weeds coated the outer walls of every single building. Even the road was broken up by roots twisting up to devour the pavement, causing the asphalt to jut out at strange angles. Because of this, carts and buggies and any other mouse transportation with wheels could not traverse the street, and thus it was rarely traveled. Even the other mice who lived in his building preferred to come in through holes in the foundation on the opposite side of the structure. The quiet was something Del adored about the studio. The fact that anyone would walk on this side of the building, *his* side of the building, was enough to pique his curiosity. He peered out the window at the street below, which was slick and glossy from the rain. Three mice walked side by side, their tiny footfalls sloshing the water that was quickly turning from a light sheen to a puddle.

Unlike himself, the three mice were all dressed very impressively. Del wore very little, even by mouse standards. His only article of clothing was a knit scarf wrapped around his neck, striped aquamarine and navy blue. It had been a gift from his mother upon being unceremoniously asked to leave and find a new home. *Happy Move Out of Your Parent's House Day. Here's a parting gift!* Despite the pretense, he loved the scarf, finding that the colors made him look quite dashing. The long ends also helped to hide his slightly large belly, provided that he wore it a certain way.

The mice on the street below looked like adventurers. *Longtails,* Del thought. In the lead was a male mouse with dark steel armor. A large battle-axe was strapped to his back, and though he wasn't much bigger than the other mice, his attire and dark chocolate-colored fur made him seem far more imposing than his comrades.

Next to him on the left was a mouse dressed in a fancy blood-red coat with white trim on the collar. He wore leather boots and wrapped his white gloved paws around the hilt of a rapier, whose sheath hung from a large black belt. He had white fur and a red fedora with a white feather pluming out of it.

To the right of the armored mouse was the ladymouse who had spoken, and Del could see that she was stunning, despite a scowl which sat firmly on her face. She had golden-blond fur and wore a simple red traveling cloak with the hood over her head, delicately tied under her chin, with pre-

19

cut holes that allowed her ears to pop out. The cloak fell over her shoulders, covering the top half of a dark leather tunic. Del immediately noticed the old mouse-sized book which was strapped onto her back like a backpack, hanging just above her long slender tail.

Del kept an eye on them as they passed, walking calmly through the center of the street below. He longed to get back to his book, but it wasn't every day that a band of Longtails traveled along the very street he lived on.

"Come now, Denya," said the white mouse in all red. "Must you always be so negative? The rain can be quite refreshing."

"Easy for you to say," remarked Denya, the ladymouse. "It'll be the first bath you've had in weeks."

"How rude!"

"Quiet down, you two," said the armored mouse in front. "You'll call unwanted attention to us."

"And what are you so worried about?" asked the white mouse. "This is a residential street. At worst, we'll distract some old ladymouse from her laundry. Then again, we wouldn't want to be the culprit in the case of the overly-soapy knickers."

"A mouse reported seeing a *slender* on this street," said the leader.

"Bah! Probably saw her own shadow. These mice are always looking for a bit of excitement in their tragically boring lives. Face it, Roderick, this mission is just an excuse to get you out of the Council chambers, so the Council doesn't have to listen to your-"

"To my what, Arthur?" Roderick interrupted.

Arthur suddenly quailed. "To your much better ideas on how the Council should be run, of course."

"Of course," mocked Roderick. He eyed their surroundings, seeming not to mind the rain wetting his fur. "Still, this street seems fairly unused. If there were trouble, this would be as good a place as any to hide it in plain sight."

Del saw something out of the corner of his eye. It was like a shadow, moving so quickly he almost missed it. His eyes darted around in the rain, trying to make out the shape which had appeared behind the mouse trio, trying to catch its movement once more. Perhaps it was another mouse, or something washed away by the rain. But as the shadow bolted once more and his eyes caught a glimpse of it, nothing could prepare him for what he saw. He let out a little squeak, but quickly covered his mouth, as if the thing down on the street might hear him.

Creeping from behind an overgrown car onto the backside of a toppled truck with a bed of marigolds blooming from it was a slender, dark-brown creature, three times the height of the mice it stalked. On its head, it wore a pair of leather goggles, and strapped to its back was a pair of menacing curved blades.

"A *mink*," whispered Del to himself. The creature looked like a hunter, stalking its prey in the night. His mind flashed to images of assassins he'd read about, trying to pinpoint which of them this mink reminded him of. Deadshot? Deathstroke? *The Terminator?* He gave his head a quick shake. *This is no time to be daydreaming.*

The mink followed the three armored mice, who seemed completely unaware of its presence. The rain and wind were the perfect cover for its approach. *But how was a mink even here? On this very street? His street?* Verden was like a fortress, impenetrable to outside animals. That was why few mice ever left. It was the safest place in the world. Or so Del thought.

He was suddenly overcome with something he had never once in his life felt before: the need to do something for someone else. It was beyond comprehension. He hoped that the trio of mice would notice the oncoming attack before it was too late, but the mink was edging closer, and the mice were still arguing among themselves, completely oblivious.

"We won't be able to spot anything useful until the rain lets up," offered Denya. "And if the drops get any bigger they'll wash us away. Perhaps a local mouse would let us take shelter, just until the storm passes."

"I'd rather be washed away then continue this pointless mission," said Arthur. "Honestly, what's next, taking mouse pups for a walk? Folding underwear? This is beneath us. *All* of us."

"Oh, shut it, Arthur," snapped Denya. "All you ever do is complain. It is our job to do as the Council asks. Not the other way around. Honestly, you Scarlets just want everything you do to be so dramatic, waving your fancy sword and magic around like you're putting on a show all the time."

"I take offense to that comment. We may be overly dramatic, but Concoctors like you are essentially glorified chefs."

"How dare you! We are vital in making potions and poultices and remedies and . . . and . . ."

"As if that takes any skill. It's no wonder you like these city missions. Maybe next week the Council will have us baking cupcakes."

"Why you little—"

The mink was almost upon them now. Every part of Del which told him to stay inside, to not get involved, to leave dangerous tasks to others, suddenly turned off. It was like a light switch had been flicked by some invisible force. And even though he was completely aware of it happening, he was powerless to stop it. He took off, moving faster than he'd ever moved before. He pulled himself up to the latch on the window and frantically spun the handle to create a small crack. Rain blew into the room, and onto his book, drenching the pages of his beloved comic. He reached out a paw in desperation, as if the water on the book was actually causing *him* pain. But looking down at the mink, he knew there was no time to save the graphic novel. Feeling like he was leaving a wounded soldier on a battlefield, Del forced himself to abandon his comic. He jumped through the cracked window out into the cold, wrapping his scarf tightly around his neck as its tails whipped in the wind, trying his best to resist looking back.

There was a wooden electrical post leaning up next to the building where it had fallen long ago. Electricity no longer pulsed through its wires, and probably hadn't for some time. Del ran on all fours, heading for the post, hoping to traverse its wires to make his way down and warn the mice. But for every single step he took, the mink seemed to take five. It moved like a viper, slithering from one shadow to the next. The assassin's paws reached behind, unsheathing the two sharp daggers.

Del pounced from the building's awning to the electrical post and then, throwing one end of his scarf over the wire and catching it in his other paw, he leapt from the awning, swinging from the wire as gravity pulled him haphazardly towards the earth below. Adrenaline raced through him. His mind focused on one pressing thought: *Warn the mice. You must warn the mice. You're swinging from these wires like Spider-man . . . I mean . . . warn the mice!* Just above the mice, he released his grip on one end of the scarf and fell. The mink was already upon them. It raised its daggers, ready to strike. A crack of thunder bellowed through the heavens as Del landed between the mink and the mice, splattering a small puddle of water in all directions. For a brief moment, he imagined he was Batman, leaping into the scene with lightning at his back, like he had seen on the cover of *The Dark Knight Returns*.

"Stop!" He held out his paws as if he could literally stop the attack. It was foolish. So foolish. He knew this for a fact. He was neither Batman nor Spider-man. He was Del. A no one. A nobody. With his paws outstretched and the blades stabbing for him as if in slow motion, he closed his eyes and awaited the end.

But the end never came.

"What the—" gasped Arthur, spinning around.

"How..." exclaimed Denya.

Del peeked his eyes open, the way he had when marathoning his apartment's collection of horror films. He was terrified of what he might see, but some sick part of him wanted to see it anyway. He felt light-headed, as if his strength was being leached away. His whole body was growing weaker by the second. The water from the rain had stopped between himself and the mink and, to Del's great surprise, had become a wall of solid ice, encasing the daggers and freezing them in place.

"W-what devilry is this?!" screeched the mink in a high-pitched snarl.

Roderick, never one to miss an opportunity, unleashed the axe from his back and lunged over the ice wall. He gave a mighty swing and then plunged the axe squarely into the confused mink's head. Hot red blood sprayed against the ice wall, splattering across its pristine surface.

Del tried to catch his breath as the mink's lifeless body fell to the ground in front of him. Everything was spinning. The ice wall collapsed, becoming water once more, soaking his already damp fur. It was as if the cold water was swallowing him. His body felt heavy as his vision began to blur.

"He doesn't look so good," said Arthur. Del couldn't tell which direction the voice was coming from. It sounded far away, and then Del felt his legs give out. As he fell, his final thought was of his book, left open and rain-soaked back in the studio apartment. It was such a shame, because he had really been looking forward to reading it. He thought he might be dying, but what hurt the most was knowing that his book would probably be too damaged to read. And wherever was he going to find *another* copy of *Locke and Key Volume One*? The world fell in on itself as he toppled to the ground and everything went dark.

CHAPTER TWO

The Home of the Longtails

Roderick entered a large domed chamber. Shafts of light spilled through stained-glass windows, filling the room with a dazzling array of colors and illuminating rows upon rows of long, wooden, human-sized benches. Small ladders had been built from the floor to the tops of these benches to allow for mice to crawl up and view the front of the room.

In a past world, this place would have been a courtroom. Now it was the deliberation chamber for the governing body of mice, The Council of Five. The mice who founded Verden had made up the original Council. After a long and arduous journey from the north to discover the city, they became its leaders, debating and dictating how mouse life was to be lived. As time passed, these responsibilities were passed down to those with a knack for politics. There was a fair bit of democracy within the Mouselands, allowing lesser mice to have at least some say in who represented their best interests. The Five were typically the eldest and wisest mice with the most pull in the community, no longer chosen based solely on the length of their tails.

The five mouse leaders sat atop a large wooden desk at the front of the domed room, bickering over a land agreement made with the raccoons that had been stuck in deliberations for over a season.

"We should show a sign of force," bellowed Kashryn, a fat gray male mouse, known through the land as one the greatest fighters in recent memory. While the entire Council had a say in the missions, promotions and additions to the Longtails, Kashryn handled the more day-to-day matters. In many ways, the Longtails saw Kashryn as their commander. They were, for lack of a better term, a military force, tasked with everything from investigating ne'er-do-wells in the Mouselands, to escorting sensitive material across enemy territories. They were even tasked with fighting to protect the Mouselands, should it ever come to that, and fortunately it rarely did. Most squabbles were settled in musty rooms by older, wiser animals, and not on battlefields. But the fact remained that should war ever break out, it would be Kashryn who led the charge. "We've allowed the raccoons to take advantage of our good nature far too long."

"The last thing we need is a war," said Batilda, the most prolific Violet in all the land. Her fur had once been brown, but an overexposure to the forces of magic had caused it to turn a grayish-blue color over the years. Small splotches of brown still dotted her fur. Of all the mice on the Council, her ears were the largest, and many mice in the city suspected that she could hear a mouse pup crying from a mile away. This was not true, but Batilda never said otherwise.

"War can be very good for business," said Otger, a two-toned mouse whose upper half was a chocolaty brown, while his lower half was white. His whiskers were bent and jagged, making it look like several thin, gray lightning bolts were exploding from his cheeks. He was the owner and operator of the Verden Treasury, a labyrinth of tunnels which served as the sole place for mice to stash their chez and other valuable possessions.

"Wars cost far too much money for that to be true," argued Meadow, a golden-colored mouse who represented the interests of the working mice in the farmlands and mills just south of the city. "We'd have to raise taxes just to be able to afford such a venture."

"Exactly my point," sneered Otger.

"The farmers and miners would never be able to afford such an increase," Meadow retorted, scowling at Otger, whose eyes glistened greedily at the prospect of more chez.

"We have a visitor," Rowena, the eldest and wisest of the mice on the Council, said as she noticed Roderick approaching. She bowed her wrinkled face to look down on him from the desk high above where he stood and pointed at him with a gnarled wooden staff. "Sir Roderick, to what do we owe the pleasure of your visit with this Council on this fine morning?"

"Forgive the intrusion," he said with a slight bow of his head. "But my team and I have just returned from investigating the *slender* sighting reported several nights ago. While combing the streets for clues, my band and I were attacked." Roderick waited a moment to make sure he had their attention. All five mice leaned forward in their chairs and focused intently on him.

"Attacked?" snarled Kashryn accusingly. "By whom?"

"I think you'll be more interested in *what* than *whom*." Roderick paused, remembering the previous night. "The attacker was a mink assassin."

There were grumbles of dismay from the Council. Meadow let out a slight gasp, cupping her paws over her mouth.

"Upon searching the body," continued Roderick, "we found this." Roderick pulled a piece of cloth from his pocket and presented it. The cloth was forest green with a symbol drawn onto it in dark crimson blood, dried with age. The symbol was that of a large paw, like a bear's footprint. In the center of the paw was an open eye which resembled that of a snake, its pupil thin as a knife's edge.

"We've seen this before," said Meadow. "A season ago, when the grain merchants were being attacked on their way to the city. That symbol was branded onto the dead bodies that were left behind."

"But weren't those attacks attributed to mice?" asked Batilda.

"They were," said Meadow. "An accusation which none of us took lightly. After all, it is rare indeed for mice to attack each other. Still, the weapons used were too small to be wielded by any other creature. Yet oddly, there were never any suspects."

"Oh, there were plenty of suspects," said Kashryn. "Just not enough proof to convict them."

"But if mice *did* attack the merchants, identifying themselves with this symbol, and now we are finding it on a mink . . . are we suggesting that mice might be working *with* minks?" asked Otger in disbelief. "The very idea is preposterous!"

"To assume anything would be foolish," said Rowena, silencing the others. "For now, we will need to investigate this symbol and this assassin further." She smiled down at Roderick. "Though the news you bring is unsettling, we thank you for it all the same. And we welcome you home. Go with the blessings of the Council." They turned away from him, presumably to continue their discussion, but Roderick stayed where he was, awkwardly awaiting another opportunity to speak.

"You are excused, boy," growled Kashryn, not liking mice who overstayed their welcome.

"There's . . . something else," said Roderick.

*   *   *

In Del's dream, he was flying an invisible jet next to Wonder Woman, who had made him her sidekick. He had a cape and his very own lasso of truth. Suddenly, a mink the size of Godzilla attacked the plane, causing it to crash into a haunted house, where he was served red bean buns and told that the key out of the house was hidden inside one of the buns. He didn't know what red bean buns tasted like but had always seen them in Japanese comics and wanted to try one someday. The filling tasted like licorice in the dream, but as soon as he swallowed his first bite, it burst into flames. A rushing river swallowed him, ripping through the house and pulling him into darkness. In the blackness, two blood-red eyes stared at him. *"I found you!"* growled a low voice.

He awoke in a warm, mouse-sized bed inside a wood-paneled room, which looked to be the inside of a slightly ajar desk drawer. A candle next to his bed cast long flickering shadows on the wall, and the smell of warm bread permeated his nostrils. He tried to sit up, but a sudden stab of pain in his back and chest made it impossible. *Why do I feel like death?* he wondered. He never exercised, save for running to his bookshelf to get the next volume of whatever he was reading. And he certainly hadn't gotten into any scuffles or brawls lately. Yet his head felt as though some larger mouse had beaten him with brass-knuckled paws. *This must be what Batman feels like after a particularly challenging battle with Bane.* He desperately hoped that Alfred would show up to fix him up.

"Oh! You're awake!" The face of a chubby, brown ladymouse peered down at him from the drawer opening and grinned. "We thought you might go on sleeping forever. Sleeping Beauty, we called you." She chuckled at her own joke, then squeezed through the opening and dropped to the floor of the drawer. She had a thick build and wore a white cloak. Del noted the thin gold necklace she wore, signifying she was a Gold, a healer. It was believed that they had the ability to cure mice of ailments, or even to extend the lives of those on death's doorstep, by bargaining with the spirits. They couldn't cheat death forever though. Time eventually ran out for all mice, and no amount of bargaining would save them.

"Never treated your kind though. None of us have," said the mouse. "Figured it was best just to let you sleep. Had no idea using a power like yours could be such a physical strain."

Del felt himself getting lost as he tried to follow her words. "A power . . . like mine?" he asked. Was she referring to his uncanny ability to memorize the names of every elf, dwarf and hobbit in *Lord of the Rings*?

"Oh, sorry. Don't like it to be called a power? Golds can be picky that way too. We always just say, *our blessing.* I mean to say . . . well, whatever you did to call on the elements to stop that mink. Do you prefer to *call on the*

33

elements, or would you rather *bargain with the elements?*"
She huffed, trying to calm herself. "Sorry, dear. I don't
mean to ask so many questions. It's just quite exciting. A
Trelock! Here! Now! Thought they were a myth, we did. A
story to tell little mouse pups before bed. A fairy tale. Can't
blame you for staying hush-hush about it though. Soon as
word gets out, you'll be quite famous, I suspect."

Del found most of what she was saying to be gibberish.
Power? Elements? Trelock? Had this Gold perhaps spoken
with the spirits of the past one too many times? Had she, in
fact, lost her grip on reality?

"Umm," said Del, finding his voice to be raspy and
weak. "Not to be rude, but I have no idea what you're talking
about. I haven't called *or* bargained with any elements. I
don't even *know* any elements *to* call."

The Gold blinked curiously at him. "Oh. I'm so sorry,
dear. I just assumed you knew . . ." She straightened up,
putting on her best 'this-isn't-super-awkward' face. "Why
don't we start over?" She placed herself in front of him and
smiled warmly. "How are you feeling?"

Every muscle in his small body ached. "Sore," he
groaned. He felt his stomach growl. "And hungry. But
mostly confused. Where am I? Who are you? How did I get
here?"

"One at a time, my boy," she said. "First, let's ease some
of the pain." She held out her paws and closed her eyes.
"*Heilen!*" she called out, and an orb of golden light filled her

paws. She then placed this on Del's chest and the light dissolved into him. His body suddenly felt warm like a summer day after eating a bowl full of honey.

"Better?" she asked.

"Much," he said, letting out a sigh of relief.

"Now, as to your other questions," she said. "I am Lady Talbith, and you are in the Gold's healing chambers within Longtails Central." This was the main building where the Longtails received training, missions and aid if a mission had not gone well. It had once been a place of law for the humans, but now, the mouse military force was proud to call it home. "You were brought here by Sir Roderick and his band of Longtails when you fainted after stopping a mink assassin from killing the lot of them. It's all very exciting stuff. Do you recall?"

This was all the nudging his memory needed. Everything rushed back to him. The rain. The mice on the street. The mink and the wall of ice halting its blades.

"I do," shuddered Del. "But I'm afraid you're wrong about that last part. I didn't stop the attack. The rain froze the mink's daggers in place, and then that Woodcutter killed him. I just warned the mice. That's all."

"Oh?" giggled Talbith, as if he had said something very naive. "I suppose the rain froze all on its own in the middle of a storm on a warm spring night? Tell me, have you ever seen rain do that?"

"Well..." His voice trailed off in thought. He'd recently read a book about something called 'global warming,' but even that probably couldn't instantly freeze rain. No, she was right. Rain didn't just freeze in place at the perfect moment. But it was just as improbable to think that he had frozen the rain. *It must have been one of the three other mice.* Surely one of them had magic that they had executed just as he had jumped in to warn them. The Scarlet, perhaps. "It wasn't me," he asserted. "I don't have any powers. Or skills. Or . . . powers." *I already said that.* "I'm boring, really. I'm like Harry Potter before Hogwarts."

"Who's Hairy Potter? And why is he called that? Is he really *that* hairy?" asked Talbith, curiously.

"No!" cried Del. "He wasn't anything. Just like me!"

"You'll just have to take that up with the others then," Talbith sighed. "After all, they're quite certain you're a Trelock. I've never seen Sir Roderick be so certain of anything before. And he never takes anything at face value."

"I don't know what a Trelock is, but I promise you that I am not one," scoffed Del. His thoughts drifted to the book still laying on his windowsill, probably soaked through by now. He yearned to get back to it and arguing with this ladymouse was killing precious reading time. "Come to think of it, I'm feeling a lot better. That little glowy thing you did must have done the trick. Now if you'll just show me the door, I'll get out of your way and you can get on with . . . well, whatever else you do here."

"You're awake!" exclaimed a voice from behind Talbith. Del looked up, rolling his eyes at his bad luck, to see a familiar face—the white mouse in all red. He searched his memory for the mouse's name—Arthur. "Pretty exciting, eh, Talbith? We found ourselves a little Trelock out among the common folk."

"I'm *not* a Trelock!" yelled Del.

Arthur grinned deviously. "Right, of course not. I'm *not* a Scarlet either." He winked with incredible exaggeration. "I'm more of a magical polar bear." He chuckled to himself. Del instantly realized that he was dealing with someone who very much enjoyed the sound of his own voice. "It's alright, kid. You're with friends here," comforted Arthur. "No need to hide your identity."

"I'm not hiding my identity!" Del snapped. "I'm not Batman." He realized instantly that this reference would be lost on any mouse other than himself.

"First, you're not a Trelock, now you're not a bat. I'm going to need you to work on your cover story, little mouse," teased Arthur.

"I want to go home," said Del, who was not at all amused by the banter with Arthur. This, he reminded himself, was why he avoided other mice.

"You can't just leave!" barked Arthur, finally taking Del seriously. There was no more evidence of levity in his voice or in his pale face. "Do you have any idea how incredible it is that we found you? Your abilities would be invaluable to the

Longtails. You'd be on the shortlist for the most prestigious bands. *Leave?* I daresay, that would be like shutting the door on your destiny!"

"I don't want to join a Longtails band! I don't want a destiny!" squeaked Del. "I just want to sit on my windowsill and read my book. I just want to go home."

"BOOKS?!" Arthur was at his breaking point. "Minks are crossing our borders, bypassing our defensive walls, and attempting to assassinate mice right under your *lovely windowsill*, and you're thinking about BOOKS?!"

"That's enough, Arthur," said a low, domineering voice. They all turned their attention to the gap in the drawer to see Roderick. He stood stoically, no longer wearing his armor, but still commanding attention to himself. A cream-colored brown tunic hung from his shoulders, and he wore a woven cord tied around his waist like a belt. He eyed Del and his expression softened slightly. "I understand you want to go home. You are not imprisoned here, so if you wish to leave, we will allow it. But at the very least, I ask that you take a short walk with me first."

Del thought for a moment and then nodded. Saying '*no*' to this mouse wouldn't be so easy.

*   *   *

The halls were filled with painted portraits and clay sculptures of legendary mice straight out of Longtails history. Each stood noble and proud in their respective works of art. Del felt as though these great mice were looking down on him as he walked along the red-carpeted floor next to Roderick, who was just as imposing.

"Ever since mice came to Verden, the Longtails have protected them. Countless threats have fallen upon our lands, many of which you probably never even knew existed, and we've stopped them—every single time." Roderick spoke gently, but his voice was big enough to fill the hall.

"That's an impressive track record," said Del, feeling ashamed of not wanting to be a part of something so prestigious. "You're like the mouse Justice League."

Roderick eyed him curiously but continued on. "You have a gift. Perhaps not one you expected or wished for, but a gift nonetheless. A gift that, if developed, could become quite strong. We haven't ever seen a Trelock in these halls. Not a real one at least. Plenty of mice have claimed to be, only to be disproved. In fact, until last night, I had assumed them to be tall tales, concocted by false prophets and storytellers. The legends would have you believe Trelocks were mythical in nature. Have you ever heard the story of the Trelock who fought a giant mutant hawk?"

Del shook his head no. He was surprised not to know this story, since he had probably heard more stories than most other mice.

"The Tale of Princess Montalani," continued Roderick. "She called upon Earth, Wind, Fire and Water to destroy the evil Rakval who threatened to block out the sun with its wings. None of it is true, of course. I've done enough research to know. Princess Montalani wasn't even alive at the same time as Rakval. But her story lives on nonetheless."

Del stopped in his tracks, causing Roderick to stop as well and look back at him. "But it *is* just a story." Del bowed his head ashamed for allowing himself to believe that there might have once been a real-life superhero among mouse-kind.

"A story which has inspired hope for generations. All tales are based on some form of truth. Legends and prophecies foretell the coming of a mouse who will commune with the spirits of nature in order to save us all from destruction." Roderick looked Del up and down. "I don't know how much stock I put in saviors, but what you did that night, controlling the water to your will, that is not something that just any mouse can do."

Del shook his head vigorously. "You're wrong. I'm not some powerful warrior. I wasn't bitten by a radioactive spider. I can't fight mutant hawks. I never have, and I never will." He took a deep breath and then let out a long sigh. "I'm sorry, sir, but you've got the wrong mouse." He hesitated, then made up his mind. "I'd like to go home now."

Roderick stared at him for a long moment, taking in all his features, before giving a gentle nod. "Very well. A deal's a deal."

"Thank you," said Del, managing a weak smile. He turned to leave.

"The elements *are* real, and they are calling to you," stated Roderick, making sure to get the last word in. "And the elements have a way of getting what they want. You can deny them for now, but eventually, you might find them unavoidable. As the Longtails say, sooner or later, everyone answers the call."

"I'll keep that in mind." Del walked back down the hall the way they'd come and followed it until it turned. He descended a long set of stairs which then led him through a large set of doors to the outside. He continued on, putting as much distance as possible between himself and the home of the Longtails. Distance between himself and his so-called destiny. Distance from a life he knew he wasn't ready for. He had indulged in his small slice of adventure. Now, it was time to go home.

CHAPTER THREE

Barrel-Fist and the Copper Clan

A soft knock broke the silence as Denya rapped on the door to Roderick's quarters. He looked up from a scroll where he was carefully writing curved letters with a feathered quill. A gentle smile curled across his muzzle, the kind a father gave his pups. She stood in the doorway without her red cloak, but still wore her leather tunic, her Concoctor's book slung sideways on her back.

"Permission to come in, sir?" she asked. It was a formality. She knew he'd never turn her away. Though he was the Alpha of their band and she a mere Scrapper, they regarded each other more as family.

"You should be resting," he said, placing the tip of the quill into a jar of black ink so that the feather stuck straight up from it.

"Can't," she said. "It's been a troubling couple of days." She entered the room and sat in a chair opposite of where Roderick sat at his desk.

His room was simple. Though he had garnered many awards and decorations from the Longtails, he chose only to display the first one he'd received so many seasons ago. The little medal hung in a glass case behind him. His armor and axe were secured at the side of the room, leaving him wearing a loose white button-down shirt and gray pants. Even unarmed, Denya knew that he could still win any fight. In her eyes, he was invincible.

"Yes," said Roderick. "It truly has. But the revelation of a Trelock is something that should bring us all hope. The world is changing. Mother Nature herself is sending us a gift for whatever darkness lies on the horizon."

"Seems to me that Mother Nature needs to work on her selection process," said Denya with an air of annoyance in her voice. "The way I hear it, he couldn't wait to go home and read."

"Reading is good for the soul," Roderick remarked mildly.

"I love a good book as much as anyone, but that's irrelevant when minks are at our front door."

"Perhaps," he conceded. "But then we all have our ways of coming around to the Longtails, don't we?" He eyed her with a knowing look, as if to say *you should know*.

She let out a short burst of laughter. "Point made. What are you working on so late?"

"I'm drafting a letter for young Del."

"To convince him to join us?" She waved her paw across the air as if she could see the newspaper heading in front of her. "*Ten reasons to join the Longtails!*"

"More to comfort him," laughed Roderick. "He'll come around to the Longtails sooner or later. Eventually everyone answers the call."

Denya shook her head. She'd only heard him say those words a thousand times.

"But this letter is meant for a later time. He is of a class that this world has not known in your lifetime or mine. The road before him is going to be filled with perils and tough choices. He will undoubtedly fail many times before he succeeds, and I like to be prepared for such occasions. Think of it as pre-planned guidance." He smiled, celebrating his own wit, but then it faltered slightly. "Would you do an old mouse a favor?"

"You've been my Alpha so long, I don't even know how I could decline that request," Denya responded. She had great respect for him as her Alpha, as the captain of any Longtails band was titled. In many ways, he'd been like a father to her. Or at the very least, she had felt closer to him than she did to her actual father. She was concerned for him though, as lately his thoughts seemed to be elsewhere. He'd become distant, and his words had become vague and cryptic.

"Should something happen to me," said Roderick lightly, though his words lacked levity. "I'd appreciate you giving this to the young mouse. But only when he's ready. That's very important. Support, if offered at the wrong time, can do more harm than good."

Denya studied his face, trying to figure out what he wasn't saying. Part of her could sense that there was more to all of this than a simple letter. However, she knew better than to pry. "How will I know?" she asked.

"Oh, you just will. I trust your judgment unconditionally."

Denya let out a hearty, boisterous laugh. "Now that is a lie if I ever heard one," she said. "Fine, I'll deliver the letter should something . . . happen. But I imagine I won't have to."

"Oh?"

"You are a stubborn old mouse," she said, with a glint of trouble-making in her eyes. "I imagine you'll stay alive for many years to come, just so you can tell me my recipes are missing the most important ingredient."

"And what is the most important ingredient?" he teased.

"*Patience* is not an ingredient!" she retorted.

This time it was Roderick's turn to laugh.

They continued to talk like this for some time, joking until it was late in the evening. Eventually, Denya yawned and excused herself, but not before asking, "Any word on our next mission?"

Roderick laced his fingers together and leaned his elbows on his desk. "Until he is safely within these walls and learning to control his powers, Del Hatherhorne *is* our mission."

"So, the Council wants you to keep tabs on him?"

"They want us to rest and await orders."

"So they don't *know* we'll be keeping tabs on him?"

"My dear Denya, you could fill a book with things the Council doesn't know."

*   *   *

Locke and Key Volume One was completely, thoroughly, and undeniably destroyed when Del finally arrived home and laid eyes on it again. Soaked beyond recognition, the pages had crinkled, and the colors had bled, merging the images and text to a point of no longer being legible. Del thought, in that moment, that funerals ought to be held for books.

Now, days later, Del laid on his bed reading *Bleach,* a comic book—or *manga*, as they were called in the faraway land of their origin known as Japan—in which an ordinary boy who sees ghosts has risen to the challenge of fighting dark spirits. Though Del was happy to be home with his books, movies, and video games, he couldn't help but wonder if he'd made the right choice.

Over a day had passed now since he'd left Roderick standing in the hallway, but he still couldn't get the conversation out of his mind. Worse still was the fact that he felt restless and suddenly had the overwhelming urge to be outside. Twice in the last day he had gone down to the market, perusing the goods, wares and odd foods, only to come home empty-handed. He'd never before desired to simply walk around aimlessly, yet now it seemed to always be on his mind. He found himself listlessly losing his place in his books and looking up at the clouds. He noticed how nice the warmth of the sun made him feel. It was all quite unnerving.

Even his neighbors in the apartments across from his and down the hall were surprised to see him. Two young pups playing with a ball, who lived on the floor below, asked him if he was new to the building. This spoke to how rarely anyone had seen him since he'd moved in several seasons ago. Worst of all, he found himself wanting to *play* ball with them. Thinking back on it made his skin crawl.

It was as if something had been awoken in him by Roderick—giving him a taste of something more than he could ever get from simply shutting himself inside all day. He found this very annoying. After all, he had yet to see anything outside that was more exciting than battling monsters in *Final Fantasy*, or re-reading his favorite book, *Ready Player One*, for the twenty-third time.

No, he had done the right thing. *He had.* He wasn't a fighter or an adventurer. He didn't know the first thing about surviving in the wild. If anything, he was doing them a favor. They would have been weighed down by his inexperience. And he wasn't exactly brave either, the single occurrence with the mink assassin being an exception. He hid from danger. He avoided confrontation. He didn't even like squabbling with his brother and sister. Anytime one of them had gotten mad at him for playing with a toy they wanted, he had simply let them have it. The Longtails certainly had no room for a pushover like himself.

Outside, the sun was setting, casting long shadows across the apartment. It helped add to the general spooky feeling of reading a story about ghosts and spirits. And that was exactly what he intended to do. *Read your book, Del,* he told himself. *Stop looking at the sunset and read your book. Focus!* Even his thoughts were more combative than he cared for.

He turned the pages and focused on the eyes of Ichigo Kurosaki, the main character of the series. Despite his obvious shortcomings, Ichigo had such confidence in himself and his abilities. Del wondered what that felt like. He wasn't particularly athletic or overly smart. He had always been one to sit back while others in his family had gone on to accomplish great things. There were hundreds and thousands of mice, and the way he saw it, nothing made him particularly special. Then again, deep down, did he really want to be special? Was he so used to being average and being told that he was average that at some point, he had just given up on being anything but that?

Questions swirled around in his mind, and after several pages he realized that he hadn't actually read anything at all. His eyes were simply moving over the words and images while his brain puzzled over other thoughts. Annoyed, he flipped the pages back, this time determined to comprehend the words on the page.

Ting. Ting. Ting. A strange sound hit his ears from the direction of the apartment door, which might as well have been part of the wall. He'd never once opened or closed it. Rust had rendered the deadbolt permanently locked, and besides, he had plenty of other routes in and out of the apartment via mouse-holes. He rolled onto his side to face the door and listened for the source of the sound. The rhythmic metallic clink seemed to be getting faster, like the sound of a fan or engine revving up in slow motion to a steady rotation. He couldn't quite place it though. It was a completely new noise in the typically quiet building. Sure, there were families living in other units above and below him and even some on the same floor, but he rarely heard so much as a peep from them.

The sound grew faster and closer. He could hear it zipping back and forth from one end of the door's bottom edge to the other. Del focused his eyes on the lower portion of the door, waiting for some clue as to what was causing the noise. Suddenly, his bubble of solitude broke as loud shots of rapid gunfire filled the air. Bullets sprayed through the bottom half of the door, tearing away at the wood.

Del dove for cover, leaping behind his book as though it might actually be strong enough to protect him. He peeked out just as the bottom fourth of the door was dismantled by bullets. Dust and debris flooded the now empty space between what was left of the door and the hardwood flooring. In the aftermath cloud, Del could just make out a slender shadow stepping through the opening.

As the dust settled around him, it revealed a mink standing on its hind legs, with completely jet-black fur, except for a small patch of white on its chin. Del immediately noticed the mink's right forearm and paw were missing, and in their place was a six-barreled Gatling minigun. It attached just above where the mink's elbow should have been. As the mink stood in the doorway, the barrels began to spin down slowly, smoke drifting up from them.

The mink wore a device on the left side of its face with a red reticle eyepiece over its left eye. Light from the red lens pulsed as the beast surveyed the room. It wore a red bandana tied around its neck, like a bandit out of one of the old human Westerns Del had watched. Across its shoulder, a long chain of shining ammo wrapped itself all the way down across its chest and waist and then back up to its shoulder again. It wore black leather pants held up by a sash, which was tied so that the loose end draped down its left leg. Its feet were bare except for the white bandages they were wrapped in.

"We know you're here, little mouse," said the mink. His voice was scratchy, as if something were caught in his throat. "We can smell you."

Several more minks with brown fur filed in behind him. These looked more like the one Del had seen on the street before. They had daggers and swords in their paws and wore orange bandanas around their heads. Copper-colored clay was smeared onto their faces and chests in harsh lines, like war paint. He could just make out a symbol branded into the left shoulder of every single mink—a bear paw with an open eye in the center.

"Coppers!" barked the gun-armed leader. The other minks stood at attention. "Find him." Del curled up into a small ball, hiding behind the book as the minks spread out, starting their reckless search of the room. They knocked over books, and displaced video game discs that Del had foolishly left out. He was breathing fast, trying not to make any noise, but knowing that sooner or later they would find him. He had to get out of the house, and he needed to do it fast. Even if by some miracle he had been the one to freeze the water that night, something told him he would be hard-pressed to repeat such a trick. Night was falling outside, giving him the slight cover of shadows. In an ironic twist of fate, he was now being *forced* to go outside.

With the minks walking along the floor just below him, he stealthily made his way to the side of the bed closest to the window. It was still propped slightly open. He'd liked the way the breeze felt after he'd come home. *Stupid breeze,* he thought. *Stupid Mother Nature.* Still, he couldn't deny that the opening gave him a way out. If he could get to it, he might be able to sneak through without the minks noticing. He could then make his escape while they continued to search the room well into the night. He didn't love the idea of them destroying his collection, but he liked it a lot more than the idea of the minks destroying him.

He waited for the one nearest him, next to the bed, to look away and then scampered across a broken nightstand against the wall, over to the ledge nearest the window. He needed to jump to the curtains if he had any hope of getting to the window from where he stood.

He pulled back on all fours, readying his jump. He could vaguely hear Arnold Schwarzenegger's thickly-accented voice in his head, yelling *"Get to the choppa!"*

"Hello, little mouse," said a voice right behind him, rudely interrupting imaginary Arnold. Del turned to see a blade coming down on top of him. There was no time to react. He held out his paws on pure instinct.

CLANG!!! Metal hit metal as a mouse-sized suit of armor appeared between Del and the mink's blade. Del looked up, his body shaking in fear. The suit of armor turned its head and Roderick looked back at him.

"Run!" he barked at Del, before turning back to face the mink again. He gave it a hard shove backwards, then swung his axe at the creature which was much larger than his small mouse body.

"Barrel-Fist!" shouted the mink. "They're up here!"

Del didn't need to be told twice. He turned and leapt for the curtain, grabbing hold of it with all four paws. The revving noise could be heard once again and moments later, bullets were spraying through the curtain fabric all around him. Barrel-Fist, the minigun-wielding mink, was onto him, running for the window at full speed and shooting in Del's direction.

Del dodged the bullets, swinging along the curtain ruffles the way Spider-Man swung along webbing, landing on the window ledge and then sprinting for the open window. He turned back to see that Roderick had caught up and was right behind him. The mink he'd been fighting lay dead atop the nightstand, blood pouring from an open wound in its chest.

"Go!" yelled Roderick, and as he caught up to Del, he grabbed the young mouse by the scruff, and together they hurtled through the open window, emerging into the cold night air.

As they fell, Roderick swung his axe, hooking it onto a downed wire—effectively transforming it into a zipline—and swung them precariously from it until they landed, rolling clumsily onto the pavement of the street. Del glanced up, and despite his head spinning from the fall, he could see the minks parading out of his apartment window in full pursuit.

"Coppers!" yelled an angered Barrel-Fist, addressing the company of minks. "Prove your worth! A bucket of coin to whoever takes down Night-Terror's killer!"

Del made a quick assumption that Night-Terror was the mink currently bleeding out on his nightstand. Several of the minks dropped down to the street in front of them, some wielding dual daggers, others carrying crooked swords and long knives. They were all naturally taller than the mice, which made them that much more terrifying. Del felt his paws grasping at the street beneath him, trying desperately to crawl away from the attackers who were closing in right on top of him. Suddenly, a metal-clad arm was around his chest. Roderick was pulling him away from the minks.

"Get up, boy!" he commanded.

Denya appeared from behind, flying over them in a horizontal spin. Her paws briefly dug into two satchels at either side of her waist. In a split-second, she whipped her paws out, flinging two small black orbs at the cluster of minks. A moment later, a deafening explosion erupted into fire and smoke, just as she landed on the street. "Take that, you filthy *slenders*!"

Roderick pushed Del towards her. "Get him out of here!"

Several minks burst through the cloud of smoke. Denya fell back, grabbing a hold of Del's arm and helping Roderick to pull him away from the battle. Del wanted to run, he really did. But fear had crippled him. He couldn't think, feel or move. It was as if Scarecrow—one of Batman's notable villains—had used his fear gas on him and now all Del could do was watch the horror unfold. Roderick and Denya had essentially become the Batman and Robin to his scared, generic Gotham citizen.

He'd read countless comic books about brave heroes who rose to the challenge when faced with impossible odds. He had always wanted to believe that if presented with this kind of situation, he too could rise above his fear to fight back. But the truth was just as Del had always known. He was not a hero. The closest he had come was attempting to warn the Longtails of the assassin, but it had been a fluke. When it came to facing death head-on, he hadn't fought back; he'd cowered and been saved by an unexplained ice wall. For all he knew, Iceman—a prominent member of the X-Men—had swooped in for a quick cameo, hoping to spice up the otherwise trite tale of Del's life.

Del wanted to run. He wanted to run and hide and never come out again. He just couldn't convince his legs to make this dream a reality.

Bullets flew past the minks as Barrel-Fist erupted through the cloud of smoke, grinding his sharp teeth as he caught a glimpse of Del and the other mice. A mystical light in the form of a bright-blue, illuminated sigil appeared between the mice and the minks. It glowed in the darkness of the night, deflecting the bullets like a shield. Del was sure that this time he had nothing to do with it. Arthur arrived, holding out his left palm to reinforce the barrier.

"Lovely show, Denya, but I think your muffins are finished baking. Might want to take them out of the oven while I take it from here," quipped Arthur with a wry grin.

Denya rolled her eyes. "I'm gonna put your *face* in an oven."

"Save it for later," barked Roderick.

Arthur grabbed the sword hilt at his waist and pulled the blade from its sheath. It was a thin rapier which glistened as though it had just been freshly polished. "Watch now, young Del," he said proudly. "Witness a true hero of mice."

"More like a true moron of mice," Denya bit back.

"Enough!" bellowed Roderick, who clearly did not find their squabbling to be very amusing.

Arthur scoffed and took off towards the minks as Roderick and Denya continued to pull Del towards a pigeon tied to a broken-down automobile that had been overgrown by foliage decades ago. Pigeons were the best means of transport for the mice, but they were highly unreliable, and so only the most experienced mice could ride them. They were also near-extinct due to being hunted for sport by the hawks to the south. Great care was taken in employing the birds, for fear that one might be killed in battle. The pigeon was fitted with a saddle and reins in order to make it possible to ride. It stared down at them with beady eyes, seemingly confused by the loud noises and yelling, but not at all concerned. Pigeons, who had not been radically affected by the high radiation levels now permeating the planet, were not all that intelligent.

Further down the street, several mice who had been looking out from nearby buildings locked their windows and closed their blinds, trying to keep out the commotion. On the back side of the building, whole families were now evacuating their homes and taking their mouse pups to safety. Nothing was as terrifying as an onslaught of minks in the middle of the city. Though Del did not care for his neighbors enough to get to know them, he was glad to know that they were smart enough to get out before things got worse. Luckily, the minks were too focused on the mice fighting back to notice those who were sneaking off into the night.

Arthur's sword moved like lightning, jabbing one mink in the eye, and slashing another across the throat. In between parries and stabs, he summoned balls of blue fire, hurling them at any who dared get near him. Fur erupted in flames, and mink screams reverberated down the street. But despite his best efforts, there were simply too many of them. As Arthur fought back the horde, Barrel-Fist broke away and charged for Del and the others.

"Where do you think you're going?" Barrel-Fist yelled, fury in his black eyes. He aimed the minigun arm, ready to mow the mice down, mere steps from the pigeon.

Roderick turned to Denya, his whiskers bristling. Del was still shaking, trying to compose himself even a little.

"Take care of Del," Roderick ordered. "Get him out of here alive. He's more important than you can imagine."

"Roderick," she pleaded. "What are you—"

But he was already running. With a giant leap, he hurled himself towards Barrel-Fist and just as the gun fired, he slammed into the mink, knocking him off his feet, and sending the bullets spraying into the night sky. They toppled across the street, a blur of metal and fur. Denya and Del looked on in horror, waiting to see who would come out on top.

Barrel-Fist's slender frame rose up, a large bloody gash cut across his exposed eye. Roderick lay squirming under the mink's foot. Denya gasped. Barrel-Fist laughed. It was a cold, mocking laugh, full of malice and victory.

"I've had quite enough of you, little warrior." He raised his gun-arm and aimed all six barrels at Roderick's chest. With one final sharp-toothed grin, a short burst erupted from the gun, firing a single bullet deep into Roderick's chest.

CHAPTER FOUR

The Death of a Hero

Denya screamed. A blood-curdling scream that silenced the street around them. Reality seemed to slow from a high-speed chase to a crawl. For the briefest of moments, she believed that she was having a nightmare. Only a nightmare. But when the scene before her kept playing out, and she didn't wake up, the possibility of a bad dream seemed less and less likely.

Arthur broke away from a circle of charred mink corpses and bolted towards Denya and Del. Del's whole body was shaking. His tail quivered. His paws were raised instinctively to his face and shaking. He had never seen a mouse killed before. Until the mink assassin several nights before, he had never seen any real death. That image had been bad enough, but this . . . this was haunting. He felt detached, as if he were floating above it all, watching helplessly. His body was heavy, like a weight tied to him that refused to come undone. He wished he could leave it behind and float away, but it held him firm to the ground, forcing him to live out every second—millisecond—of this moment.

"Pitiful," spat Barrel-Fist. Reaching down with his only paw, he dug his claws into Roderick's scruff and lifted the mouse's limp body, like a puppet without a master, off the ground. He waved it in the air mockingly so that the other mice could see. "Longtails. Bah. How quickly they fall. Was this mouse the best you had? The Longtails' finest? I, for one, am very disappointed. Here we've been sneaking around the city like vermin. If this is all you've got, we should've come sooner. We should've come during the day. We should've *knocked*."

"*You* are vermin!" shouted Denya, tears streaming down her face. "You all are. Vile. Rotten. *Slenders*." She growled the last word. "You disgrace him with your filthy paws." She sneered. "Or should I say . . . paw?"

Barrel-Fist grunted. "You can have your precious Alpha back. He's of no use to me. Then again, he wasn't of much use to you, either." He tossed Roderick's body towards them like a sack of seeds. It flew through the air and tumbled in front of the mice.

Denya ran to him while Del crawled along the rough pavement, pulling himself towards the limp body. He hadn't known him for long, but Roderick had been kind to Del.

He'd believed in Del. Del didn't even believe in himself, and yet this mouse who had only just met him did.

"No, no, no," pleaded Denya, cradling his head in her arms.

The sound of a weak cough came from Roderick's body. It was strained, but they all heard it. To Del's surprise, Roderick still lived. He took in short, labored breaths as blood seeped from the wound in his chest.

Del approached the old mouse. Sliding in next to Denya, he placed a paw on Roderick's arm. It was already cold to the touch. "Why?" he asked in barely a whisper. Even as Roderick lay dying. Even though any words he spoke might be his last, Del had to know. "Why protect me? Why die for me?" It didn't seem fair. Roderick's life was far more valuable than his own. He was a high-ranking officer in the Longtails. He commanded respect simply by walking into a room. Del was just a shut-in. No one relied on him. No one put their lives in his paws. He contributed absolutely nothing to mousekind. And yet . . . Roderick was the one with a bullet in his chest.

"I couldn't let them kill you. You're too..." he trailed off, coughing. "Important."

"I'm not," cried Del, tears pouring down his furry cheeks. "I know you want me to be, but I'm not. I'm no one."

"For now," said Roderick weakly. "But someday you will be, and all of this...will not be in vain." He heaved another cough and then smiled solemnly up at Del. "Your tale is just beginning. Mine . . . is at its end . . ." His eyes closed, and then he said no more.

"So. Very. Sad," mocked Barrel-Fist, stretching out each word. He melodramatically pretended to wipe fake tears from his eyes. "Truly, my heart aches. Either that, or I ate a bad piece of meat earlier." He gathered himself and cleared his throat. "Now, which one of you is next? Volunteers? Or should I pick a name out of a hat?" The other minks snickered at their leader's wit.

"No," whispered Del. He could feel heat rising in his chest, anger pumping through his veins. *Is this what hatred feels like?* He wasn't sure. He'd never hated anyone before. Unless you counted Professor Umbridge in *Harry Potter*, but who wouldn't hate such a horrible witch?

No, this hatred was real. He could barely even look at Barrel-Fist without feeling an unquenchable thirst for revenge. He couldn't—wouldn't—watch another mouse die trying to protect him. The loathing ignited within him, overflowing in such a way that he couldn't control it. His teeth clenched. His paws became fists. His eyes narrowed. He felt like Bruce Banner as he was about to become the Hulk. Even if he wanted to stop the transformation, he couldn't.

In his mind, a thousand voices collided. He could hear the very air around him buzzing. He glowered at Barrel-Fist with eyes that were no longer his own. Something else was coursing through him, using his body as a shell to exact judgment. His eyes turned completely black, and he lost all sense of himself: his fear and pain and sadness. All of it was replaced by a twisting wrath. He yelled, like a warrior crying out for blood, and charged at Barrel-Fist.

The mink was not threatened in the least. He grinned gleefully, ready to take down his second foolish mouse of the night. "Looks like we have a volunteer after all, boys!" he declared to his fellow Copper Clan members, who had all stopped to watch their leader, in awe of his mouse killing expertise. They cheered, like the audience of a Roman fighting pit. Their beady eyes fixated on Del—the slave—and Barrel-Fist—the vicious lion, eager to see which one would emerge victorious.

"Don't!!!" cried Denya, but her warning fell on deaf ears.

Del launched into the air, higher than he'd ever jumped before. So high, in fact, that he hovered over Barrel-Fist for a moment. And as he looked down at the mink, reeling his fist back to strike, he saw the beast's expression change from a smile to confusion and then to surprise.

Barrel-Fist tried to raise the minigun arm to meet Del's attack, but the heavy, metal weapon rendered his movement a fraction too slow.

A glowing black aura burst from Del's fist as it connected with the mink's gun-arm with explosive force. Barrel-Fist was blown backwards, his thin body skidding down the broken pavement of the street. Streams of black lightning surged around Del like a shield, frightening the onlooking minks. They huddled together defensively. Del landed nimbly on the street, his head cocking to the side. His blackened eyes peered curiously at the fallen mink leader.

Barrel-Fist pushed himself up from the ground. His body was sore and bruised, and patches of his fur were singed where the black aura had touched him. But he would be damned if he was going to let a mouse get the better of him. He wiped the blood from his wounded eye, patted his singed fur, wiping away some of the black energy which had stayed on him like shimmering oil, and aimed the minigun at Del.

"I'll give credit where credit is due," he yelled. "You are much more impressive than the old timer. Your death will make a fine sacrifice to the Blight."

Del held out his paws to his sides, holding the air around him as if it were something he could grasp. The buildings on either side of the street shook, as if being ripped from their foundations. Loud crunching, creaking and snapping sounds echoed in the street, and the ground shook as if an earthquake were tearing it apart.

Barrel-Fist froze, glancing upwards as debris began to fall from above. The tall buildings on either side leaned into the street, like concrete and metal giants awakening from a long slumber. He realized with mounting anxiety, that they were going to collapse onto the street where he stood.

Barrel-Fist leveled his eyes at Del, not sure whether the mouse could even hear his words—not sure if this monster was even a mouse anymore. Its power was more that of a God.

"Time to go boys," Barrel-Fist yelled. He motioned for his companions to follow, and together the minks ran for safety. They made their way to the end of the street, heading for the city gates, leaving their slain brethren behind to be buried beneath the falling buildings.

And they weren't alone. Mice ran alongside them, choosing to follow the minks, rather than wait around for their homes to collapse. It was a mass exodus, where species no longer mattered. Only the will to survive.

There was a thunderous crack from above. With a symphony of crashes, bangs and booms—the creaking and the wrenching of steel—the buildings crumpled inwards, crashing first into each other and then falling to the street below, separating Del, Denya, Arthur and Roderick's body from the fleeing crowd of minks and mice beyond the rubble.

For several minutes, no one dared move. Dust and debris settled and an occasional beam broke, creating another small song of destruction. But at last it ended, and the street lay silent once more. Denya and Arthur stared in shock at Del whose paws remained at his sides, his head bowed, as though he might be sleeping or praying. It was Arthur who broke the silence.

"Wow," he muttered. "Someone has got some serious anger issues."

"All the stories about Trelocks . . ." Denya trailed off, not sure whether to be impressed or mortified. "They said they were powerful, but this . . ."

Suddenly Del collapsed, his body's control returning to him. Denya ran to him and put her arm around his shoulder to steady him. She expected him to be unconscious, like the previous time he had tapped into his power. But to her surprise, he was sobbing. His tears rolled to the ground, creating a small puddle.

"Why?" asked Del through the tears. "Why? Why? Why?"

"There, there," said Denya, patting him on the back.

"Roderick should have left me alone. He should have left me to the minks."

Denya bit back tears of her own for her fallen mentor. There would be time for that later. Denya considered herself an emotional mouse, but she was good at hiding it, choosing instead to express her pain in private. That was something Roderick had taught her at a young age. *We all feel loss and grief on the battlefield. The trick is to not let that stop us from performing our duty. There is a time and a place, and they both start when the job is done.*

"Roderick had a way of seeing things in others that not even they could see in themselves," she said softly.

Del looked at the pile of brick, concrete, glass and rubble all around of him, the culmination of two city buildings toppled on top of one another. "I didn't mean to do all of this," he said. "I could see myself doing it, and I didn't want to, but I couldn't stop it." To him, it was like watching the villain in a comic book do something horrible to the hero. His heart ached to stop the villain, but the words just kept coming. The story just kept happening. His power had rendered him powerless. "Why couldn't I stop it?"

"Trelocks are a complete mystery," said Arthur, approaching from behind as he sheathed his blade. "I expect the only mouse who can answer that question will be yourself."

As if Del could not feel any worse, he noticed several mice crawling out from the rubble of the building, pulling one another out of the fallen buildings. Apparently, not all of his neighbors had left in time to avoid the calamity. The pieces of the wreckage were big enough that most of them were able to squeeze through to safety, but Del still couldn't help thinking that he had ruined their lives. Worse still were the looks they gave him as they emerged. Their faces were all painted with the same emotion: Fear. They trembled at the sight of him, and mother mice pushed their pups behind themselves protectively.

"The other tenants," said Del. "I've destroyed their homes. I've..." Grief filled his heart. "I've destroyed *my* home. My books. My games. My bed. How..." He broke down sobbing again.

"There, there," sighed Arthur, patting Del on the back. "I'm sure no one even noticed it was you." It was a nice thought, even if it was a complete lie. He leaned down next to Denya, putting a paw on her shoulder. "Get the boy out of here. Take Roderick's pigeon. I'll stay here and help the mice. Speak with the Council when you return. We'll need a place to give them food and shelter."

"I'll send help," Denya replied. Then in a whisper, "Try to smooth things over."

"Oh, trust me. I'll say it was a freak tornado before I admit to a mouse having this kind of power."

"A freak tornado?" Denya was not impressed with the makeshift lie.

"Not believable enough?" asked Arthur charmingly. "I suppose I could always blame it all on the minks." He put on a fake voice, as if telling a story. "Those dastardly *slenders* and their terrifyingly efficient building-crusher!"

"That'll have to do." Denya watched several more mice crawling out of the wreckage, some of whom were already crying over the loss of their homes.

"Really? A tornado is far-fetched, but the building-crusher gets the seal of approval?"

"As long as the mice don't know it's Del, I don't care what you tell them," snapped Denya.

"Fair enough, love." Arthur turned to look back at Roderick's body, lying motionless in the street. "You'll take him with you, yes?" he asked, his charming demeanor slipping away.

"Of course," sighed Denya. "He deserves a proper burial."

"He deserves a statue. A painting in the hall of heroes. A medal of the highest honor." Arthur choked back a tear, wiping his eyes. "A truly heroic mouse . . . right to the very end."

"He really was." Denya wrapped her paws around Arthur and hugged him. She was not someone who hugged easily, preferring other mice to be kept at arm's length, but she suspected Arthur needed it just as much as she did. They'd both lost their Alpha, their mentor and their hero. It was a brief moment, but necessary for both. She pulled away and helped Del to his feet, walking him towards the body of her fallen friend and the bird that would carry them all home.

But as she secured Del and their Alpha to the saddle, she couldn't help but ponder something. It was like an itch on her back that she couldn't quite scratch. *Why had the minks targeted Del?* she wondered. *How had they known* exactly *where to look for him?* They hadn't ransacked the building. They hadn't searched. They had gone right to him. Roderick, Arthur and herself had watched it happen. They'd assumed they had time—the time it would take for the minks to locate the right apartment, the right mouse. But they had known right where to go. And this wasn't even counting the bigger question of how the minks had gotten past the city wall. The line of thought sent a shiver down her spine, and she couldn't help but wonder what other questions would arise before the mystery of the minks was solved.

* * *

"Prison," concluded Otger. The five mice of the Council glared down at Denya from their roost. She'd been summoned to speak before them regarding the events surrounding Roderick's death as well as the fate of Del Hatherhorne and the mice who had once resided on his city block. Four days had passed but in Denya's mind, it felt like only minutes. Pain tore at her heart every time she imagined Roderick's eyes closing for the last time. He'd believed in her when no one else had, not even her own parents. In many ways, Del was as much to blame for his death as the mink who had killed him. Del's choice to not join the Longtails, where it was safe, had led to the minks attacking his home. Still, despite this fact, she couldn't stand by quietly in the face of Otger's verdict.

"Prison?" questioned Denya, trying to keep her cool but failing miserably.

It was late in the day. She was exhausted. Her restless sleep had been interrupted by a messenger informing her that Roderick's office was being cleared out. Since his death, she'd avoided the room that once felt so much like home, but her promise to him came before her emotions. She charged right into the room and swiped the sealed scroll meant for Del—for when he was ready. Then she'd watched them take everything from the room, leaving it bare, as though he had never even existed.

Deliberations had gone on for hours now. *How did the minks get in? Did Roderick know the attack was coming? Why didn't he tell anyone? Why was a band of Longtails watching Del when no one had asked them to? But how did the minks get in???* Judging by the foul expressions on the Council's faces, they were not in the mood to quibble or question further. They were ready to dole out justice.

"He saved our lives! Arthur and I would be dead had he not intervened," she protested, ignoring her better judgment.

"He saved you *while* destroying the homes of dozens of other mice," snapped Otger, pushing up the spectacles on his nose angrily. "Do you have any idea how much chez it's going to cost us to relocate all of them? To care for, house and feed them in the meantime?"

"His abilities are untested and he's untrained," Denya fought back. "He doesn't know his own strength. No one does! This is uncharted territory for all of us. That night, he wasn't even in control of his own actions. He was in shock." Her words caught in her throat. "We all were."

"This would seem even more reason to detain him," Batilda piped up, stroking her chin with her paw as she deliberated. "Perhaps he is too dangerous to let loose back out into the world." Unlike his first visit, Del had not been allowed to leave the Longtail's building. Officially, he was being called a 'special guest,' though the only thing 'special' was that he was asked to stay in his assigned room at all hours of the day and given food through a small hole in the padlocked door.

"Batilda has a point," Kashryn said harshly. "This mouse could be even more dangerous than the mink problem, if left unchecked."

"Just imagine if he should create more destruction," fussed Meadow.

"Just imagine if he should fall into our enemy's paws," warned Kashryn.

"Just imagine," interrupted Denya, "that he's as special as Roderick believed he was. Just imagine if he really could control his abilities? Roderick knew that Del was important. He knew that Del was going to change this world for the better."

"Roderick, Roderick, Roderick," nagged Otger. "That old sod—may he rest in peace—was full of big ideas and no evidence to support them. Now, I know that he's no longer here to defend himself, but that doesn't make his belief in some unforeseen darkness on the horizon any more plausible. What's here and now is that boy, and he is a menace to society!"

"He needs training, not prison!" shouted Denya, at her wit's end.

Rowena held a wrinkly paw up to silence them. "It seems we have a visitor."

Denya turned as the other Council members looked down to see Del standing unassumingly at the entrance of the long room. He was accompanied by two guards who were there more for everyone else's protection rather than his own. In the large doorway, he looked tiny and frail. His paws fidgeted with one another as he struggled to look up, lost in shame and nervousness.

"Have you anything to say for yourself?" asked Rowena kindly, with a smile which revealed what few teeth she still had in her mouth.

Del took a few steps forward. The guards followed suit, careful not to lose sight of him. "I'm . . . sorry for the trouble I've caused," he mumbled.

"You'll have to come a bit closer," interrupted Rowena. "These big ears aren't as effective as they used to be." She gave one of her ears a flick with her paw, then nodded to the guards. "Let him approach. He's a scared young mouse, not a raving psychopath."

"That is yet to be decided," grumbled Kashryn.

The guards backed off nonetheless.

Del approached the tall Council bench, stopping to stand next to Denya. He looked over at her, and she nodded encouragingly.

"I think about what I am, and I'm scared," he said, trying to sound at least a little confident. "I imagine this must be what the X-Men felt like at first, before they met Professor X and learned how to control their mutant abilities." He realized that this probably made little sense to the Council, but often times Del found that he was most comfortable relating his thoughts and feelings to those in comic books, regardless of whether or not anyone else would understand. He cleared his throat and continued. "If I'm being honest, I want nothing to do with minks or magic or fighting. I've always thought those things were more exciting to read about than to actually . . . do." He took a deep breath and then stood up straight. "But Sir Roderick believed that I was special. So much so that he gave his life for me. I can't just ignore that. So, while I can understand why you might want to throw me in a cell and toss away the key, I'd like to apologize for my actions . . . and to propose another option."

The Council members stared down at him curiously.

He took a deep breath, hoping he would not regret his next words. "I'd like, with your permission of course, to join the Longtails."

"Preposterous!" yelled Otger. "One more instance of loss of control here and he could destroy our entire military defense force. Can you imagine how much money that would cost us?"

"I'm inclined to agree," added Kashryn. "I can't think of a single band who would want a ticking time bomb on missions with them." The Council members all grumbled in agreement among themselves.

"Well, I think Del's proposal is quite brave," remarked Denya, silencing the elder mice. Del gave her a sheepish smile. He had not expected her to come to his defense so quickly. Even he had thought the idea to be ludicrous, but it seemed his only option other than life in prison. "Not only that," she continued. "I think it's quite smart. We'd be able to keep an eye on him. And who better to train him to control his strength than us? Yes, he is a risk, but if he can learn to use his power with control, imagine what an asset he'd be." Denya took a step forward, emboldened by her own speech. "Most importantly, Del joining the Longtails is what Roderick would have wanted."

"Pish posh," said Otger, unimpressed. "Decisions made on the desires of dead mice are foolish and pointless."

"I happen to agree with the young ladymouse," said Rowena. She gave Otger a sideways look. "And I'm *not* dead. Not yet anyway."

"I agree as well," said Meadow with a kind smile. "This mouse has a beautiful spirit, and to lock that away in a dungeon would be like putting a rose in a room with no windows."

"Oh, give me a break," grumbled Otger.

"I'm afraid I'm still on the fence," Batilda murmured. "Young mouse." She addressed Del. "You do understand that joining the Longtails requires venturing into dangerous territories, fighting any creature that would cause our people harm, and sacrificing one's life for the very livelihood of all mice?"

Del gulped down his hesitation, then nodded. The thought of dying was not one he was eager to entertain. Yet, in his mind he was indebted to Roderick, whether or not the Woodcutter was gone from this world. "I do," said Del. "Roderick told me that his story had come to an end but that mine was just beginning. I'd like to think he wanted a story worth telling. My story up to this point has not been that way, but if you'll have me, I'm willing to give it my all." He turned to Denya, speaking his next words for her ears more than anyone else. "I'm not very athletic." He patted his round stomach. "But I've got a sharp mind. I can read all sorts of human languages, and I'm good at remembering small details. Even ones that seem silly. I can literally tell you the names of every member of the Green Lantern Corps."

"What is a *Green Lantern Corps*?" asked Denya.

"All in favor of letting this boy join the Longtails?" interrupted Rowena, before Del had a chance to launch into a diatribe about the harrowing adventures of Hal Jordan, Earth's greatest Green Lantern.

Rowena herself was the first to raise her paw, followed by Meadow. Batilda thought for a moment and then raised hers as well, but she stared down at Del with piercing eyes, as if threatening him to not prove her choice a poor one. Kashryn thought long and hard and then let out a low grunt before raising his paw.

"Whiskers to the fire," he grunted.

"All against?" asked Rowena.

Otger, to no one's surprise, raised his paw. "I hope you're all happy," he growled. "I can practically hear the chez draining from the treasury."

"It is settled," said Rowena, a smile wrinkling her cheeks. "Welcome to the Longtails, Del Hatherhorne."

Del exhaled a breath he hadn't realized he was holding. He thanked the Council and then excused himself. He quickly ran from the room and promptly threw up what little breakfast he had eaten. Who would have thought he could get himself into so much trouble in such a short amount of time?

*   *   *

The following evening, a burial service was held for Sir Roderick. His body was laid out on a bed of ferns, that had been positioned to look like wings. The deceased was then burned, and as the embers floated up to the sky, it was believed that the mouse's soul left this earthly plane and soared up to traverse the heavens. From above, the dead were able to look down and offer guidance to the mice they'd left behind. Del wondered if Roderick would look down on him with pride or shame.

Tomorrow he would be officially inducted into the Longtails. He would train in survival skills and basic weapons handling, but there was little the mouse teachers could do to educate him on his own innate abilities. He was one of a kind. The Longtails strongly believed in learning on the job anyway. Therefore, shortly after his induction and preliminary training, he would be assigned to a band at the lowest rank. He would apprentice to the mice in his band, learning their ways and earning his right to be a full-fledged member. This meant that the predominant part of his training would occur in the field and on assigned missions. Young mice in training were called Rooks, and though he was older than most when they joined the Longtails, he was no less a novice.

"He was a great mouse," said Denya, who appeared by his side.

"Yeah," Del replied, mostly because he wasn't sure what else to say.

"You didn't really know him, though," said Denya, a coldness to her voice he hadn't heard before. "I stood up for you today because it's what he would have wanted. But make no mistake, you still have a lot to learn and a long way to go before you'll be worthy of his sacrifice." She attempted to stifle tears that were beginning to collect and fall from her eyes. "Honestly, you may never be."

Del bid a silent farewell to any hope that Denya might be his friend.

"You'll be joining our band," she continued. "I just found out. We're getting a new Alpha too. One chosen especially for your . . . special needs."

"They've found someone to train me?" asked Del, cautiously excited.

"Or to stop you if you lose yourself in another fit of destruction. It's hard to say. He's from the mountains to the south. Mice out there are trained killers. I heard they have to take down a deer all by themselves as a rite of passage."

Del swallowed his fear and tried to suppress the urge to throw up again. He hoped he was not the next monster on this mouse's hunt.

"The team's going to be completely new, it seems," she continued. "Don't get too comfy, Rook. I'll be as hard on you as Roderick was on me." She bowed her head towards Roderick's body, which burned silently. A crowd of Longtails stood in a large circle around it, their heads bowed in solemnity. "His training was effective because he didn't accept mediocrity. And I will be no different. As far as I'm concerned, if you don't at some point regret turning down prison as an option, then I'll have failed you as a mentor."

She turned to Del, whose eyes were wide open. He was trying to look brave, but his quivering whiskers betrayed him. He didn't dare tell her he already regretted his choice a little.

She shook her head and sighed. "If you'll excuse me, I need to pay my respects. I'll see you after your introductory training, provided you don't topple another building right on top of yourself during it." She moved towards the inner circle to be nearer to Roderick. He watched her as she knelt down next to the smoldering corpse and said a silent prayer. A single tear rolled down her furry cheek.

She was right. He was a long way from deserving the sacrifice Sir Roderick had made for him. His thoughts drifted to a favorite character of his, Izuku Midoriya from *My Hero Academia*. In a world where almost everyone developed super powers, Midoriya was born with no abilities at all. Yet he did everything he could to become a true hero, despite the odds. He worked harder than all the rest.

Del had a power inside of him. He didn't know how to use it or what it meant for his future, but he could no longer deny it. If he could give it his all, just like Midoriya, then maybe, just maybe, he could learn to control his power.

He pushed the hopeful thought aside and bowed his head, silently wishing Sir Roderick Kegglefite happiness and peace in the next life.

Roderick had said that his story was ending and Del's was beginning. But that wasn't quite right. Roderick was off to join the mice in the heavens, and Del was leaving his old life to join the Longtails. It was not a beginning nor an end, but a new chapter.

For both of them.

CHAPTER FIVE

The One-Eyed Demon

"We're quite fortunate that you were able to take on the Alpha role of this band on such short notice," said Rowena, adjusting her spectacles as she peered down from the Council desk. Below the five members stood a solitary mouse. And though they were the leaders of the realm, some of the Council—namely Meadow—found this particular mouse to be imposing.

His attire, like that of all those who followed the way of the Demon, was strongly inspired by traditional Asian attire. Long ago, a nomadic group of mice had stumbled upon what they believed to be a monastery in the Grizzly Hills to the south. In reality, it had served as a human dojo for a myriad of martial arts. After researching the ways of the people who had once studied there, they had adopted many of the traditions into their own culture. Since then, the nomads had divided into three clans: the Demons, the Ghosts, and the Ascended.

As a Demon, he wore a black haori jacket, with fine golden embroidery on the arms and down the seams, over a black kimono and matching hakama pants. On his back was sheathed a long, gently curved katana, its handle sticking out over his shoulder. A wakizashi blade, much smaller than the katana, hung from a sash at his waist. He also wore a pair of black sandals, despite the fact that mice rarely ever wore shoes, for fear that it would make running or climbing too difficult. Perhaps his most distinctive features though, were his coal-black fur and the eye patch which covered his left eye. His dark fur and clothing made him look like a walking shadow.

"I needed a change, you needed an Alpha," grunted the mouse in a gruff voice. "Just good timing, I suppose."

"Yes . . ." Rowena responded cautiously. Most mice were in awe of the Council. This one just seemed bored. "You understand the mission then?" she asked. Meanwhile, Meadow attempted to cower as subtly as possible behind her.

"We're escorting a honey merchant to his home at the Tower of Toleloo," replied the Demon. "Seems pretty cut and dry to me." It was as if the objective of the mission was so simple that it barely needed doing. Despite his demeanor, escort missions like this one were an important part of the Longtails' duties.

"And that is precisely what you will tell your band," remarked Kashryn, leaning forward.

The Demon peered up with his one eye. At last, something had piqued his interest.

"Your mission is actually two-fold," clarified Rowena. "But the first part is more of a cover. This next bit is your *real* mission. And as you can imagine, it is of utmost secrecy. The very existence of such a mission could raise panic in the Mouselands."

The Demon grunted, which was the closest he ever came to laughing. "A Trelock on my team and a secret mission. And here I thought this wasn't going to be exciting."

"Heed this warning," said Rowena. "You must not share your true purpose with anyone, not even your band members. We have one chance at this. Give your intentions away too soon, and you will endanger all of us. Do I make myself clear?"

The Demon made eye contact with each Council member, one at a time, then nodded.

"Then we shall proceed," Rowena declared curtly.

The Council laid out his mission for him. His *real* mission.

When a missive had arrived at the monastery, begging Kando Nakatomi to return to Verden to join the Longtails, the question that kept circling in his mind was *why?* The

Longtails had plenty of good officers who could lead a band; plenty of mice who could attempt to train a Trelock—though truthfully, he still wasn't sure he even believed one to exist. So why ask *him?* It wasn't the offer of pay or prestige that had convinced him to pack his bags and leave Handies Peak where the monastery stood. It was that singular question.

By the time he left the Council chamber, he had his answer.

*　　　　*　　　　*

Del ran haphazardly through the narrow towering hallways of the Longtails building. He passed by several mice clad in armor and others in billowing robes, and each time asked them for directions to the Briefing Chamber. They told him so many rights and so many lefts, and he followed their directions closely, or so he thought. Yet somehow, he managed to get even more lost than before.

He should have left his quarters earlier. He knew that. But the night prior, unable to sleep due to anxiety, he'd instead lost himself in the Longtails' private library on the first floor. Somehow, he had managed to dig up a copy of *Wild Times*, a book about the creation of an old comic book studio called WildStorm, which had created some of his favorite comics. He had continued late into the night, searching through old tomes chronicling magic and warriors of past ages. All of these books were covered in dust and

85

looked as though no one had touched them since the times of men. Eventually, he found a book which appeared to be a strategy guide for playing through *The Legend of Zelda*. It wasn't quite the same as playing the game, but the vivid imagery and solutions to several puzzles helped Del to calm his nerves regarding the first day with his new band.

His course work over the last few weeks had been a whirlwind. He learned everything from the Longtails Code and their history, to basic survival skills, such as tying knots, erecting tents and foraging for food. Del found that he excelled at anything involving books or the memorization of information, but utterly failed when it came to actual survival skills. It was only by the thinnest strand of hair that he had passed his final tests, and thereby earned the right to start training with his band. He was grateful and comforted by the fact that he would no longer be scrutinized by the instructors, looking down their long noses dismissively at him, or fellow students, who were much younger than him and laughed at him when they thought he wasn't looking.

That comfort was fleeting as it was soon replaced by fear and anxiety. Being late on his first day was not going to sit well with Denya and whoever had been chosen as the team's new Alpha. *Why even get a new Alpha?* Del happened to think that Denya would've made a fine Alpha herself. She seemed confident and had a good head on her shoulders. He thought she was the most impressive ladymouse he'd ever known in real life, not that his knowledge of ladymice was extensive or anything.

At long last, he found the designated room and marched in, hoping to not make a scene as he adjusted his new green traveling cloak and old knit scarf. He didn't carry a weapon. He had failed miserably with each one he had tried during his training. It had been decided that he was safer to himself and his band without one, for the time being. There was already abundant uneasiness that he might bring down another city block; accidentally cutting someone's paw off didn't need to be added to the list of concerns. His instructors claimed that not having a weapon would force Del to hone his natural skills more quickly. He was not so optimistic.

The room was round and cramped, built inside the wall to be mouse-sized, as opposed to the building itself, which was originally used as a county office by humans before they'd gone extinct. Wood paneling adorned the walls as well as several shelves filled with old, yellowing scrolls. In the center of the room was a round table made of birchwood, upon which sat a map of the Mouselands and all the connecting territories.

Denya scowled at him with her arms crossed. This seemed to amuse Arthur, who leaned against the wall at the back of the room, chewing on a piece of bread.

"You're late," she said.

"I know," Del replied. "I got lost."

"In the wild, that's how you die," snapped Denya.

"We ought to put that on the recruitment posters," Arthur interjected giddily. He seemed to be in a much better mood than Denya as he held up a paw, imagining a make-believe advertisement out loud. *"Get lost in the Longtails. In the wild, that's how you die!"*

"Remind me not to be near you before I've eaten my morning coffee bean," said Denya, pulling a withered black bean from her side satchel and taking a bite out of it. Del noticed the leather book hanging sideways on her back over her tail.

"What's in that book?" asked Del, hoping to distract Denya with questions. "I must say, I do love a good book. If I'd known we could bring them along—"

She glared at him, and he abruptly stopped talking. She rolled her eyes. "If you must know, it is my collection of recipes."

"Recipes?" Del echoed. "Like, cooking recipes?"

"More like recipes that'll save your life when a snake bites you." This answer came from a deep voice coming from the room's entrance. They all became silent and looked towards the doorway where Kando stood, filling the passage with his girth. He wore a scowl across his black face. Del swallowed loudly, internalizing his fear. *How did he lose one of his eyes?!*

"Don't you mean *if* a snake bites us?" Del asked hesitantly.

Kando merely stared at him, unamused.

"Sir!" Denya and Arthur saluted, holding their right arms laterally across their chests with their elbows bent and their paws made into a facedown fist. They bowed their heads slightly as a sign of respect. Del, noticing this, followed suit.

"You're meant to kneel," said Denya through gritted teeth.

"You're not kneeling," he whispered back.

"I'm not a *Rook*," she hissed. Del quickly got down on one knee.

The Demon's face was expressionless as he addressed them. "My name is Kando Nakatomi," he said. His voice sounded like something heavy being dragged through gravel. "As of right now, I am your new Alpha." He stepped up to the map atop the central table. "Our mission is simple. We are to escort a honey merchant back to his home in Toleloo. His sales this season were exceptional, so his honey jars will be empty, but residue on the jars will still create a scent which might attract unwanted attention. We are to see to it that the merchant arrives safely home. That is all." Kando glared at the map, as if pondering the route they might take.

"Toleloo?" asked Del. "You mean, the great mouse tower?" He'd never been there, of course, but supposedly, scientifically-inclined mice with a thirst for knowledge had commandeered a tall skyscraper, overgrown with the roots of a huge tree, and turned it into a labyrinth for all forms of creation and research. Technological salvage from the old world was often brought there to be studied and reverse-engineered, eventually giving way to the creation of something new.

At the top of the tower was said to be a huge beehive from which mice harvested honey. This honey was shared throughout the Mouselands, but was also used in the tower for medical research, due to its powerful curative abilities. Besides the medicinal benefits, the honey tasted incredible and was used by chefs to create delicious culinary dishes.

"Rooks may only speak when spoken to," said Kando coldly. "Prepare yourselves for the travel north. We'll all meet with the merchant at the Northern Gate. Adjourned."

"Excuse me, sir," Denya interrupted. She suddenly felt quite nervous.

Kando shot her a piercing glare with his singular eye. "What?"

"Oh, it's just that, perhaps you could tell us a little about yourself. I find it helps to know a bit about each other. Helps us to work together." She smiled, hoping that might help her case. She desperately missed Roderick, but that didn't mean she wouldn't do everything in her power to make this new team work. It was what he would have wanted.

"Don't mind her," said Arthur. "She's a sap, that one. Always getting on about her feelings."

Kando glared blankly at Arthur. Silence fell over the room. As if no one had spoken, Kando turned and exited.

"Well, he seems like a pleasant chap," remarked Arthur sarcastically.

Denya sighed. "The first time we met Roderick, he was hard on us too. I'm sure Kando will soften up after a while."

"Or he'll slit our throats in our sleep," replied Arthur.

"Would he really do that?" asked Del, terror in his eyes.

"I wouldn't be surprised," said Arthur, trying to put on a creepy voice. "He comes from Handies Peak. The mice up there bathe in the blood of their enemies. For all we know, *they're* the ones helping the minks get into the city. Dark deeds in the dead of night. Collusion with the minks and porcupines of the south. Trading secrets for poppy seeds. Trading lives for a drink of fine wine. Perhaps he was sent here at our time of greatest uncertainty to throw us off the trail and quietly exterminate the legendary *Trelock*."

"Oh, Arthur, do you ever shut up?" asked Denya, annoyed by his ramblings.

"Is any of that true?" asked Del. His tail was shaking nervously. "Would mice really work with the minks? Do you really think they'd send a mouse to get rid of me? I thought I was supposed to be safer here."

"The only thing real that comes out of Arthur's mouth is his foul breath," said Denya. "He's just trying to scare you. Come on. We all need to prepare for the journey."

She left the room, followed by Del, who looked back just in time to see Arthur breathing into his paw and smelling it, then shrugging. Apparently, he didn't see the problem.

*   *   *

At the north, south, east and west city limits, large gated walls had been built to keep out unwelcome guests and to help monitor anyone coming in or out of Verden. These massive walls encircled the entire city. While high enough to keep out smaller animals like porcupines or ferrets, it stood little hope against larger animals like wolves or moose. Luckily, most of those animals were not natural predators to the mice and kept to their own lands. The wall had never been attacked head-on to test its strength, so it was perhaps more symbolic than anything else to the mice within its walls that they and their pups were safe.

Del didn't have much in the way of belongings, due to his house having been destroyed. He had only the cloak on his back, a small pouch for water, and a satchel filled with bread, fruit and nuts for the journey ahead. His scarf was his only true possession, and it hung loosely around his neck, a warm reminder of the life Del was leaving behind.

As he approached the Northern Gate, he saw Denya speaking to an old mouse who was leaning against a long cart filled with empty glass jars, speckled with the last golden remains of the honey they once held. The cart was fastened to the backs of two gigantic beetles standing side by side. Though Del knew that these pack animals were docile so long as you didn't spook them, they looked quite threatening with their large tusks and glossy black shells. Denya wore a brown tunic and a red traveling cloak; her book was strapped to her back as usual.

"'Tis mighty kind of you Longtails to assist me back to the tower," said the old mouse. He had gray fur, and his back was hunched over slightly. A large set of glasses balanced atop his nose and he wore a blue apron tied around his back and neck. Despite his old age, he was fairly muscular. In fact, Del got the feeling that the old mouse was capable of wheeling the cart of jars all by himself, without the help of any beetles.

"No need for thanks," said Denya kindly. "It is our pleasure to serve." She turned and noticed Del approaching. Her smile immediately faded. "Looks like you managed to not get lost this time, eh, Rook?" she mocked.

"Ah, a new recruit," said the old mouse. "I remember my first days of honey gatherin'. My master scrutinized my every movement, day and night." He leaned towards Del as if to tell a secret. "But it made me the fine mouse you see today."

"Rook, this is Sir Inneous Cromwell, the mouse we'll be escorting on this mission," said Denya importantly.

Inneous Cromwell gave a frail wave of his paws. "Blech! No need for such formalities. Call me Crom. That's an order!" He gave an exaggerated salute.

Del's mind immediately thought of Conan the Barbarian, who worshiped a god named Crom. *Get to the choppa!* Why couldn't Del think about Arnold without that line? Maybe this too was a symptom of being a Trelock.

"If that's what you'd prefer," said Denya.

"What if we call you Inny?" came the cool voice of Arthur. "Or perhaps Wellkins?"

"Arthur DeGandia!" exclaimed Crom. He gave Arthur a big hug. "As I live and breathe."

"Not for much longer, I'd say, eh, old chap?" said Arthur, plucking a gray hair from the mouse's head. Crom let out a hearty chuckle.

"Whiskers to the fire," scoffed Denya, realizing she'd be sharing the road with the two of them for the next several days.

"It's noon," said a gruff voice. They all fell silent and turned to see Kando approaching them. He was eyeing a small golden pocket watch, which he quickly returned to his coat pocket. "We should be leaving."

"Punctuality!" exclaimed Crom. "I like that in a mouse. Let's get to gettin' then." He stepped up onto a little wooden seat and gave the beetles a thwap of the reins. They immediately started scuttling forward.

Kando handed a small scroll to the gatekeeper, a large mouse clad in heavy metal armor. Del thought he looked like Alphonse Elric from the manga *Full Metal Alchemist*. Alphonse was a human whose soul had been transmutated through alchemy and bound to a hollow suit of armor. Unlike Alphonse, though, the gatekeeper's flesh and blood body was clearly visible within his metal armor.

The gatekeeper quickly scanned the scroll and then handed it back. He gave a wave to several mice atop the wall and within moments, the gate began to lift out of their way, clearing the path with a heavy groan.

"Pleasure seeing you again, Crom," said the guard heartily.

"Pleasure's all mine," replied the old mouse.

"This one here sells the finest honey in the Mouselands," said the guard to the band, not speaking to anyone in particular. "But watch out. It filled me so well, I had to nap to recover. Better than any draught or sleeping potion, I'd wager. Dreamed of bees buzzing and sugar canes, I did."

"Happy to hear you enjoyed it!" exclaimed Crom. "I'll be sure to bring more next time."

With a wave to the guard, the group filed through the gate. Del gave one last look back at the city he'd spent his whole life in. This would be the farthest he'd ever been from home. He was Samwise Gamgee following Frodo to Mordor. He only hoped he'd live to make it back in one piece.

CHAPTER SIX

A Feast for Shrikes

The world beyond Verden's walls wasn't much unlike the world within it. Man-made homes were smaller but still lined the streets in parallel rows. The overgrown foliage was far worse though. Trees had burst through the pavement, devouring cars and structures. Several houses were completely demolished by tall trees which had grown right through their connecting rooms and roof. Leaves and branches blanketed the sky so that the sun came down in infrequent shafts, making everything seem darker and more dangerous. Del's eyes couldn't decide what to focus on. Everything around him was completely new. He'd seen trees, houses and cars before, but never outside the safety of Verden's walls. Was there really danger around every corner as he'd been told? He wasn't sure. Now and then he heard the sound of a bird cawing in the distance, and sometimes a cricket chirp would break the eerie silence. Each time this happened, his fur would stand on end for a short time. Other than that, the only sound was the steady rolling of the cart wheels, the skittering of the beetles pulling the cart, and Crom, who liked to regale them with stories, even if no one particularly wanted to hear them.

"When I was a young mouse, I used to come out here with my buddies and play in the abandoned cars," said Crom. Kando soldiered forward while Denya and Arthur walked on either side of the old mouse's cart, listening to him with one ear and listening for danger with the other. Del was in charge of bringing up the rear and making sure nothing got the jump on them. It was more responsibility than he'd ever been given in his entire life. Kando was right. They were going to get bitten by a snake, and it was going to be his fault.

"Whole mess of wires and metal in those things. We'd play hide-and-seek, and sometimes you couldn't even find yourself. My friend Racatel got stuck in a pipe inside one of them things. Took us a whole day to get him out. Thumping on the metal. That was the trick. Had to lead him out with the noise. Poor thing was so traumatized, he joined the Golds just so he could pray all day. He's a high-ranking member now, but I'll bet you five chez he still sleeps with the candles lit."

"Any life path is better than no path, I suppose," remarked Arthur.

"I suppose," sighed Crom. "But Racky used to be so full of the adventurous spirit. Sad to see it go to waste, but then again, growing up is all about change. I don't suppose anyone thought I'd end up a honey peddler, but here I am. I've been buying honey off the harvesters in Toleloo and marching it down to Verden ever since I can remember. Well, me an' my wife Delilah, that is. She prefers the business side more'n me, though—balancing the books and what not. I like the part which requires the talkin.' The wheelin' and the dealin', if you know what I mean." He chuckled to himself. No one was surprised to find that he preferred the talking part of business.

Crom looked around at his captive audience before focusing his gaze on Denya. "You look awfully familiar, young ladymouse," he said.

"Just one of those faces," she replied, averting her eyes.

The foliage surrounding the path they were following steadily became thicker. By midday, barely any sun managed to sneak past the thick blanket of leaves above them. Del noticed that there were no more birds singing or crickets chirping. There wasn't even a breeze. It was as if the world was holding its breath. Suddenly, Kando held up a fist, halting the group.

"Bathroom break already?" asked Arthur, grinning deviously.

"We're being watched," said Kando, staring up into the trees above.

Everyone in the party immediately looked up towards the treetops. Arthur placed a paw on his rapier. Denya shoved her paws into her satchel. Kando rested his free paw on the hilt of the katana on his back. They waited. Nothing happened.

"You sure about that?" asked Crom. "I don't see nothing."

"*Anything*," corrected Arthur, as if it were second nature.

"Eh?" asked Crom.

"You don't see *anything*. It's the proper way to say it."

"Quiet," snapped Denya. Her ears perked up, listening intently to the world around them.

"Where are we right now on the map?" asked Kando, his eyes locking on Del, who had been entrusted with the map. Map duty, he was told, was often given to the Rook so that they could better learn the lay of the land and its various paths, trails and roads.

Del clumsily pulled a scroll from his pack and stretched it out in between his paws, his eyes darting around as he tried to pinpoint their exact location. "We should be just south of Toleloo," he replied. "Hmm, that's weird." He felt his stomach drop. "I was sure we were supposed to take a left at that last fork."

"Where *are* we, Rook?" pressed Kando, who looked as though he might use his sword on Del instead of whatever was waiting above.

"We turned left when we should have gone right." He gulped, averting his gaze from the other mice, who might as well have been shooting poison out of their eyes at him. "That would put us..." He traced the path with a claw. "Here." His expression turned grim as he looked up over the top of the map at Kando. *The Thorn Bush.*"

"Everyone needs to find cover," Kando snapped.

"The Thorn Bush?" Denya asked. "You mean, shrike territory?"

"Now!" barked Kando.

At his command, they all bolted towards a nearby car with green vines and small white flowers growing from its dashboard. Del brought up the rear of the group, staying behind the cart as the beetles leading it scurried towards the derelict vehicle. There was a sudden whoosh of air as a shadow passed over them. Was it a bird? *Or a plane?* Del cursed his overactive imagination. It was definitely too small to be a hawk or an owl, let alone *Superman.*

Slam! A small bird, only slightly larger than a sparrow, crashed into the honey cart, toppling it over sideways. It had gray feathers, a white underbelly, a black band accentuating its eyes, and black-edged wing tips. Crom went skidding across the pavement along with the jars, which clinked loudly as they rolled. The beetles fell over themselves trying to escape, all twelve legs flailing wildly.

"Stay low!" yelled Denya

Del dashed for Crom instinctively. The old mouse lay on the ground grabbing at his knee with one paw and shoving a honey jar off of himself with the other. "My leg!" he cried. "I think it's broken!"

Del knelt down and put an arm under the mouse. "We need to get under the car," he said. Denya was making a run for them. A shadow appeared overhead, and Del looked up just in time to see a shrike diving towards them with open talons. There was a loud *bang* as one of Denya's bombs hit the shrike from the side and knocked it off course. It toppled sideways and hit the ground, rolling a few times before righting itself. It quickly stood up, shook off its wings and took off once more.

Del lifted Crom, allowing the older mouse to lean on him for support. "I've got you," said Del, not entirely confident in his statement as his legs rattled beneath him.

Crom smiled at him. "Thank you, lad," he said.

"Can you walk?" asked Del.

Crom didn't have a chance to answer. Instead, he cried out as a shrike grabbed him around his midsection and yanked him into the air. Del, holding on tightly, lifted skyward with them, hanging on for dear life.

"Del!" cried Denya from below, reaching out to them.

They ascended quickly, much faster than Del had thought possible. He had always wondered what it felt like to fly. So many superheroes did it all the time. Now he knew. It was absolutely terrifying. He would mark it off the bucket list and then throw the bucket list in the garbage.

"AHHHHHH!" Del screamed.

"Gah!" choked Crom. Del stopped screaming and looked up at the old mouse. One of the bird's talons was buried in Crom's side. A small stream of blood trickled from the wound and fell behind them as they flew.

Del tried to focus. Had he read anything about birds of prey? He *had* read *Birds of Prey,* the iconic comic book series originally featuring a partnership between Black Canary and Barbara Gordon. It had eventually featured several other awe-inspiring female heroes as well. *Not those Birds of Prey!*

He shook off the thought and tried to be more specific with his memory recall. He needed to know about shrikes. Hadn't one of his classes over the past few weeks mentioned birds? Yes, as he thought more about it, an image of old Professor Milton came to mind, standing in front of a board displaying several different birds of varying sizes, all lined up next to each other.

Del closed his eyes, visualizing the words under the relatively small drawing of a shrike. *Shrikes are birds of prey but not in the same sense as hawks or eagles*. He could just make out a small notation written hastily in white chalk: *They often toy with their food before impaling it on any available sharp point. They then feed on the body over time.*

Del opened his eyes. He turned his head as much as he could while still holding on, searching the ground for any obvious sharp points. Not far off, he saw it—a thorn bush. Its twisting, curling branches were covered in sharp, menacing spikes. He stifled his breath, trying not to vomit all over Crom and their attacker.

"It's taking us to that thorn bush!" he shouted to Crom. "It's going to drop us into it!"

"Wouldn't it make more sense just to eat us?" asked Crom, his voice noticeably weaker.   "Where's the fun in that?" asked the shrike, speaking for the first time. Her voice was high and shrill with excitement over the dark deed she was about to perform. To her, this was all a game.

"We're actually having more of a private conversation," retorted Del. "If you don't mind."   It was one of the wittier things he'd ever said, and he couldn't help but wonder if Arthur was rubbing off on him.

"What a coincidence," cackled the shrike. "I'm about to have a *private* dinner." Del rolled his eyes. If Denya were there, she would never have allowed such banter in the middle of a life or death flight. He took a deep breath, then crawled up Crom to the shrike's bony leg. He opened his mouth as wide as it would go and imagined a delicious red apple, before biting down hard.

*   *   *

A blood-curdling screech rang out from above as Denya and Arthur watched the shrike that had taken Crom and Del veer sideways, losing control and flapping frantically as it tried to stay airborne.

"We have to help them!" shouted Denya.

"We have to help us first," replied Arthur. His sword was drawn as he looked up at the watch of shrikes circling them. With every swoop and dive, the vicious birds were attempting to hook their talons into the mice. The two of them leapt out of the way, hopping back and forth across the pavement like rabbits. Denya dodged one bird by rolling towards the car, but another shrike immediately converged on her, its talons outstretched. She shielded her face, ready to take the attack.

The cruel sound of tearing flesh filled the air as blood splattered the ground, filling her nostrils with a putrid coppery smell. The shrike pursuing her crashed into the ground in a flurry of feathers, it's body sliced in half through its midsection. Kando stood over the bird, his katana held firmly in both paws. He glared at Denya. His chest rose and fell easily beneath his black kimono, as if he were enjoying a gentle breeze, rather than fighting for his life. Blood dripped from the blade, forming ripples in the already spilled pool at his feet. He flicked his wrist, sending the blood flying from the blade, leaving its edge clean.

"Stop hopping around like a cricket and fight back," he said. Denya could sense his shame in her. She gave herself a brief moment to process the feeling, then stood up straight.

She nodded, trying to ignore the warm, splattered blood of the shrike that had doused her fur, then reached for her pack and pulled out two small bombs. Looking up to the sky, she reeled back her paws and then hurled the bombs at the shrikes, catching two as they converged on Arthur.

"*Firenze!*" Arthur yelled, holding up his free paw and shooting out a blast of blue fire. The spell knocked several shrikes out of the sky. As another descended, he spun his rapier and stabbed it up into the shrike's chin while smoothly sidestepping its open beak. He quickly pulled the sword free, letting the bird's momentum send it careening to the ground.

Scarlets were known for their versatility of skill. Many mice referred to them as battle mages because they could fight with both a sword and magic at the same time. They were a jack of both trades, but a master of neither. Arthur was considered one of the stronger members of the class, but even his magic had its limits. As the shrike onslaught continued, he felt his body start to tire and weaken. Wielding the sword drained his muscles; wielding the magic drained his energy. He was burning the candle at both ends and the wax was almost gone.

The watch circled them like a tornado of black and gray feathers. The three mice backed into one another, creating a defensive circle.

"Well, this is a bit of a predicament," said Arthur.

Kando looked up at the birds with his singular eye, assessing the situation. "The odds are against us," he said. "But that doesn't mean we've lost."

"Looks pretty hopeless to me," said Arthur. "Perhaps if we surrender, they'll go easy on us."

"Longtails do not surrender," Kando stated bluntly. He thought to himself for a moment, muttering rapidly as he worked to devise a solution, then suddenly looked up, as if inspiration had hit him. "Denya, do you have any Light Paw Solution?"

Denya rummaged around in her satchel, pulling out a small vial filled with a white cloud. "Right here," she said.

Light Paw Solution was a difficult concoction to mix, and a bizarre one to use. After drinking it, a mouse was able to defy the normal rules of physics for a short time. She'd made the solution months ago but had yet to find a reason to use it, other than floating around like a balloon when no one was watching.

"DeGandia," snapped Kando, referring to Arthur by his last name. "Do you know the Vortex Incantation?"

"Know it?" Arthur snorted pompously. "I wrote a dissertation on it."

"Knowing it will be plenty," said Kando. "I've got an idea."

*   *   *

The screeching shrike shook its leg, desperately trying to get Del to stop biting him. All the while, the bird flapped erratically closer and closer to the thorn bush. Biting her leg had caused her to release Crom but being so many feet above the ground still meant that Del had to grab Crom with his paw, while holding onto the bird with his teeth so that they didn't plummet to their deaths. Del did the only thing that made sense in the frenzied moment. He bit down harder.

The shrike screamed yet again, then spun wildly, until at last they crashed into the thorn bush, precisely what Del was trying to avoid. The force of the collision ripped the bird's leg from Del's jaws, and flecks of blood and skin came off in his mouth. A thorn branch smacked him across the chest as he continued to fall, causing him to release his grip on Crom. With nothing left to hold onto, he haphazardly grabbed a thornless section of branch and swung himself upwards, narrowly avoiding a menacing black thorn below him.

With his body no longer in freefall, Del panted heavily, trying to catch his breath while forcing himself not to run away and hide. Not running away to hide took a great amount of effort. His instincts were begging him to scurry to the nearest hiding hole and wait for all the commotion to pass. But Crom was still in danger. He couldn't just leave the old mouse. He thought of Roderick, who was brave in the face of danger. *What would Roderick do?*

Del carefully pulled himself up, over and under the branches, searching for any sign of Crom. It didn't take long to locate the honey peddler, hanging limply from a cluster of thorn-covered branches. Blood trickled down from his body like rain droplets long after the storm has finally subsided. A slight rise and fall of his chest told Del that he was still breathing, but just barely.

"Crom!" Del swung his way through the branches, narrowly avoiding all the thorns which seemed to be beckoning him to fall upon them. One snagged at his shoulder, ripping at his flesh and another, at his knee. But he kept moving forward. Finally, he reached Crom and cradled the old mouse's head in his paws.

"Talk to me," Del pleaded. Crom had cuts, scrapes and gashes all over his body. The scene reminded Del of how Captain America had looked after his death at the end of the Civil War—the comic, not the movie. The only thing that was missing was a red, white and blue shield laying over the mouse's chest.

"It's not good, m'boy," said Crom. His voice was barely a whisper.

"We'll get you out of here," said Del. "I'm sure Denya and the others are coming to help us right now. Just hang on."

Suddenly, the thicket around them thrashed wildly. Del grasped onto a nearby branch, cutting his paw on a thorn. He turned to see the enraged shrike twisting its way through the brush to get to them. If ever the phrase *you should see the other guy* applied, it was then. The shrike was bleeding from its head, back and wings. It looked as though it had gotten into a fight with a blender and lost. Yet somehow the bird was still standing, and it had no intention of dying before getting its revenge.

"Surprise!" she screeched. "Didn't think you'd get away so easily, did you?"

"Not really," Del sighed, pulling on Crom to get him free of the thorns. "But I was hoping we might just go our separate ways... agree to eat other rodents."

"Aw, but I've got my heart set on eating YOU!" She flapped her wings viciously, tearing at the branches, thrashing and twisting towards them, despite the thorns digging mercilessly into her feathers.

"Come on, come on, COME ON!" yelled Del, carefully lifting Crom off the thorns. With a sudden lurch, Crom's skin pulled free of the thorns and they both fell backwards. Del held desperately to Crom with one paw and to a bare branch with the other. "I've got you!" Crom didn't respond. Del pulled him, heading for the light coming through the brush, away from the shrike. He hoped the light would lead to someplace safer.

He forced their way through the branches slowly but surely. The bird was getting closer but so was the light. They were almost free. Crom cried out in pain. At least he was still alive. Del wanted to stop to check on the peddler, but there was no time.

The shrike's beak snapped greedily at their tails. Suddenly, Crom wouldn't budge. Del turned to see Crom's shirt snagged on a thorn, effectively trapping them. He looked up at the blood-thirsty bird and held out his paw.

If there was ever a time to use his power, it was now. He knew that. But knowing something and doing it were very different things. He had no idea how to access his power. No idea how to actually call the elements. No idea how to do anything that could save them. He imagined fire spewing forth from his paw to destroy the bird and the bush. Or maybe ice which could cut down the bird or block its attack.

But he couldn't focus on conjuring a wall of fire or ice, because the only image in his mind was that of his mother: looking on proudly as his brother showed her his most recent blooming flower and as his sister showed her the acceptance letter welcoming her to start working in the libraries. And then his mother looked at Del, and the pride vanished from her expression, replaced only by disappointment. And why wouldn't she feel that way? He was disappointing.

The bird snapped its beak at them and Del shook off the thought. If he was going to shoot fire at the bird, it was now or never. He yelled the only thing he could think of that might summon fire.

"Flame on!" he cried, channeling the Human Torch.

But nothing happened. He was not the Human Torch. He wasn't even the Mouse Torch. He was more of a Mouse Unlit Candle, and there was no room in the Fantastic Four for an unlit candle. For all intents and purposes, he was powerless. The bird screeched and freed herself from the thorns pressing in around her. Her body crashed forward, taking both herself and the mice by surprise. Her beak came at them like a bulldozer. A ripping sound declared Crom's freedom, and the two of them were shoved through the last branches into the sunlight. They fell a short distance, then toppled to the ground.

Del had lost all sense of direction. He could just make out their shrike pursuer sticking out of the bush above them. He scurried away, but stopped, noticing that the shrike was no longer moving. A thorn had impaled the center of the bird's head. Its eyes had gone empty, and its beak drooped open. In her quest to eat them, she had killed herself, completely by accident.

Del let his head fall back as he laid on the rocky ground. He should have been happy to be alive, yet all he could think about was the image of his mother's disappointed face. She'd known he would never amount to anything. And now he knew it too. He was going to get himself and the others killed.

*   *   *

Kando reached for the bottle of Light Paw Solution, popped the cork from the top, and took a hearty swig of the cloudy mixture within. A rope had been tied around his waist in order to make sure he didn't simply float away. Denya gripped the tail end.

"Cast the spell," Kando commanded. "Aim it for the center of the flock above us."

"I'll be defenseless while casting," warned Arthur, sheathing his rapier and bringing his paws together, one palm on top of the other in front of him.

"I'll cover you," reassured Denya. At that moment, a shrike swooped down on them. Denya took one hand off the rope and whipped a bomb at the bird, knocking it off course. She didn't mention to the others that her bag was growing increasingly lighter, her stockpile of explosives rapidly depleting.

Arthur nodded, then began an intricate dance with his paws and fingers, whirling them over, under and around themselves so that it appeared as if he were giving himself a secret handshake. *"Virbel Gravitas,"* he said, igniting the spell. A black swirling mass appeared between his paws. As the distance between his palms became greater, the black mass grew. It was like a black hole was forming in front of him. *"Crescere!"* he said gently, as if the sound of his voice might have an effect on the spell. The mass expanded.

Another shrike attacked. Kando dodged out of the bird's path, then swung his katana in a sweeping upper-cut, lopping off its wing. The bird shrieked in agony and crashed into the pavement. "Anytime now!" he yelled at Arthur, his patience waning.

"Ready!" yelled Arthur, the mass barely contained in his small paws.

"Ready!" confirmed Kando.

"*Ascender!*" cried Arthur, hurling the black vortex up at the birds. The vortex had its own gravitational pull and quickly tugged the birds off course. A mixture of beaks, feathers and talons collided at the epicenter of the vortex and a raucous chorus of agitated caws filled the sky.

Kando readied his sword for a swing and closed his eyes. Then he flung his body and the katana into a whirling spin and leapt up into the center of the vortex. He was a mouse-sized buzz-saw, slicing mercilessly at the birds as the vortex pulled them to him. Blood and feathers rained down on Denya and Arthur.

As the vortex faded, Denya tugged at the rope, pulling Kando back to the ground. Any bird still able to fly took off, soaring away from the terrifying band of mice. Most of the shrikes fell to the ground, their bodies sliced in ways that made it impossible to survive. Kando landed softly, flicked his katana to clean the blood from it once more, then sheathed the weapon on his back.

Denya's heart sank as she took in the scene of death around them. She understood that the shrikes had meant to eat them, but something did not sit right with how the battle had ended. Kando had killed almost the entire watch. No, not just killed, *massacred*.

She was no stranger to violence. In the wild, it was often kill or be killed. But the Longtails always strived for peaceful and diplomatic solutions first. And even if that didn't work, they usually took more of a defensive stance, protecting themselves and others while causing the least amount of harm.

She felt her breath leave her chest, sorrow welling up inside her. She believed that all life was precious. Yet here she had aided the ending of many lives at once. Whole families of shrikes would now suffer because of her team's actions. She buried her emotions, remembering that first and foremost, her duty was to follow the commands of her Alpha.

"I suppose the shrikes will think twice about attacking us from now on," said Arthur. He was trying to be his normal sarcastic self, but Denya had known him long enough to hear the unease in his voice. "I imagine we'll become a cautionary tale for future generations."

After this, there may not be *any future generations*, thought Denya.

"There are far more where those came from," said Kando coldly. "They'll be back."

"Help!" called Del. They all turned to see him limping towards them down the street, carrying Crom over his shoulders. The honey peddler was covered in blood and his gray fur looked dull and matted. Denya ran to them and helped to lay Crom on the ground. She then pulled a vial full of red liquid from her satchel and poured it down his throat. He took a weak breath.

"Will it save him?" asked Del.

"It'll keep him alive for now," said Denya. "But he needs more healing than a potion can give him."

"Then we've no time to lose," said Kando. "Rook, gather the honey jars onto the cart and secure the beetles."

Del nodded and limped off towards the jars strewn across the ground.

"I'll help him," said Arthur, moving to follow Del. Kando grabbed his arm, stopping him short.

"You will do no such thing," said Kando.

"The boy is hurt. He can barely walk. It'll be faster if I help."

"He will do it on his own, and you will help get the peddler secured in the cart." They glared at each other, sizing each other up.

Finally, Arthur pulled his arm away, turning back towards Crom. "Yes, sir."

Del found that the movement of lifting the jars back into the cart actually helped his muscles to stretch and relax. By the time he was done, his limp was all but gone. He found the beetles hiding behind the flattened tire of a car. They were shaken and took a fair amount of coaxing to get back to the cart, but they were otherwise unharmed, thanks to their armored bodies.

"The tower isn't much further," said Kando.

"You hear that? You're going to be just fine," said Denya, brushing a paw over Crom's forehead. She wasn't sure she believed it, but hope was all she had to offer him. They'd need to hurry on to Toleloo if they were going to have any chance of saving him. She said a silent prayer that they'd make it in time.

CHAPTER SEVEN

The Tower of Toleloo

The Tower of Toleloo came into view long before they ever reached it. Even from far away it seemed massive, but as the band approached, it seemed to grow larger, and larger and larger still. Just when Del thought a building couldn't stretch any further into the sky, they'd walk for a time and he'd look up to find that the building had grown even more. In many ways, it reminded him of the tower from *The Lord of the Rings*, in which Sauron's eye resided. Not in shape, necessarily, but in the way it loomed menacingly over everything around it. It was the sole skyscraper in the area, surrounded by a large field and a few dilapidated single-story buildings.

But it wasn't *just* a building. An equally gigantic tree had interwoven itself up, in and through all 56 stories of the steel structure, so that it appeared as though the tree and the

117

building were one and the same. At the very top of the monolith was not Sauron's eye, but a flourish of branches and leaves, an awe-inspiring treetop which replaced the roof of the building. Because of this, it looked like the strange offspring of Stark Tower and the Tree of Life. It existed in a place between technology and nature.

Toleloo was like a fortress or a shrine, procured in the name of progress. Within its walls, science was pushed to new, often terrifying, heights. Magic was tested and twisted, revealing new spells and incantations. Despite its frightening nature, many mice called Toleloo home. And while new forms of destruction were created within its walls, it was also the birthplace of innovations in farming and sustainable energy. Verden may have been the heart of the Mouselands, but Toleloo was its ever-curious brain.

As the band approached, they came to a low, defensive wall made up of metal pillars placed every few feet, which shot several strands of electricity back and forth between themselves, making it a fence you'd only cross if you wanted to be struck by lightning. They walked to a gate which gave passage through the wall and waved to a mouse wearing a black leather coat and thick goggles. He held a small gun, a weapon not customary to mice in Verden. Unlike most guns, this one did not look like it shot bullets. Where a barrel should have been, there was a round metal orb. The gun itself was bulbous in nature and looked more like a toy than a weapon.

"Hold and state your business in the great Tower of Toleloo," the mouse ordered. His fur was white with gray spots, and his whiskers were clumped together in a great arch which peaked at his nose, making them look more like a fancy mustache.

"We are Longtails from Verden. We're on our way to bring this honey peddler home," said Denya, motioning to Crom.

"Looks like he was run over by a racoon's Slicer," said the guard as he glanced at Crom's battered body. The old mouse was breathing, but just barely.

"Our chap here is badly injured," said Arthur. "A nasty run-in with shrikes during our travels. He needs medical attention."

"A likely story," the guard scoffed, seemingly unconvinced. Del became acutely aware of how very beaten and battered the entire group of them looked. Longtails were meant to be proud and respectable. Their band looked like a ragamuffin group of scavengers, covered in dirt and dried blood, their shoulders slumping from exhaustion. "Any of you bringing in poppy seeds under those fancy outfits? Unauthorized weapons? Any plan to cause trouble in town?" asked the guard, eyeing each of them suspiciously in turn.

They all shook their heads and mumbled a collective "No, sir."

"Figured that'd be the answer, but we like to be safe." Suddenly he held up the gun and aimed it at them.

"Wait!" yelled Del, but he was too late. A blast of cold air hit them, sending a chill down Del's spine. They all glowed a gentle blue and then returned to their original color. Crom was the exception. He glowed a bright red before the color faded.

"W-what was that?" Del asked, afraid that he might explode or die of radiation poisoning at any moment.

"That gun is a truth ray," said Denya. "They use them to make sure no one is coming into the city that means to do other than they've declared."

"Fortunately," said the guard, holstering the weapon, "you all pass."

"Why'd Crom turn red?" asked Del. Kando shot him a menacing glare, making Del wish he hadn't asked.

"Mouse has got a fever, from the looks of it," the guard replied. "Probably doesn't even know where he is. Being in that rough of shape throws off the mind, messes with the results." The guard patted the gun. "But we don't typically scan residents of the tower anyway. It's you lot I've got to worry about."

He turned and typed in a code on a small monitor to the left of the gate. The monitor flashed green and the gate swung open. Kando, Arthur and Denya entered, with Del bringing up the rear as he guided the beetles and cart behind him. Crom continued to lay disturbingly still on the seat of the wooden cart, buried beneath several blankets to keep him warm.

Kando placed a paw on the guard's shoulder and spoke softly to him. "Send word to Inneous Cromwell's wife."

Inside the gate, the air smelled musty and tasted of various flavors. Hints of honey were permeated by a dash of smoke and something sour. They followed a dirt path towards the tower, and before long they reached the entrance without further delay. They entered through an enormous revolving door which turned automatically as they stepped inside it. Del picked up the pace so as not to be crushed by the door as it came up behind them.

"Wow." Astonishment washed over him as the door spun to reveal the interior of Toleloo. Somehow, unbelievably, it was even more spectacular on the inside than it had been on the outside. Somewhere in his head, Doctor Who was chuckling to himself. *It's bigger on the inside.*

The tower stretched high above them, further than he could even see with his small eyes. He looked up through the center of the building. It had been gutted from the entry floor all the way up to the top of the building, where a swarm of bees gently buzzed around a honeycomb. A network of cables and hinge-based pulley systems were set up throughout the tower in an interconnected system of lifts, built for raising and lowering mice to the floor of their choosing. A cacophony of noise flooded the air: metallic clanks, steam whistles, digital beeps and boops, jangling bells, rhythmically-beating hammers, an occasional small-scale explosion, and shopkeepers—shouting out sales and specials in the hopes of enticing customers to their booths. Del had a hard time distinguishing between all the sounds, with so many hitting his ears at once. He was reminded of young Clark Kent, before he became Superman, who had to try to filter out all the noise that bombarded his super hearing.

And there were lights. So many colors and sizes of lights. Red, green, white, yellow, all flashing, twinkling and filling the air with a strange sort of haze. It was as if Toleloo were challenging the sun for who could be brighter, and Toleloo was winning!

The tower was multi-purposed as a research center, a market, and a network of homes. The ground floor was filled with shops of all shapes and sizes: minimal makeshift stalls, pubs, inns and restaurants built of stone atop a dirt-covered marble floor. You could buy anything your heart desired: pots for cooking, books for studying or leisure, fine jewelry, garments made of only the finest cloth, or the perfect potion. It was all available—provided you had enough chez in your pockets.

The next fifteen floors above the market were settlements of small homes—mouse-sized, unlike Del's human-sized apartment—all built into the trunks of the tree. The tree ascended through the building from five separate trunks, which all converged in the center of the tower around the thirty-sixth floor, braided together, and then parted ways again at the forty-third floor to ascend to the upper floors and tree tops.

Everything above floor 17 was dedicated to the pursuit of science, magic and knowledge. This was by design, so that any toxic fumes from experiments or spells gone awry would not affect the homes below. Instead, it all billowed upwards and filtered through to the lush leaves of the treetops, which absorbed the gasses and purified the air, replenishing the oxygen. It was a perfect ecosystem.

Del had never seen so many mice and so many systems all functioning so perfectly together. A mouse piling books onto one of the pulley-driven lifts would lower himself two stories, leave, and then be replaced by another mouse with several sizes of mushrooms in their paws. This mouse would go up to another floor and be replaced by another mouse going about his own unique business. No one ever seemed to run into each other despite the constant flow of traffic. It was chaotic perfection. Del thought of his books and the many descriptions of places like New York, Tokyo and Hong Kong that he had read, and couldn't help but wonder if this was what they had been like.

"Crom!" a voice squeaked from the crowd in front of them. A frail old ladymouse in a sky-blue dress weaved through the crowd. Her fur was also gray, but with a golden hue to it. She was frantic, flailing her arms and waving at them as she ran. Wet patches soaked the fur under her overly large eyes; she had been crying since word of her husband's injuries had reached her. "Where is he? Is he okay? Where's my husband?"

"You're Crom's wife?" asked Denya. Del noticed that she frequently took the lead when it came to speaking with common mice. He'd read several books about role-playing games which humans once played, and he imagined that if she were a character in one of these, she'd have a high Charisma score.

"Yes. Delilah Cromwell," she said with a hurried tone. "Is my husband alright?"

"He needs medical attention," Denya warned gently, leading Delilah to the cart.

"Oh, Crom!" she exclaimed, running over to him. She hopped up to the seat of the cart, pushed aside several layers of blankets, and cradled him in her arms.

"If you can direct us to the nearest healer . . ." said Del meekly, wanting to help but not wanting to interrupt her grief.

"Of course," she said, attempting to be strong. She quickly mumbled directions to the Canticle Hall, a local Canticle outpost which housed several Golds. Del led the beetle-driven cart further into the hustling, bustling crowd, as they escorted Delilah and Crom to a lift, where a mouse in an eggshell-white robe assisted them in moving Crom. Del went to grab Crom's pack from the cart, hurrying so as not to delay the lift. Perhaps there was money or food in it that they would need later on, and it would be a shame for Delilah to have to leave her husband's side to retrieve it. As he grabbed the satchel, there was a soft thud as something fell from inside and hit the dirt-covered floor.

"Come on, Del," he muttered to himself, noting how much he hated it in books when characters spoke to themselves. "Can't you do anything right?" He reached down to pick up the fallen object. It was a small, elongated, arrowhead-shaped, bronze emblem, small enough to fit in the palm of his paw. It seemed completely unremarkable save for the bear paw with a snake-eye embossed in the center of it, which was enough to make Del's breath catch in his chest.

Del was still examining the emblem when the lift groaned behind him and started its ascension, leaving him holding Crom's pack. Denya, Arthur and Kando had also stayed behind, and stood watching the lift rise away from them. The three mice let out a collective sigh of relief. Whether Crom lived or died was now out of their hands. They'd done everything they could.

"Welp, I've had about enough adventuring for one day," said Arthur. "I think I'll go find a couple of gents to play a round of cards with."

As they turned towards Del, he quickly pocketed the emblem in his cloak, placing the pack back into the cart. He considered telling them about the emblem, but he hesitated. The very thought of it sent a shiver up his spine, like some sixth sense telling him to keep the information to himself. After all, why would Crom have something with the same symbol branded on the minks who had attacked him? He couldn't just go making accusations without knowing all the facts. And if he *was* going to accuse Crom of something nefarious, he needed more proof first. The others, especially Kando, already saw him as a screw-up. He couldn't even read a map correctly, and that one mistake had nearly gotten them all killed. How could they even trust him now? He wasn't about to hand them one more reason to discredit him. Though he couldn't figure out when to speak, when to bow, or how to use his mysterious powers, *this* he would get right. He had to. A mouse's reputation was at stake, and not just his own.

"All the knowledge and culture you could choose to seek out here, and you're going to go gambling?" scoffed Denya.

"Of course! Don't you know a city's underbelly is far more thrilling than its top-side," replied Arthur, before winking at her and then sauntering off. He was almost instantly absorbed by the crowd.

"We should find the inn and get some rest. Not to mention a good rinse," said Kando. "The journey today was harder than expected." He turned to Del. "You are to take the cart to Crom's home first." He handed Del a folded piece of paper with several numbers and letters written hastily upon it: an address. Some of the ink was smeared by tear drops, which he assumed were Delilah's. She'd written the note right before jumping on the lift. "Is that understood?"

Del nodded, fearing that Kando could somehow read his thoughts. The black mouse glared at him for a long moment, but Denya interrupted the stare and Del was thankful to her for it.

"I thought perhaps we could have a word," she said to Kando. She knew her place and calling Kando out for his earlier actions in front of the entire band was unacceptable, but she hoped that a private conversation might be less frowned upon.

"It's late," said Kando. "We can talk tomorrow." Denya was visibly disappointed by this response. Kando sighed. "You think I should have spared the shrikes."

She was startled that he was so perceptive.

"But you know as well as I that it was us or them."

Del stayed off to the side, not wanting them to know he was listening. He pretended to be checking on the empty honey jars, making sure they were accounted for and secured in the cart.

"There was a better way," she replied. "It might have taken more thought or more cunning, perhaps even an actual conversation. But we could have found a better way. Tensions will rise between the mice and the shrikes now. That path will forever be more treacherous."

"We shouldn't have even *been* on that path," growled Kando, shooting a harsh look in Del's direction.

"Which just strengthens my point. We walked into *their* territory, and when they defended it, we slaughtered them. What we did may have made sense in the moment, but that doesn't make it any less wrong."

Kando closed the space between them in the blink of an eye. "Do not try to teach me about *right* and *wrong*," he said harshly. "What happened back there was not a choice between right and wrong. It was a decision between living and dying. And since you are still standing here, able to lecture me, *your superior,* then I'd say we picked correctly."

Denya stood her ground. "The Longtails are better than that. We ask questions first and attack as a last resort."

"Perhaps that way of thinking is what got your last Alpha killed."

Denya froze. It felt as though a knife had just been shoved into her heart. She was rendered speechless.

Kando backed away. "We return home at dawn. No need to waste any more time here than necessary." With these final words he trudged away, leaving her holding back her emotions once again.

Del approached her cautiously. "You okay?"

She took several long breaths and then turned to him, her face rigid and unfeeling. "You heard him. Get the cart to the Cromwell's and then return to the inn." She glanced sideways. A quiver in her voice betrayed her composure. "Come on. I'll walk with you."

"Something tells me he'd want me to do it alone," he said, kicking at the ground bashfully.

"Probably, but I've obeyed enough orders for one day."

*   *   *

Denya accompanied Del to the upper floors, where Crom and Delilah lived. Their home was built into one of the massive tree trunks in the side of the building. It was a quaint cottage with a roof made of hay and walls made of smooth, gray pebbles.

They hitched the beetles outside, making sure to leave some seed for them to feed on, and parked the cart beside the house. Then they departed to the lowest level of Toleloo once more.

The two mice barely spoke as they checked into the inn, booking separate rooms. Denya resisted the urge to slam the door in Del's face as she locked herself in for the night. She wasn't mad at him. Her mood was just foul in general.

The inn was built of smooth gray rock and gave off the cozy feeling of a cottage in the woods. Twinkling lights on green wires hung from the ceiling of the inn's lobby, and painted portraits of mice adorned the walls. In the corner was a fireplace, kept alight for warmth rather than light, and around it were several round wooden tables.

Upstairs, Del's small mouse-sized room paled in comparison to the human-sized studio apartment he'd once called home. Still, there was a small straw bed which was comfortable to sit on, a little wicker chair, and a wooden desk for study. A light bulb hung from the corner of the room, illuminating the space.

Del sat at the desk and pulled the bronze emblem from his pack. It didn't seem to have much use. Anyone else might have scrapped it. But the symbol, and the minks he had seen it on, would haunt him for the rest of his life. He knew, deep down, that there was more to this arbitrary arrowhead than met the eye. He fiddled with it, twirling it this way and that in his paws. It seemed to be fairly thick, yet not heavy at all. Perhaps it was hollow? He couldn't be sure. There were little circles engraved into the back, and he gave them each a soft push with his paws.

SHWOOM! The emblem sprang to life as a faded blue image projected from it. Del fell out of his chair backwards, horrified. A holographic, life-sized mink was looking back at him. Somehow, Del got the impression that Obi-Wan Kenobi was not this hologram's only hope. Still, he would have much preferred to see Princess Leia staring down at him.

"Operative Two-Nine-Four," said the mink, sounding quite official. "The Blight has need of you."

Del's blood went cold. *The Blight.* The gun-armed mink had mentioned this as well. Del sat very still, leaning onto the two hind legs of the chair, awaiting the next words from the mink hologram with bated breath.

*   *   *

Kando wandered through the market on the ground floor, sliding through the throng of mice and blocking out the cries from merchants of their low prices, latest deals or newest products, which they always claimed were nearly sold out. At the far east side of the tower, he found a large tree root which housed a small pub. Pushing through the saloon-like swinging door, he found a large, dark, musty cave filled with the faint scent of mead. The lighting was low and infrequent, creating long shadows and several dark corners where one could disappear from the world. It was exactly what he needed after the long day of travel.

He walked past several tables full of rowdy mice, and approached the bar, ordering "whatever you have that's strong." The bartender, a slim mouse with glasses and only one of his front teeth, filled a dusty flagon with pumpkin mead and slid it to Kando, who placed five chez onto the bartop. He nodded thanks to the bartender, and then went to sit at a small table in the back corner of the large space, one of the few not overflowing with mice drunkenly gambling and swearing at each other. He wasn't here to socialize. In fact, he was barely here to drink. Kando was here to listen. All the gossip of the world found its home in places like this, and he was keen to learn what secrets were being kept at the great Tower of Toleloo.

The Council had trusted him with a secret. Escorting the honey peddler, even though it had gone terribly, had only been a cover mission. They were here—no, *he* was here—to investigate something far more nefarious.

He sat for a while listening to mice play rowdy games of Rat-Bite Five, a card game which Kando did not know the rules to but understood that losing meant flipping a table and attacking the winner. This happened no less than four times before a conversation caught his ears.

"Heard about that mink attack in Verden?" A mouse with a scar across his face was addressing his table companion, another mouse who was busy drinking his third flagon of mead. "Heard they killed a Longtails Alpha. Awful business, that."

"Minks," scoffed the drunk mouse. "Bloody mercenaries. Got bored killing off the rats and had to pick on someone else, I suppose."

"You think they're doing it for sport?" asked the scarred mouse. "I don't buy it."

"You don't buy anything!" chortled the drunk mouse. "Seems I'm always footing your bill."

"Har har har." The scarred mouse was not amused by the joke. "I mean it! Minks don't do nothing without getting paid for it."

"You think they killed the rats for money?" asked the drunk mouse.

"Certainly didn't need that many rats to feed themselves. Had to be another reason."

"Minks don't need a reason to kill. They just like the smell of blood. Simple as that." The drunk mouse paused, then waved the scarred mouse closer.

"But suppose," he said in a hushed voice. Kando leaned forward, his ears perking up ever so slightly. "Just suppose they *were* killing for money. Makes you wonder who's paying them."

Kando logged the conversation away in his mind. It was definitely food for thought. The shrill voice of a ladymouse caught his attention.

"Keep your paws off the goods," she snapped, pulling another intoxicated mouse's paw off her tail.

"Just had to see if it was real!" chuckled the mouse. He had a big round belly and a tuft of fur under his chin. "Some mice in this city got them fancy metal arms and tails now."

"Do I look like I've got money to buy a metal tail?" she asked. "But if you wanna donate to the cause..." She gave him a wink, and three other mice at the table laughed. The big-bellied mouse tipped the waitress as she picked up some empty flagons off his table and turned towards the bar. "Thanks, honey."

Kando kept an eye on her as she went to fix up several more drinks. She was uniquely colored, with a face that was half black and half white, split so that when she was in profile, she looked like a completely different mouse on her right side than on her left side. She wore a white blouse and a green and gold plaid skirt underneath a pumpkin-orange apron. She turned to the other barmaid, a large, round-faced ladymouse with long, frizzy fur, which made her look even rounder than she actually was.

"Bunch of morons, eh?" she asked with a smile.

"That they are," replied the plump ladymouse. "But if that bunch of *morons* is our biggest problem, I'll take it. I hear they've got minks down in Verden."

"I'd say their real problem is worse than minks," said the barmaid. Kando let a rare smile slip across his muzzle as he sipped some of the mead from his mug. He was curious to hear what this barmaid had to say about the great mouse city. *What does she think is worse than minks? A systemically low tipping rate?*

"What's worse than minks?" asked the plump maid, rubbing a white cloth over the bar to clean it.

"Minks are bad, but you *know* they're bad. What scares me are bad *mice*." The barmaid let out a shudder. "Harder to tell the good ones from the bad when they're your neighbors."

Kando's head tilted. When the Council had told him his actual mission, he had thought them a bit mad. Overly cautious, at the very least. One thing that was certain about mice was that they were incredibly single-minded in the way they worked to aid each other. Everyone and everything else was the enemy. Mice would never turn on each other. But that word they had used still hung in the air, as if it were a bad smell in his clothes which he couldn't seem to get rid of: *Traitor*. However overly suspicious he thought the Council was being, Kando was not one to turn down orders. He had assumed he would find nothing, and that the mission would be a simple one. Yet, if this lowly barmaid was saying what he thought she was saying, perhaps it was not such an implausible concern.

"What are you on about, 'bad mice'?" asked the other barmaid.

"Well, the way I see it, they've got a big wall up around the city, right?"

"Right."

"Well someone had to let those minks in."

"Now, there you go, looking for something dark and twisty. Mice make mistakes, ya know? Maybe one of them guards simply fell asleep on the job."

The flagon in Kando's paw dropped to the table, spilling its contents all over the wood. He barely noticed. He was too consumed by what she'd just said. She was right. The minks wouldn't have been able to just waltz into Verden. It was guarded at all sides and the minks were too big to have been able to simply climb the walls without anyone noticing. If her deduction was accurate, the mink attack had been an inside job. Perhaps the Council's suspicion was not so far-fetched after all.

He stood and walked to the bar, never taking his eyes off the two-toned barmaid. He pulled a single chez from his pocket and laid it on the bar.

"Can I help you?" she asked, unfazed by his imposing nature.

He found himself at a loss for words. She wasn't some tactical strategist or a wise old mouse. She was no more an expert on mouse politics than any other mouse in the bar. Yet somehow, she had managed to consider something Kando hadn't even thought of.

"I couldn't help but overhear your conversation," he said.

"You mean you couldn't help but eavesdrop?" she replied, rolling her eyes.

"Call it what you must," he said. "You really believe a mouse let those minks in?"

"I surely do. I've always found that the simplest solution is usually the correct one."

"But . . . to what end?" Kando hated that he was asking a barmaid such questions. Yet something about the ladymouse captivated him.

"How should I know?" she asked.

Kando sat down at the bar. "Your theory seems plausible. That's why I'm sitting here. But if you can't back it up with proof, then it falls apart rather quickly. If we assume a mouse is behind the mink infiltration, then we have to have a motive."

"Well, there's a pick-up line I haven't heard before," said the round barmaid, picking up several flagons and heading out to the tables where other mice were laughing and jeering boisterously at each other.

"Look, I don't know why some mice do what they do," continued the two-toned barmaid, lowering her voice. "But my Mom always taught me to look past the obvious and search for what's hidden beneath. Minks sneakin' into a city to kill mice is what you'd expect from *slenders*. But which mice let them in, why and how—that's the real mystery, ain't it?"

"Your Mom sounds like a smart lady," said Kando.

"Not smart enough to still be alive," snapped the barmaid.

"Death comes for all of us, even the wisest," said Kando solemnly. He was taken aback by an unexpected memory and straightened himself up. "So, if you were this so-called mouse who let in the minks, how would you do it and where you be by now?"

"I don't know how, but I do know I'd get as far away from the scene of the crime as possible," she said. "I'd leave the city before anyone knew I was involved."

A thought slithered through Kando's mind, like a snake slithering beneath dry leaves in autumn. A dark and terrible thought. A thought so twisted that even he didn't want to believe it. He wanted the thought to be wrong. It was too coincidental, too horrible. Something about the statement made by the round-faced barmaid earlier came back to him suddenly. It hit him like a blow to the chest. *Simply fell asleep on the job.* His heart raced and his mind swirled. No, not *simply fell asleep.* That was too much of a coincidence.

"Thank you," he said. "You've been very helpful." With a final look at the barmaid, he stormed out of the bar and into the night.

*   *   *

Del waited silently, but the hologram merely looked back at him, unmoving. *Maybe it needs a response?* He'd read plenty of comics with high-tech computers which could be conversed with. Maybe this was one of those.

He cleared his throat. "The . . . Blight?" He wasn't sure if it could hear him or not. He stood, sat his chair back upright and re-seated himself.

"He requires another offering," the hologram suddenly continued. "As you know, our supply of rats has dwindled. Their numbers have been depleted by his hunger, but we must not despair. We have been working to satiate his need for rat flesh with their cousins, the mice. I know this will be difficult as the mice are *your* kin, but sacrifices must be made if we are to please him. If not, his wrath will be..." the mink paused. "Most severe." The mink closed his eyes for a moment, then reopened them and continued. "In one week's time, we will come to the Northern Gate of Verden at nightfall. Make your way there and find us a way to enter safely. Up until now, a single assassin has been able to gain access to the city without your help, but the situation has changed. Our new target requires...a larger show of force. We will be led by our best warrior, Barrel-Fist, along with his finest assassins, the Copper Clan.

"We just received news by a reliable source that there is one mouse in particular with enough power to satiate his hunger and strengthen him for many seasons to come. Barrel-Fist will acquire this mouse, and the Blight's hunger should diminish for a time. After this, we can work out a less . . . difficult solution." The mink paused briefly. "I know this is not ideal for you, but it is the only way to guarantee your safety and the safety of your wife. Should you fail, *he* will hold all who bear the mark accountable." The mink got closer so that he was staring right into Del's eyes. "Your sacrifice will be remembered in the new world. Do not fail us." The recording ended, and the mink disappeared.

Del let a breath out which he hadn't even realized he was holding. What did all of this mean? Who was the message meant for? He suddenly felt as though he were being watched, as if he knew too much, and now some secret organization was coming to capture him. *All who bear the mark. The Blight. Barrel-Fist.* All of it seemed to add up to two horrifying conclusions: They were after him and a mouse had let the minks into the city. Del gasped. *It couldn't be. Could it?* "Crom . . ." he whispered under his breath. His mind flooded with questions. He threw on his cloak and tightened the scarf around his neck. Then he pocketed the bronze emblem and marched out of the room. He would tell Kando about the emblem. Del would tell him everything. He had to. But first, he needed answers.

CHAPTER EIGHT

Betrayal

Del arrived at the Canticle Hall much faster than he expected to. It was a beautiful white cathedral built into the side of the tower on the sixth floor. He knew he was foolish to go alone, but he wanted to believe that his hunch was wrong. If he *was* wrong, waking Denya up to lead her on a wild goose chase would only make him seem even more incapable than she already thought he was.

Spiraling golden designs laced along the trimmings of the building and interwove with the nearby tree branches, as if they were all part of a single entity. Golds drew their power from their spirit as well as the spirits of those around them, so it only made sense that organic architecture was a part of their central hub within the tower. Natural surroundings allowed the Golds to bridge the gap between reality and the spirit world. Back in Verden, the Golds kept a large garden full of flowers and crops, which was the perfect place to sit and reflect after a long day of honing their craft. Del walked up a wide set of ivory steps and pushed open a heavy wooden door with etchings depicting trees to find a large, sparsely-lit foyer.

A frail young mouse dressed in a simple white robe was dusting the many bookshelves that lined the walls. She must have been half his size, and he could only assume that she was one of the apprentices who came to the Hall at a young age to learn the art of healing and protection.

"Oh, hello, sir," she said, turning to him and bowing. "Do you require healing or medical attention?"

"No, not injured," he said, hoping to put her at ease.

"That's a relief. All are welcome to commune with the spirits here of course. But most mice prefer daylight hours."

"I'm actually looking for someone," said Del. "Inneous Cromwell, a honey peddler. He was brought here earlier today. I wanted to check in on him."

"That is kind of you," the young mouse replied. Del suddenly realized that Crom might not have survived, in which case all of his questions would go unanswered.

"It's been a rough day for Mr. Cromwell, and he will need to endure many more challenging days ahead," she said. "But the Golds attending to him do believe he'll make a full recovery."

Del let out a breath. "That's a relief." *Unless he's a traitorous slender sympathizer.*

"Are you one of the Longtails?" she asked, eyeing his cloak.

"Er, yes," he said. It still felt strange to answer *yes* to that question. "I'm a new recruit."

"I'm new here as well. My name's Tilly." She bowed again solemnly.

"Nice to meet you. I'm Del."

"A kind name. You know, my teachers say that being the new mouse here doesn't last forever, but it certainly can feel that way sometimes." She chuckled to herself.

"That's for sure," said Del, grinning. He wondered if she dealt with the same feelings of inadequacy from her superiors as he did from his.

"I'll take you to Mr. Cromwell," she said politely. "If he's awake, you're free to speak with him. Only a short visit though. He needs his rest."

"This won't take long," he said, trying to sound reassuring. He didn't want her to pick up any hints that he was hoping to question Crom, rather than console him.

He followed Tilly down a long hallway illuminated by a string of lights hanging from the ceiling. He'd seen characters in comic books hang lights like these around pine trees in the winter time, while celebrating a human holiday called Christmas.

Christmas was not a mouse tradition. Mice celebrated Yalda, the longest night of winter, which marked the halfway point of the cold season. Ghost stories were told on the eve of Yalda, spooking young mice and haunting the dreams of all. The next morning, presents were handed out, symbolic of the gifts that spring would soon bring. Del always enjoyed the stories more than the gifts. Stories were invaluable, priceless things, and no amount of them could ever be enough.

Tilly stopped in front of a small door and pressed it open gently, peeking inside. "A guest to see you, Mr. Cromwell."

Del heard a muffled voice from within the room.

"His name is Del of the Longtails." She turned to Del and nodded, smiling. "Very well. He says you are welcome to enter. Remember, only a short time."

"Thank you," said Del, darting into the room readily, as though Crom might bolt at any moment. The old mouse was in no condition to run though. He looked terrible, as if he hadn't eaten or slept in weeks. He was tucked under a mountain of blankets, next to a window overlooking the interior of the tower; the sheer quantity of lights beaming from inside the tower made it hard to believe that it was actually late into the night.

"So, we meet again, m'boy," Crom said weakly. "I was just thinking, I never got the chance to thank you for saving my life." He coughed loudly, wheezing for air as he cleared his throat, trying to catch his breath. "Not many mice would have done what you did for me. That took real gumption."

"It was nothing," said Del. "Seeing others in trouble lately has sort of triggered something inside me. I can't help but try to stop whatever terrible thing is happening. I've got this . . . drive to help those in need, and so many questions about this power everyone keeps telling me about, and I can't seem to control either of those things."

Del slowly moved closer to the bed. Nothing about Crom screamed traitor. He was still the same kind old mouse they'd met back in Verden. He needed to make Crom feel comfortable enough to confide in him. He needed Crom to trust him. "I read once that we subconsciously take on traits of the characters in books we read. These traits can have long-lasting effects on our lives. Maybe all the super hero comics I've been reading finally flipped some light switch in me. Maybe not. I don't know. I don't need to be a superhero. I just want to feel worthy of being in the Longtails."

"As far as I'm concerned, you already are," said Crom with a weak smile. He raised his paw to Del. Del took it gently and felt the honey peddler give his paw a gentle squeeze. "You're a good kid. And coming from an old fuddy-duddy like me, that means something."

Maybe Crom wasn't what Del thought? Maybe Del had let his wild imagination get away from him? He had read a lot of *Teen Titans* recently. Perhaps he was projecting the story of Tara Markov, a Titan who turned out to be only part of the team so that she could destroy them, onto Crom. He reminded himself that real life was not a comic book and let his shoulders slump. He peered down at his paw nestled in the paw of a kind, old mouse who just wanted to sell honey. But no matter how much he wanted Crom to be good, he couldn't ignore what he saw branded on the mouse's inner wrist: a bear paw with a snake-eye at its center.

His eyes darted up to Crom in disappointment. "You did it, didn't you?" he asked shakily. He could feel fear and anger boiling up inside him.

"Did what m'boy?" asked Crom, not giving any hint that something was amiss.

"You worked with the minks," said Del, an accusation rather than a question. "You let them into Verden. You betrayed everyone. They wanted to take me . . . and you let them."

The smile faded from Crom's face. "I . . . I don't know what you're talking about."

Del's mind whirled as everything fell into place before him. It was like finding out that Professor Quirrel had been harboring Voldermort all along and Snape was actually the good guy. He raised his free paw up to his mouth in horror. "The honey you gave the guard. He said it made him take a nap. That's when you did it, isn't it? That's how you got them in. But why?"

Del suddenly felt Crom's grip on his paw tighten. Crom let a long sigh escape his lips. "Looks like the cat's out of the bag. Seems you're smarter than I gave you credit for. Well, maybe not that smart. After all, I didn't actually *open* the gate. That nasty business fell to another. Tell you what. I propose a trade. You guarantee my safety, and I'll tell you everything. What do you say?"

SLAM!! The door erupted off its hinges as Kando burst into the room with Tilly in tow, begging him to wait outside. Kando's katana was drawn and pointing directly at Crom.

"Step away from him, Del," Kando commanded, his words cutting the air like a harsh wind.

"*Two* mice found me out," Crom murmured, coughing. "I really did let my guard down on this one."

"Shame we brought you all this way, just to return you back to Verden so that they can hang you for treason," said Kando.

"He has information about who opened the gate," begged Del. "If we offer him protection—"

"We've got him cornered. He'd say anything to get out of facing justice," snapped Kando. "Making deals is above our pay grade. If he wants to trade accusations for mercy, he'll have to take it up with the Council."

"But we could know *right now!*"

"You shouldn't have come here alone, Rook."

"They came for me!" Del was furious now. "They tried to kill me and killed Roderick instead. I deserve to know *who*. I deserve to know *why*."

"This mouse is a traitor to the Mouselands. Any *truth* he shares could just as easily be a lie."

"Lie?" grinned Crom. "Me?" He stared into Del's eyes, as if speaking only to him. "Sooner or later you're bound to realize there is only truth. *The* truth. *The Blight*. This world was his long ago and it will be his again. All will bow before him. Many already do. Even those you wouldn't expect." His eyes narrowed. "Even your closest allies."

"What do you mean? What is the Blight? Which allies?" Del demanded. "Tell me what you know! Tell me who tried to kill me! Tell me why Roderick is dead!"

The window next to the bed suddenly shattered. Glass poured down onto Crom. Del pulled back, wincing away from the glass. When he looked back to Crom, he saw a red feathered dart with its tip buried into the old mouse's neck. His eyes were still open, staring up at Del, but there was no doubting that Inneous Cromwell was dead.

"No!" squeaked Del.

"An assassin!" yelled Kando. "Get down!"

But Del had no intention of getting down. He leapt to the window, searching for the attacker. In the center of the tower, not far from them, he could just make out a cloaked rider atop a large honey bee, flying towards an opening several floors up from them.

"A rider!" he exclaimed. "We have to catch up with him!" He turned back to Kando, who looked furious.

"It's too late," the older mouse snarled.

"Then what?!" yelled Del, moving towards him. "We're just going to let him get away?!"

Kando suddenly grabbed Del by his scarf and pulled him close, growling at him as if he might throw Del out the broken window. "We're not going to lose all our senses simply because some Rook forgets his place. That's what we're *not* going to do. You are a new member to this band, to this *order*, and I am your superior, your *Alpha*. Do you understand me?"

"Y-yes sir," squeaked Del, terrified.

"Good." Kando released him. "Now, it's been a long night. We'll get some rest and regroup in the morning. Whoever did this is someone who was in the tower long enough to steal a bee, a big one at that. Things like that don't go unnoticed. There's bound to be a trail, with that assassin waiting at the end of it." He glared at Del, daring the young mouse to argue that this plan was anything less than satisfactory.

"Okay," said Del. "Yeah."

"I'm going to investigate here for a while," said Kando, eyeing the dead body. "Go back to the inn. And stay there."

Del nodded, bowing his head in shame. With his tail between his legs, he left the room, giving Crom's body one last look. The peddler's last words haunted Del all the way back to the inn. *All will bow before him. Many already do. Even those you wouldn't expect. Even your closest allies.*

Someone had helped Crom get the minks into the city. Someone had opened the gate. Someone had lead the minks right to his front door. And if they could find Del once before, they could find him now. There was only one way he would ever feel safe again.

He needed to find the assassin.

CHAPTER NINE

Beekeepers at the Top of the World

Tension permeated the air. Denya and Arthur were being chastised for not having kept an eye on Del, and Del was being berated for having run off on his own to question someone he knew to be a potential traitor. They all sat at a rounded table near the hearth, in the lobby of the inn. With the night behind him, Del had thought that perhaps things would calm down in the light of morning. He was sorely mistaken.

"You could have been murdered," Kando barked at Del. Next, he scolded Denya. "You should have kept an eye on him. And *you*," he growled at Arthur. "No mouse should *ever* consume that much alcohol, least of all a Longtail. The Tower guard found you passed out in an alley." Arthur, meanwhile, looked as though he might pass out again at any moment. Dark bags hung beneath his eyes, and his whiskers drooped onto the tabletop.

"In my defense . . ." started Arthur weakly. He paused, closing his eyes to ponder his defense. They all waited for the end of the sentence, but the next thing out of his mouth was a soft snore.

"Wake up!" snapped Denya, slapping him on the back.

"I don't know her! It's not my baby!" Arthur shouted, his eyes popping open in surprise.

Kando was completely and utterly ashamed of all of them. Del thought that if they were the Justice League, Kando would be Batman after they'd let Metropolis fall into the hands of General Zod. But for once, Del was too upset to be cowardly in the face of such rage.

"None of this matters," he squeaked. They all turned towards him, surprised that he would dare to talk back. "Crom was a traitor, and now he's dead. Whether I was there or not, that wouldn't have changed. What matters is that there are more mice like him, and they want to capture me to feed to the Blight, whatever that is. We need more information, and our only lead is Crom's killer, who took off on a bee and is probably long gone by now. We don't even have a way to track him. You can yell at us all you want, but you're really just giving him and the minks more time to plan their next attack. But I guess that doesn't matter, because it's not *you* they're after!" Del was standing now, breathing heavily as he stared down Kando.

No one spoke. Silence filled the air like a thick cloud. Kando's nostrils flared.

At last, Denya cleared her throat. "There actually might be a way to track the killer. Provided the assassin got the bee from the hive at the top of the city, that is."

"Go on," Kando ordered, but didn't take his eyes off of Del.

"You sure you don't want to yell at us a bit more?" asked Arthur. "I really think you were just hitting your stride."

Kando shifted his glare from Del to Arthur.

Arthur quailed in his chair. "Denya, dear, I think you ought to do as he says."

Denya sighed. "The bees here are special," she started. "They're not a naturally occurring species. The scientists in the tower bred them to be bigger than any other bees in the world, so that they could produce more honey at a faster rate. They call them *gigabees*. In fact, they're big enough for a mouse to ride, as you two saw last night—though few do. Their brains are also larger, which makes them easier to train. As you can imagine, these gigabees are fairly valuable since they represent a significant investment for both the scientists and the honey harvesters who care for them at the top of the tower. Because of this, a tracer is implanted into each one when they're still larvae. Thing is, most mice don't know this. It's something of a trade secret kept between the gigabee breeders and the honey harvesters."

The other three mice looked at Denya curiously. Del was impressed that she knew so much about the gigabees. Arthur was so interested, he'd even managed to keep both eyes fully open for the duration of her explanation.

"And how do you know this . . . trade secret?" asked Kando.

Denya took a deep breath, and suddenly she looked like an ashamed pup trying to hide the fact that they'd just broken their mother's favorite vase. "My parents . . . are beekeepers."

"No wonder you're so uncouth," chided Arthur. "Might has well have been raised in a barn."

Denya gave him a shove with her paw, which in his current state was enough to topple him out of his chair and onto the floor. "Ow!" he shouted, trying to right himself.

"Wait," started Del. "Your parents are beekeepers *here*?"

Denya rolled her eyes. "Yes."

"And you weren't planning on sharing this information?" asked Kando stiffly.

"It didn't seem all that important until now," said Denya. "And my parents and I aren't exactly close. I would have easily gone this whole visit without even thinking about them."

"This is why Crom thought you looked familiar," said Del. "He knew you because of your parents."

Denya nodded. "I guess so. Though honestly, I don't remember him at all. I was pretty young when I took off."

"The timing of all of this isn't ideal, but I think it might be time for a little family reunion," said Kando. Del couldn't help but notice that Kando seemed to soften slightly, as if he actually felt badly for Denya.

"I was worried you might say that," murmured Denya.

"Everyone should get their affairs in order," Kando instructed. "We'll meet back here in an hour and head up to the hive."

The four mice stood and made for the stairs up to the inn's many rooms, but Kando grabbed Del's arm, stopping him in his tracks.

"Need something . . . sir?" gulped Del, nervously. He was much less willing to speak his mind when it was just the two of them alone. It was like being in a room alone with Batman.

"At what point had you planned on sharing *how* you found out about Crom?" he asked, casting a suspicious gaze on Del.

Del slowly pulled the bronze emblem from his pocket and held it in his palm to show Kando.

"It's a holographic message," Del explained. "It shows a mink ordering Crom to find a way to get the minks into the city, so that they could come and find me."

"Where did you get this?"

"It fell out of Crom's bag when he was being loaded onto the lift yesterday."

"And you didn't tell anyone?"

"I couldn't . . ." Del sighed. "I got us lost in the woods, nearly got us killed. I had to be sure it was something worth mentioning. You hate me enough as it is. And Crom seemed like such a good guy, I couldn't just report him for having something suspicious without checking it out first."

Kando's hold on his arm tightened. "You may think you can do whatever you want just because you're a Trelock, but you can't. This is not a solo mission. We work *together*. It's the only way we survive."

Del felt anger rise in his chest. "Oh, so now you care that I'm a Trelock? Now you want to bring it up?"

"What is that supposed to mean?"

"I don't think I can do whatever I want because I'm this . . . thing! I'm scared out of my mind. I'm supposed to learn to use this power, and I don't know the first thing about it. You want us to survive together so badly, then maybe you should stop telling me that everything I do is wrong and actually teach me how to do something right!" Del yanked his arm free. "But I guess yelling and being mean and intimidating is easier than all of that."

He turned and stomped up the stairs, leaving Kando speechless.

*　　　　*　　　　*

An hour later, the four mice departed from the inn and made their way towards the network of lifts which would take them to the top of the tower. The ascent required them to switch lifts no less than four times, as no single lift went from the main level all the way to the top. Denya explained to them that this was done to alleviate risk for both the mice riding the lifts, as well as those who performed maintenance and repairs.

"So, you grew up here?" asked Del.

"Yes," she replied softly.

Kando was leaning against the lift's outer railing, silent and brooding, seemingly lost in his own world. Arthur was holding onto the opposite side, trying to keep himself from throwing up his breakfast, which had been a mug of pumpkin juice and a single piece of bread to absorb the residual mead in his stomach.

"Why did you move to Verden?" Del asked.

"I wanted to be a Concoctor." Concoctors were artists of alchemy. They mixed herbs and essences to create potions of healing, strength and manipulation. They were also able to use sand, flint and chemicals to create bombs, explosives and noxious gasses. "When I was little, Mom and Dad always expected I'd take over the family business. But while they were teaching me to harvest honey, I'd sneak off to ask the scientists questions about which herbs mixed well with which gels. I wanted to put two things together and create something new. Not clean up after mindless gigas."

"That still doesn't explain why you left," said Kando, who was apparently listening after all. "Toleloo is the best place in the Mouselands to learn Concoction."

"Yes, but despite what you might think, this tower isn't *that* big," she said, a tinge of bitterness in her voice. "Mom and Dad had a talk with the local scientists and forbade them to teach me how to concoct anything. So, I packed up and moved to the city where no one knew my parents. I could learn freely." She looked up as the top of the tower came closer into view. "And that was the last time I ever saw them."

"I'm so glad I woke up early so you could sort out your mommy and daddy issues," whined Arthur.

Denya pivoted so that she was beside him. She put her mouth up to one of his tall ears and yelled "Thank you!" into it.

Arthur winced in pain. Del thought he almost caught a glimpse of a smile briefly crossing Kando's face. It quickly disappeared as the lift neared its destination.

"We're here," Kando announced.

Del looked up to see the branches of the tree stretching out above them, reaching towards the sky and obscuring it from view. The air smelled lavishly sweet. An aroma of honey, sunny days and springtime filled Del's nostrils. It made his mouth water and his stomach growl.

As the lift came to a halt, they got their first view of the massive beehive which clung to the tree branches above them. Mice bustled briskly here and there on a large wooden platform beneath the hive. Several ceramic vats were set up under the honeycombs to catch the honey as it oozed down in fat shimmering droplets. Flying lazily overhead, gigabees filled the air with an overwhelming buzzing sound that sent vibrations through his body and down to his tiny mouse bones.

"Whoa!" Del yelled as a bee hovered directly over his head.

"Don't worry." said Denya. "They're harmless. Gigabees don't even have stingers."

"That's a relief," he replied. The four of them stepped off the lift onto the platform. Del couldn't help but notice Denya looking around nervously, as if she didn't actually want to see her parents, even though that was the entire purpose of their visit.

They pressed onward, passing by several mice who didn't pay them any attention, save for a few polite nods and the occasional tip of a wide-brimmed straw hat. Visitors were not an unusual sight in this area. Denya stopped to address a young male mouse. He was wearing gloves and scooping honey out of a vat and into a jar.

"Excuse me," she said. "Would you happen to know where I could find Gillean or Raisha Woodhollow?" But the young mouse didn't get a chance to answer.

"Denya?" They all turned to see an old gray ladymouse wearing a white dress and gloves approaching them. She seemed to tremble as she approached. "Is that really you?"

A surge of emotions rushed through Denya—anger, heartache, pain, regret, resentment, loss. She couldn't decide which one to settle on. "Hi, Mom."

The ladymouse, Raisha, approached Denya and slowly placed a paw on her daughter's face. "You've grown so much," she said. Tears began to fall from her brown eyes. Denya allowed her face to press into her mother's paw and feel the warmth and comfort in it. She hadn't realized how much she'd missed this maternal contact until now. But the feeling was short-lived. "After all these years, have you finally seen the error of your ways?"

The words landed like a blow. Denya took a step back and bit her bottom lip, wanting so much to snap and yell at her mother, just like she had done when she was a little mouse pup. But she denied herself that reaction. "I'm here with my band," she responded calmly, gesturing to the others standing several strides behind her. "Last night, an assassin killed a mouse on the lower levels. The killer rode off on a gigabee. We were hoping to track them."

Raisha's face sunk. This was not what she had been hoping to hear. "Oh," she murmured weakly.

"We need your help," said Denya.

Raisha nodded, wiping the tears out of her eyes. "You better come inside."

The old mouse led them all to a cottage built into one of the lower hanging branches of the treetop. Above it was a rich golden honeycomb which glistened with honey as the gigabees tended to it.

The interior of the home was spacious enough for two mice to live and appeared well-tended. For Del, any home that was actually mouse-sized felt cramped, and no matter which way he turned he always managed to bump into something. But he couldn't deny that this one had a warm and welcoming ambiance. The sweet scent of honey filled the rooms and made him feel as though he had just stepped into a bakery or a candy shop.

There were two rooms that he could see: one a living area, and the other a kitchen. The living area had a soft rug on the floor and a cozy chair next to a couch, both of which were set around a small oak table. Various books about beekeeping were piled haphazardly atop the table. Del had half a mind to grab one of the books and start reading. It had already been too long since he had read anything other than maps and street signs, and his mind ached for the sort of stimulation only words on a page could provide.

At the far end of the room was a fireplace where a stack of twigs burned, keeping the home warm. A shelf next to the fireplace held more twigs, piled in an orderly fashion. On the other side of the room was a tall bookcase filled with everything from honey encyclopedias to the finest of mouse fiction. Pictures hung from the wall, mostly of Raisha and a male mouse, whom Del assumed was her husband and Denya's father. Nowhere was there a photo of Denya.

The kitchen had an olive-colored table in the center of it which was already set with two plates, napkins—perfectly folded into triangles—and silverware. The cupboards and drawers matched the olive theme, and several pans hung from hooks above a black stove. An antique wooden clock ticked away on the wall, under which was a line of jars filled with different-colored honey, all labeled and in alphabetical order: *Alfalfa, Blueberry, Clover, Fireweed, Orange Blossom, Sage*. Del imagined each flavor as being even more delicious than the last, and he licked his whiskers as he imagined spooning them into his mouth.

"You're all welcome to sit," said Raisha. "I'll put a kettle on."

"There's really no need for that," started Denya.

"Now, now," interrupted Arthur. "There's always need for tea." He smiled at Raisha. "As any proper lady knows."

Raisha nodded, trotting over to the stove.

"Wise words from the most proper lady among us," jeered Denya.

"I'll choose to take that as a compliment," Arthur retorted haughtily.

The mice gathered around the table and sat. Raisha brought them each a teacup and started the tea boiling in a copper kettle.

"As your daughter mentioned, we were hoping you might be able to track the gigabee that was used by the assassin," said Kando.

"Whiskers to the fire," Raisha said. "I still can't believe a mouse was killed. And so close to home, no less. I certainly hope it wasn't someone we knew. But in regards to your question: yes, we can," she admitted. "The gigas come and go, of course. There's nothing keeping them here, and often times they find some new nectar that adds an all new note to the honey's flavor." She grinned mischievously. "When that happens, we call it a seasonal specialty and sell it at a higher price. But still, we keep an eye on them, just in case they ever find themselves in trouble or, as in this case, if one disappears entirely."

"We'd very much appreciate if you could help us locate *this* one," said Kando. Del was surprised to see him acting so cordial. Maybe he was only hard on the members of his band. Perhaps civilian mice were afforded at least a little bit of kindness.

"My husband will have to help you there," laughed Raisha. "I'm not much good with the computers."

"When's he coming home?" asked Denya.

Raisha shook her head and gave a little sigh as her shoulders sank. "Funny," she said, half to herself. "We used to ask that question about you."

Denya's face flushed and her whiskers bristled.

"Your daughter's actually really good at what she does," Del interjected, hoping to help.

"Don't stand up for me, Rook," muttered Denya. "Besides, I could save a hundred mouse lives, and it still wouldn't be enough for my parents to accept my decision to leave."

"You should be home with your family," said Raisha, tears welling up in her eyes once more. "Not gallivanting around the Mouselands fighting assassins and who knows what else."

"I think the words you're looking for are 'protecting innocent lives,'" cut back Denya.

Raisha's sadness was suddenly replaced by anger. "They don't need you like we need you!" she yelled. "The Mouselands would be just as safe without you! And at least then we could be a family!"

The teapot began to whistle, steam shooting out of the spout.

"We *are* a family, and nothing changes that, but what I'm doing is more important than us!" yelled Denya, who was now standing. "Why can't you see that!?" The other mice couldn't do anything but stare at the two of them as they yelled back and forth. The whistling grew louder, filling the room with its horrible scream.

"*Nothing* is more important than your family!" cried Raisha.

"THIS! IS!" Denya shouted.

"Enough!!!" They all turned to see a dark brown mouse standing in the doorway. He wore a red vest with buttons shaped like honey pots. A white beret sat atop his head accompanied by a foul expression. Del couldn't help but think that he was the spitting image of a Hobbit in mouse form.

"Dad," squeaked Denya.

"Get out of this house," he ordered.

"Dad, we just—"

"I said, *get out*." His words were stinging and not at all jovial, in contrast to his festive attire.

"We were actually wondering if we might have a word about a stolen gigabee," attempted Arthur.

"All of you!" Gillean growled, ending any hopes of a discussion.

Arthur just rolled a 1 on Persuasion, thought Del, remembering the *Dungeons & Dragons* books he was so fond of. The four mice stood and made for the doorway, their eyes downcast and their faces filled with dejection as they left. Kando lingered, turning in the doorway to face Gillean.

"For what it's worth," he said. "Your daughter's a fine member of the Longtails."

"The Longtails broke apart our family," Gillean muttered stiffly. "So your words aren't worth much." Kando wanted to say more, but decided against it. He exited, leaving Gillean to slam the door shut behind them.

CHAPTER TEN

Confessions in the Night

The ride back to the lower levels of the tower was silent. No one dared speak to Denya, who looked as though she would use one of her bombs on anyone who tried. Kando was pensive, lost in his own thoughts as he gently stroked his chin with two fingers. Arthur fell asleep standing, happy to not have any more duties for the time being. And Del simply observed each of them curiously as though they were characters in a book.

He'd never been a part of a team, but he was pretty sure this wasn't how one was supposed to function. He'd always loved books about super teams like *Teen Titans, Justice League,* and *The Young Avengers*. He loved seeing characters from all different backgrounds find a way to work together to bring justice and peace to the world. As he looked at the mice around him now, he couldn't imagine the four of them ever seeing eye-to-eye enough to come up with a solution to the problem at hand, let alone save the world should it ever be in danger.

They stepped off the lift and headed back to the inn, where Denya shut herself up in her room and locked the door. The other three convened at the wooden table in front of the lobby hearth once more. It was only then that Del finally dared to speak.

"So, what now?" he asked.

"We've hit a dead end," said Kando bluntly. "I'll send word to the Council. I think it's best that we return to Verden and wait until another lead presents itself."

"No!" Del insisted. Kando shot him a piercing glare.

"No?" the old mouse echoed angrily, as if fire might burst from of his mouth.

"By then it'll be too late. The assassin will have time to prepare. There might even be another attack!" Del was begging Kando to hear him. To do something. Anything.

"We have no way of finding the assassin now. Besides, if these mice really *are* after you, then you'll be safer in Verden."

"What's this, then?" asked Arthur, a confused expression on his face.

"Don't worry about it, DeGandia," growled Kando.

Del was done keeping secrets. "I found a message that told Crom to let the minks in so that they could take me to the Blight. They said it needed me to 'satiate its hunger.' They broke into Verden for *me*."

"Why weren't Denya and I informed of this?" asked Arthur, hurt that they had been left out.

"I wasn't even informed of it until this morning," said Kando. He looked furious, as though he might kill Del himself before the minks got a chance at him.

Arthur leaned back, thinking to himself.

"Besides, I assumed this information was on a need-to-know basis," said Kando.

"You told me that I wasn't on a solo mission. So, I guess everything is need-to-know," Del retorted. "If we go back to Verden, it will be like you're handing me over to them. They found me there once, they'll do it again!"

"I hate to say it," interrupted Arthur. "But I have to agree with the lad. There has to be another way about this. We could always break into the old chap's office and track the bee ourselves?"

"Listen, you two," snarled Kando, grabbing each of them by their ears. "We are part of an honorable and sacred order. We aren't vigilantes. We do what the Council asks, when the Council asks it." He shot Arthur a disapproving look. "We don't break into places to get what we want." He turned on Del. "And we don't disobey our superiors and go off on our own. We are not the wheel. We are merely a single spoke. We will return to Verden and seek the Council's advice. That is the way of the Longtails."

"Then I'm as good as dead," said Del, his anger boiling over like Raisha's teapot.

Kando squinted at him with his good eye but was not swayed. "We leave in the morning." He stomped out of the inn, slamming the door behind him. The innkeeper, a small old ladymouse, jumped in surprise.

"Never would have been like this with Roderick," said Arthur. Taking orders was completely new to Del, but he often forgot that Kando's leadership was also new to Arthur and Denya. "He always did the right thing, even if it flew in the face of the Council. I respected that about him." He fiddled with a button on his red coat and then with the small candle in the center of the table. Something was pressing on his mind.

Del sighed, feeling his frustration seep out of him like air from a leaking balloon. "Kando's just trying to do what he thinks is right," said Del, suddenly ashamed of the childish way he had yelled at his Alpha.

"Maybe," responded Arthur gloomily. "Or maybe you're not the only one keeping secrets from the group."

Del stared at Arthur in surprise. "What do you mean?"

Arthur thought for a moment, then shook his head. "Nothing. It's just . . . he gave up so easily when we were talking to Denya's parents. Big scary mouse like Kando with his one eye and his big sword, and he just let them throw us out. Let them send us on our way. It just seems...odd. Like maybe...he doesn't *want* us to find the assassin." Arthur

169

closed his eyes, and when he reopened them, his mind seemed clearer, the darkness of his thoughts melting away. He smiled his charming smile at Del. "Don't mind me. You do this kind of work long enough, everyone starts to seem suspicious. I'm sure it's just the hangover getting to me." He pushed his chair back away from the table and stood. "I'm going to get some fresh air. Think I'll go ask Mrs. Cromwell if she knows anything. Though I expect she's just as much in the dark as we are."

"Arthur?" asked Del. "Do you think I'll be safe back in Verden?"

Arthur chewed on his bottom lip as he thought. "If it were up to me, I'd find a way to catch that assassin. Then I'd hunt down whoever had it out for me. To the ends of the Earth if I had to. Only then would I feel truly safe." He paused, taking a deep breath. "Then again, Verden is incredibly well-fortified. Try not to dwell on *what ifs*. It makes life so much less fun." He patted Del on the shoulder and left the inn.

Del remained alone at the table and despite Arthur's advice, his mind wandered into the myriad of *what ifs* that he now faced. *What if he went back to Verden only to be taken by the minks? What if there was still a way to find the assassin? What if? What if? What if?*

But one question rose above the others, and try as he might, Del simply couldn't quell the thought. *What if Kando was hiding something?*

*   *   *

The moment the door closed behind her, Denya finally allowed herself to cry. And not just to cry, but to sob. Tears poured down her face in a way they hadn't since she was a pup. When she was younger, she cried over everything—not getting to stay up late or not being allowed to ride the gigabees. But when she'd left home something had clicked inside her. She'd become a different mouse. Her resolve had hardened, and her emotions had become more complex, no longer focused solely on not getting her way. Yet she always knew deep down inside herself that the stubborn brat of a pup was lingering, threatening to reemerge.

She pulled her Concoctor's book from her back and threw it onto the small wooden table at the side of the room. It landed with a heavy thud, sending a dust cloud into the air. The book was bound in thick leather with a golden stag engraved on it and held closed by a silver buckle. Its pages were yellow with age, edges tattered from years of being flipped through, often in the heat of battle. Denya stared at the knowledge-rich manual, softly illuminated by the few embers which still remained in the fireplace.

She could still recall receiving it from her Concoction master, Belanie Harwind, an esteemed professor. She was the kind of ladymouse that Denya aspired to be. Hard and unyielding, she wore a pair of goggles and a grin which said *I'm not one to be trifled with.*

"Concoction began as transmuting the known into the unknown," she used to say. "If one is to be a successful Concoctor, one must always be looking for the parts that make up the greater whole, and always searching for which parts can create an even better whole. Break down the very essence of nature in order to concoct something even greater." Denya looked up to her so much. When she finally received her own recipe book, Belanie hugged her tight and said "Now you are a true Concoctor, and a force to be reckoned with. Let no one tell you otherwise."

It was the happiest day of Denya's life. Now, she looked upon the book with dismay and regret. She loved being able to take leaves and berries and form a curative. She loved adding a slight bit of silver fulminate to a pawful of sand to create a deadly explosion. She loved tweaking a recipe in the slightest of ways, only to reveal a formula that was completely new. But only now did she really allow herself to see the cost of all this joy.

In her search to break down the ingredients of the world, she'd broken apart her family, and she couldn't simply rewrite the recipe to put it back together even better than before. She couldn't bear the thought of it.

With great rage, she picked up the book and walked to the fireplace. A shuddering breath escaped her lips. She could end this all here. She could burn the book and start over. She lifted it above her head, ready to fling it into the embers. But at the last moment, she let it fall from her paws. It bounced once on the floor and then came to rest by her bedside. She fell to her knees, placing her paws over her eyes.

Outside the window, she could hear laughter, shouting and music. She was tired of being the disappointing daughter. But she was also tired of being the overly-emotional soldier. She was tired of everything.

She turned her head to the window and wiped the wetness from her eyes. She needed fresh air. More importantly, she needed to be no one for a few hours. If she went out the door, someone would surely see her leave. They might even try to comfort her. No, better to sneak out quietly. That way, she could be alone with her thoughts. Leaving the book where it had fallen, she squeezed out the window and into the night.

*   *   *

"Back again, stranger?" teased the barmaid as Kando sat at the bar, sipping from a flagon of pomegranate ale. He couldn't help but feel that talking to her was like talking to two separate mice because of the way her face was split in color right down the center.

"Today was a bad day," he said simply.

"They happen," she said.

"I wanted to thank you for your advice the other night," he said, giving her the weakest of smiles. "You've got a good head on your shoulders. You'd make a good Ghost. Maybe even a quality Eagle, if you've got yourself as good an eye as you have a brain."

"You're awfully kind for a Demon," she said. As they spoke, she used a white rag to clean the inside of several glasses and mugs, placing them off to the side once they were dry. "But I'm no soldier. The Longtails may call to some, but not me."

"The Longtails call to each of us," said Kando. "The only thing that sets us apart is whether or not we answer."

"Wise words from a wise mouse," said the barmaid, half-jokingly.

"It appears I'm not the only one. How do you know about Demons? Most mice have never even seen one."

"We don't see many out this way, but that doesn't mean I don't know of them," she replied, eyeing his outfit and the katana fastened to his back. "Don't suppose a keeps-to-himself fellow like you would care to share what brings you all the way out here? Way I hear it, the Demons, Ghosts and Ascended stay in the mountains to the southwest, chanting mantras on Handies Peak and keeping vigil in the Grizzly Hills."

"Ha!" Even Kando was surprised to hear himself laugh. "You know more than you let on."

"My mother was obsessed with the Handies Clans," sighed the barmaid. "She used to tell me stories of their bravery before bed. She loved a good tale of the Grizzly Wars as much as she loved talking about the architecture of the temple there. 'Gold as high as the eye can see' she'd say. Honestly, she was a bit of a fanatic. And most mice, myself included, thought she was making it all up."

"Your mother sounds fascinating," said Kando.

The barmaid looked away. "She was."

Kando paused for a moment, taking the young mouse in, trying to read her. Perhaps he seemed odd to her, what with his sword and Demon attire, but she was just as strange a creature to him. "What's your name?"

"Narissa," she said.

"It suits you," said Kando, raising his glass to her.

"Are you flirting with me, Mr. Demon?" she asked with a sly grin.

Kando let out a laugh and shook his head. "No. Just making conversation. You're far too young for an old mouse like me. And besides, I've already had my great love for this lifetime."

"Only one?" she asked. "I've already had myself a few great loves."

"Bah," he scoffed. "We only ever really have one that matters. I'm willing to bet you haven't come across him yet." Kando waved a paw in correction. "Or her. I'm not one to assume."

175

Narissa laughed. "So why are you here?"

"I'm the Alpha for a band of Longtails. We came here on an escort mission."

"No," corrected Narissa. "What I mean is, why are you here and not back at Handies Peak?"

"Oh," said Kando, taking another long gulp of ale. "Verden is actually home. Or at least it's where I was born. I was recruited by the Demons at a young age and made the long journey south to the Peak. I trained and learned, and before I knew it I was fighting skunks and foxes."

"Sounds like quite the adventure," admitted Narissa.

"It was . . . for a time," said Kando. "But it was also a life filled with loss. I'd make a new friend only to see them die the next week. I got good at not feeling anything at all. And then . . ."

"And then?"

"I met her. *The one*." He took another long drink. Perhaps it was the alcohol which made him feel at ease with the barmaid. Or perhaps she simply put him at ease. Either way, he continued. "And then . . . I lost her. It was more than I could bear. From then on, I simply went through the motions. Nothing had meaning anymore. So, when the letter came, calling me to the Longtails, I left Handies Peak and the Demon Master who raised me. I left it all behind and returned to where it all started."

Narissa frowned and refilled his drink. Kando tried to stop her but she just continued pouring. "On the house," she said. "A drink for a story." When the mug was full, she set the pitcher to the side and let her shoulders slump. "A very sad story, I might add."

"It is, isn't it?" sighed Kando.

Narissa poured herself a small glass of the ale and held it up in a toast. "To the loves we've lost."

Kando nodded and held up his ale. "To Muireen." Just speaking her name made his heart skip a beat. He didn't often speak of her, but he thought of her every day.

His thoughts elsewhere, he didn't notice as Narissa stayed her paw, not drinking but simply staring at him as he took a long swig of ale. "Muireen?" she echoed.

"Muireen Lecosa," he said. "The last and only ladymouse I'll ever love." He took another drink, hoping to drown out the pain. It never worked, but it was worth a try. "So, what about you?" he asked. "What's your story?"

Narissa faked a smile. "My story is that my shift is over." She knocked her knuckles twice on the bar top. "Thanks for the story, Mr. Demon." She turned and hastily disappeared through a set of double doors behind the counter, leaving him to his nearly empty flagon.

She barged into the backroom of the pub and ran to the bathroom, taking heaving breaths as she tried to calm herself. She looked at herself in the mirror as a tear ran down the black half of her face. She repeated the name back to herself. A name she hadn't heard in ages. *Muireen Lecosa.* Even when Muireen had been alive, it was a name

177

Narissa had rarely used. After all, when she had known Muireen, she'd called her by a different name: *Mom*.

*   *   *

Denya pulled the hood of her cloak tighter over her head, obscuring her face in shadow as she made her way into the center of Toleloo's ground level. There, mice gathered on the full moon of each month to dance and celebrate their hard work and accomplishments. It was believed in Toleloo that hard work and sacrifice merited an equal amount of festivity. Lights had been strung up on poles around a large circle where mice were dancing to and fro, laughing and singing. An instrumental band was playing upbeat music off to the side of the circle. Four mice, all playing mouse-made instruments, made up the group: a violinist, a cellist, a horn player and a pianist.

"You want to know why you're not good at this whole hiding in plain sight thing?" Denya jumped, spinning around to see Arthur in his red coat and hat grinning foolishly at her. She had thought no one would recognize her with her cloak and hood on. She had clearly been wrong. "You're the only one at a party not having fun," he continued. "You stick out like a crooked whisker."

"I just wanted to get away for a bit," said Denya, embarrassed at how childish the notion sounded when spoken out loud.

"Well, I'm not going to tell," Arthur promised. For all his snide comments and sarcastic undertones, she had to admit he *was* the most charming mouse she'd ever known.

The band finished playing a song, paused for raucous applause, then launched into another tune, even more joyous than the last. The crowd of mice around them gave a cheer and several more ran out to the dance floor and began stepping in time with the music and swinging each other, paw in paw, arm in arm.

"I don't suppose," started Arthur, looking at the dancing mice and then back to Denya, "that you would care to dance?"

Denya laughed, shaking her head, both in surprise and embarrassment. "You're better off with another partner, Mr. DeGandia. I don't actually know how to dance."

"Oh, come now," scoffed Arthur. "Deep down, everyone knows how to dance."

Without another word, he grabbed her paw and lead her out to the dance floor. He showed her a quick set of footwork and then took her paws in his and began moving her to the rhythm. To her great surprise, she picked up the dance rather quickly, and before she knew it, she was keeping pace with both Arthur and the other mice.

"You're not half bad," laughed Arthur.

"You're pretty good yourself."

"Oh, I already knew that," he said with a wink.

"And still humble as ever."

"I don't get paid to be humble."

"And you only do what you get paid to do?"

"Only a foolish mouse does anything without a proper reward." He raised both their paws up high and spun her. Her cloak fluttered in the air. They both laughed and continued to dance until the song ended.

Arthur taught her different steps for each song: the box step, paw reverse, tail spin and the ear shuffle. Finally, they retired to a small vacant table lit by candlelight, one of many set up to one side of the dance floor. They sat down, and Arthur waved down a passing mouse waiter. He ordered two glasses of wine and a plate of sugar plums, a candy treat which Denya admitted to never having tried. When they arrived, she marveled at the purple pebbles which glistened as if dusted with magic. Arthur plucked one off the plate and bit into it, offering one to her as well.

She found it to be sweet and luxurious. It tasted far too lavish for her to be gobbling up so quickly. The indulgent candy felt like it should be forbidden, but the way it melted in her mouth and filled her pointy nose with its sweet scent made it a temptation she couldn't resist. "It's delicious!" she exclaimed.

"I know," he said, as if this was old news. He took another bite, finishing his off and then used a small napkin to remove the sugar dust from his paws. He then held the wine glass to his lips, sniffed the dark red drink, and took the tiniest of sips. "A good year," he said, placing the glass back on the table.

"You know, in all these years, I've never asked you why you joined the Longtails," she said, taking a much less orchestrated sip from her own glass.

"Well, then, why start now?" he asked with a smirk.

Denya rolled her eyes. "Come on. Was it just another way to earn chez for you? You said you only do things for the reward, so what was it?"

"Alright, alright." Arthur surrendered, waving his paws at her in defeat. "It may surprise you to find out that the most elegant mouse you know grew up in a dirty orphanage on the south end of the Verden."

"You lie," she said, teasing him.

"'Fraid not," he replied. "I lived with sixty-eight other little pups. We would eat our porridge and play hide-and-seek in that run-down, man-made house. Eventually, our orphan mother, Mrs. Crawley, would come looking for us, and she'd give us each a spanking across our tails with a long stick."

Denya laughed. "I can't even imagine you in such a place."

"I still remember it like it was yesterday," he continued. "One day, we were playing outside, and a crow attacked my friend and me. It ate my friend in one gulp, and when it came for me, I somehow managed to blast it away with magic. Me, of all mice. I'd never done such a thing in all my short life. Scared Mrs. Crawley half to death. I was immediately shipped off to the Spectrum Halls. I was a fast learner, both mentally and physically, which made me quite good with a sword *and* spellcasting. Before I knew it, I was a donning the red garments of a Scarlet."

"That still doesn't explain the Longtails," Denya pointed out.

"Well, that's simple, really. I wanted to make sure that I'd never end up like my friend who got eaten by that crow. I never wanted to be on the weaker side of a conflict." He removed a small bronze chez from his coat-pocket and showed it to her, flipping it between his fingers so that she could clearly see both sides. Unlike a normal coin, both sides bore the image of a female mouse's head. "I wanted to be like this coin. A winner no matter the odds. The Longtails gave me that. They gave me the chance to be a part of something more, something strong."

"So that's it?" she asked, skeptically. "You're just power hungry? Simply on a mission to cheat the odds and take everything you can get along the way."

"Hmm," he mused, replacing the coin into his coat-pocket. "I prefer to think it's more that I'm allergic to fragility. I don't need to be the most powerful, but I refuse to be weak. I never want to be on the losing side of an argument or a battle. I never want to find myself in the belly of a crow." He leaned forward and twitched his nose at her. "And you?"

"I wanted to put two things together and make something new," she said, thinking of her Concoctor's book lying discarded in her room.

"That's why you became a Concoctor," Arthur nodded. "But the question was, why did you join the Longtails?"

She thought for a moment and then laughed. "Is it terribly cliché to say that I wanted to help people?" she asked.

Arthur shook his head. "Cliché: yes, but not surprising."

She became quiet and sullen. "I miss Roderick. He always knew what to do. He would have given anything, made any sacrifice to see this mission through."

"True," said Arthur, plucking another candy from the plate. "But Kando's right. We've hit a dead end. I even went to speak with Crom's wife, but she had no idea he was part of something nefarious. If some clue doesn't turn up soon, we'll be heading back to Verden, no matter how badly Del doesn't want us too."

"I'd think Del would be itching to get back home." She took another small sip of her wine, noting how long it had been since she had drunk anything even slightly luxurious. Arthur was already several sips into his own glass.

"Oh, I forgot. You weren't there." Arthur leaned forward. "Seems our little Rook found a message from the minks to Crom. They weren't just in Verden to harass mice. They were there for him."

"What?" Denya felt her face flush.

"Now, he thinks that if we go back to Verden, he'll be in even more danger. He thinks the only way to end this is to find Crom's killer and get to the bottom of things."

"I think I might actually agree with him," she said. She glanced up to the top of the tower, thinking of her parents and the way they'd shunned her and her band, asking them to leave—no, demanding that they leave.

"If only we had a way to get that tracking information." He ate another candy and pushed the plate towards her, offering her the last one.

She let out a heavy sigh, picking up the candy and putting it half-heartedly into her mouth. The flavor tasted less sweet this time. She swallowed, then smiled politely at Arthur. "I think I've had enough hiding in plain sight for one night."

"What's this then? The party's only just beginning," Arthur laughed, peering at the mice around them still dancing.

"You stay," she said, standing from the table. She turned to walk away, but looked back "And, Arthur . . . thank you for tonight."

"My dear, you are welcome to join me in drunken frivolous exploits anytime," he said, toasting her with his nearly emptied wine glass.

She laughed before turning back towards the inn.

*   *   *

In his dream, Del was standing in a great forest. He'd never been anywhere so overgrown and devoid of human relics or machinery. In front of him stood the largest tree he'd ever seen. Its trunk was wider than any building or skyscraper he knew of, and its limbs and branches stretched so high that they touched the stars.

A sudden wind picked up, ruffling his fur and causing him to shield his face with his paws. From the tree, a flurry of leaves gusted towards him on the wind. They shifted and moved through the air until they formed a mouth and two eyes. Del looked up into the face of leaves, feeling fear seep into his skin. After all, he'd never spoken to a leafy face before.

"What are you?" asked the face. Its voice was androgynous and sounded both brash and intimidating. It was almost as if the howl of the wind were forming words.

"I'm a . . . a . . . a mouse," stuttered Del, though he had the distinct impression that the voice was speaking more figuratively than literally.

"You come to the great tree while you slumber," said the leafy face. "You are no mere mouse."

Del thought for a moment and then tried again. "They say I'm a Trelock."

"*They* say? What do *you* say?" asked the face.

"I . . . I don't know," he sighed. Thunder shook the sky above, startling him.

"To be a Trelock is to have the deepest spiritual connection with life itself," said the voice, as though this might help Del make up his mind on the matter.

"I don't feel connected to life. I don't know how to call on the elements. I barely know myself anymore." Del slumped, feeling defeated. His so-called power had only manifested twice, and then not even when he had called upon it, like when he had tried to summon it in the thorn bush. Even if he was a powerful Trelock, what good did it do him or anyone else if he couldn't use his abilities when he needed them? He didn't trust them. Worst of all, he didn't trust himself. He didn't even *like* himself anymore. He had been reduced to a petulant child: yelling at Kando to get his way, scared to go back to Verden for fear of being captured, afraid to move forward for fear of failing.

Suddenly, the leaves flew at him, and before he could move out of the way, they spun around him like a green tornado. He turned this way and that but couldn't see any way to escape. One of the leaves nicked him, slicing into his shoulder, which drew a thin line of red blood. And then, just as quickly as the whirlwind had begun, the leaves left him and went back to forming a floating face between himself and the tree.

"The blood of the Trelocks of ages past does indeed course through your veins." The leafy face somehow did not look happy about this. "One does not choose to be a Trelock. One is chosen. And there is only ever one."

"Only one?" asked Del, terrified by this revelation. "But I'm worthless at it. Don't you have some sort of . . . backup plan?"

"*You* have been chosen. Only you. But..." The leafy face turned to look at the sky above the tree. The atmosphere was growing darker as a black cloud began to consume it. "As you are, you will not be ready to stop the coming darkness."

"Coming darkness?" All of this sounded a bit like something out of a comic book to him. *The chosen one. Darkness on the horizon.* He was sure he'd read this story before. Yet now, somehow, he was at the center of it. "Then what do I do?" he asked. "What do I do when the darkness comes?"

"A Trelock is one who can tap into the very elements that make up this world. Only when you have unlocked the full capabilities of these fundamental elements, will you reveal your true power. What you do when the darkness comes is up to you. One might not choose to be a Trelock, but one must choose how to use one's power. Rise or fall, win or lose, the choice will be yours."

There was a flash of lightning and then Del awoke, his breathing labored. He abruptly sat up in his small bed at the inn. He worked to steady his breath, turning to let his feet hang off the bed.

What remained of the flames in the fireplace still gave off the slightest bit of heat, enough to warm his toes. He replayed the dream in his head, trying to decide if any of it were true, or simply a fiction created by his imagination after so many days on the road.

Outside his room, he heard footsteps creaking on the wooden floor. He went to the door and cracked it open. To his surprise, Denya was walking past his room, a contemplative expression on her face.

"Denya," he whispered. She turned to him.

"Can't sleep?" she asked.

"Bad dreams. What about you?"

"Just got back. I went out for a bit to think things over."

"Yeah, today was pretty rough," he agreed, knowing the fact that her parents were involved probably made the situation that much more difficult to stomach. "Maybe we can come up with another way to track the bee. We can't just give up, right?" Any idea was better than giving up.

She could see the fear in his eyes. Arthur was right, Del was terrified of what would happen to him. "Actually," started Denya. "I think I figured it out."

"Oh?" asked Del curiously.

"A trade," she said. "My parents will provide us with the location of the stolen bee."

"Really?" remarked Del. "What are we offering them in this trade?"

Denya's smile faded. "Me."

CHAPTER ELEVEN

Farewells

The next morning, with the entire band gathered once more around the small table at the inn, Denya told them all her intentions. Del had tried to object to her plan the night before, but she had merely wished him goodnight and then locked herself in her room.

"I'll stay here and help them with the apiary," she said. "In return, they will give you the information you need to follow the assassin."

"This is absurd," Kando argued, more emotion in his voice than any of them had ever heard from him. "You are an Scrapper in the Longtails. You can't simply run off to raise bees. We will all go back together, to Verden, and we will find another way."

Del saw Arthur flash him a quick look, as if to say, *See how badly he doesn't want us to continue on this quest?* Del had already noticed this detail himself.

"My job is to do anything in my power to ensure the safety of the mice in Verden and my band," countered Denya. "I've thought this through, and it's the only way to meet this objective. We go back now, and we risk the lives of every mouse in the city, not to mention Del's life. Taking him back there paints a target on all of Verden. I am doing this, and then you are all going to go after the assassin and cut this threat off at the throat."

There was a long silence at the table. "Well, I'm for it," said Arthur, leaning back in his chair. "It might be tough on the road with only three of us, but the Rook's gotta start pulling his weight sooner or later. Just to be safe though, I think I'll take over on map duty."

"Sorry," Del muttered.

Kando shook his head, as if trying to sort things out. "This is absurd. We should not be taking Del further away from safety. He's not ready for the dangers that are out there."

"Then teach me!" exclaimed Del, hitting the table with a fist. "I'm not safe *anywhere!* Not until I learn to use this . . . power. So, if you're as worried as you say you are about me, then teach me something!"

Kando looked at Del but gave no response. Then he turned to Denya. "You're sure about this?"

Denya nodded confidently. "Yes."

"Then we will gather our belongings here while you speak with your parents," said Kando. "Your agreement with your parents is of a personal nature. As such, we will grant you the space and the time to discuss it with them."

"Good point," agreed Denya. "I've already sent word ahead to spell out my terms. That way they won't simply lock me out when I arrive."

"Good," said Kando. "Everyone should be back here and ready to leave within the hour." They all nodded. "And Del . . ."

Del met Kando's eyes, once again feeling ashamed at his outburst.

"You're right. You do need training." Kando scratched his chin thoughtfully. "I should have started working with you when we first began this trip, but I've been . . . preoccupied."

Del's eyes flicked to Arthur's for a brief second, then back to Kando's. The Demon *was* holding something back.

"But that changes now. Once we're on the trail of the assassin and your would-be killers, I will teach you what I know."

"Thank you," Del replied. He rose from the table and left the lobby area. He headed for his room to prepare for their journey, followed by Arthur.

Denya left the inn and made her way up the various sets of lifts leading to the top of the tower. Looking around, she marveled at the city, which hadn't been home since she was a pup. The mice running about on the lower levels, playing and laughing, gave her hope of one day having her own family. The scientist mice higher up, shooting electricity between metal rods or creating small explosions, gave her hope that perhaps she could still find time for her passions.

All her life, she had wanted to do the right thing for herself. Now, it was time to do the right thing for everyone else. In this, she realized that she had finally figured out what it meant to be a member of the Longtails. Somewhere inside her heart, she felt that Roderick would have been proud of her decision.

At the top of the tower, the familiar scent of honey wafted into her nostrils as she disembarked from the lift and followed the path, that she knew by heart, to her father's workshop. She rapped her knuckles on the wooden door and then entered without awaiting a reply. Her mother and father were both there, and her mother flung her arms around Denya and began to cry.

"Welcome home, my darling," she said. Denya hugged her back. It had been a long time since she'd felt a hug that warm and tight. It was a nice feeling.

Her father beamed a rare smile. "Good to have you back," he said. As she broke from the embrace with her mother, her father handed her a small folded up piece of paper. She unfolded it to see that it was a hand-drawn map of the surrounding lands with a mark to the east of the tower.

It was far beyond the border of the Mouselands, straying into the rarely traveled outer territories. It was a place which birthed all manner of rumors and tall tales.

"Aurora," she breathed softly.

"It's been there for quite a while. I can't imagine it will move on them." He sighed. "You understand why we couldn't give this to you before," said her father. "It was too dangerous. You would have run out there and gotten eaten by who knows what. But now . . . well, we wish your friends the best of luck on their travels."

Denya peered up at him, trying to ignore the clear implication that she was not strong enough for such an adventure, and that her friends were being led to their deaths. "Thank you, Father."

She placed the paper in the pocket of her leather tunic, her paw grazing the scroll that Roderick had written for Del. *When he's ready,* Roderick had said. *He isn't ready,* she thought. *But, will I ever see Del again after I hand off the map?*

"Will you permit me to take this to them?" she asked.

Her father nodded. "We know you've made the right choice, but it certainly wasn't an easy one. Take the map to your friends. Say your farewells, and when you get back, we'll get everything else settled. But, please—" Her father's words faltered for a moment before he continued. "Do come back."

Denya gave a single nod. "I will. I promise."

She left the workshop and headed back down to the main level.

*   *   *

"Aurora?" asked Kando, eyeing the map. "What would a mouse be doing out there?"

"That's what you all have to figure out," said Denya. She turned to Arthur, who reached out a paw to shake hers. To his total surprise, she hugged him. "You've been a fine friend and fellow Scrapper," she said.

"As have you," Arthur responded. "Do promise you'll write. All these ladymice fawning over me, I'm afraid I'll need your scrutiny to keep me grounded."

Denya laughed. "I will." She turned to Kando. "Take good care of them, will you?"

Kando nodded. "Of course."

Finally, she turned to Del. "And Rook -" She paused. "Del..." She thought of the rolled-up scroll in her side-satchel. Her paw reached in and grazed over it, ready to hand it off to him. But at the last moment, she changed her mind. Perhaps she was doing it for his own good, or perhaps she simply couldn't accept that this would be their last meeting. Either way, she withdrew her empty paw from the satchel. "Continue to learn and grow. I imagine you're stronger than you or any of us realize."

Del stifled his tears and nodded. He then flung his arms around her in a hug. "Thank you, Denya," he whispered. "For everything."

Denya hugged him back and then stepped away. It was hard for any of them to believe this was goodbye.

"We should get going," said Kando. The three members of the band turned and walked away, exchanging final farewells as they left. Denya waved back, wanting so much to follow them, but knowing she couldn't.

It felt like the last day of the only life she had known for so long. But it also felt like the first day of a new one that was ready to begin.

*   *   *

The three mice pushed through the always-busy crowd until they reached the entrance of the Tower of Toleloo. Del gave one final look back at the massive tower, which had filled him full of astonishment upon arriving. Looking back at it seemed sad now: the colors less vibrant, the spectacle less awe-inspiring. He decided it was best to keep his eyes forward.

Rise or fall, win or lose, the choice will be yours, the voice in his mind said, echoing his dream. He didn't know what choices lay before him, but all he could do was keep going. He was part of something bigger now. If Denya could give up on her dreams for the mice of the realm, the very least he could do was to put one foot in front of the other.

"Aurora, eh?" asked Arthur skeptically as they stepped out into the sun. "You know, I heard they roast mice on sticks for a snack out there."

"Then we'll have to avoid fires and sticks," said Kando.

"Right you are," replied Arthur.

They journeyed south to the main gate of Toleloo, ready to pass through the electric fence once again. Del took time to breathe the fresh air, realizing he had indeed missed it while being inside the tower. The sky was full of clouds, and each of the mice wished silently that they wouldn't be facing rain on top of everything else. The guard at the main gate escorted them out and wished them well, and then they all turned eastward. There was no path to follow anymore. Mice didn't go east of Toleloo. Not unless they had a death wish.

"Everyone ready?" asked Kando.

"Ready as I'll ever be," said Arthur.

"How about you, Rook?" asked Kando, eyeing Del warily.

Del's thoughts lingered on the bronze emblem and the message it held. He needed answers, and there was only one way he was going to get them. Besides, the way he saw it, he could either die in Aurora, or die in Verden, waiting for another mink attack.

"Ready," he answered.

"Then let's move on before the weather turns."

Without any more talk, they started east. Towards the assassin. Towards answers. Towards the one place mice knew they should never, ever, go: Aurora.

CHAPTER TWELVE

Raindrops

The walk east was a long and steady one. Rolling hills and grassy knolls had taken up residence where there had once been sprawling human neighborhoods. According to Arthur, their path was weaving between the furthest edges of the Mouselands and the southernmost fringes of the Glenn: Blue Jay territory. Del truly felt as though he had left civilization behind. In Verden, at least the mice had maintained the buildings to some degree, but out here, nature had torn through and overwhelmed any signs that humanity had once existed, effectively erasing them from history.

For the most part, they walked in silence. Every once in a while, they would stop for Kando and Arthur to examine the map and make sure they were on the right track. Del was not asked his opinion on the matter. They would then continue the trek. Del was reminded of his first read-through and subsequent viewing of *The Lord of the Rings,* in which he often wondered whether the endless walking would ever come to an end. Then again, he was in no hurry to get to Mount Doom.

By late afternoon, a trickling sound filled their ears, giving them pause. "There's a river on the map that skirts by the gigabee's last known location," said Arthur, eyeing the map which was now his responsibility. "Think it's the same one?"

"According to the map, it is," replied Kando, peering over Arthur's shoulder at the wrinkled parchment. Arthur had been adding concise markings and notations to the map to track their route, ensuring they still knew where they were and how to get back.

They continued on a ways through tall, dry grass which cracked under the weight of their paws as they pushed the blades aside to clear a path. Eventually, the grass grew shorter and then ended completely, replaced by dry mounds of dirt.

They came to a cliff overlooking river rapids below it. The river wasn't all that wide, but for them, it would be impossible to cross. The water frothed and churned over rocks and boulders, sending sprays of mist into the air and making everything damp and cold.

"Path along the edge looks walkable!" Arthur shouted over the roaring of the river. "Maybe we could follow it all the way."

Kando looked up at the sky to get his bearings, but a blanket of clouds obscured the sun from view. "We should wait until the clouds clear so we can be sure we're heading in the right direction." He looked at the dry ground around them and nodded. "This is a good time and place to get some rest and eat something." He peered at Arthur. "Set up camp."

"Shouldn't the Rook do that?" asked Arthur, grinning devilishly at Del.

"He's coming with me. We'll find some berries or mushrooms to eat with the bread we purchased from the inn," replied Kando.

"Aw, a private adventure then," grumbled Arthur.

"Do as you're told," was the Demon's only response. He turned to Del, who slumped his shoulders in an attempt to make himself look small enough that Kando might ignore him. He was unsuccessful.

"Come," Kando ordered.

Arthur set to work on digging a small fire-pit into the plateau overlooking the river. Del anxiously followed Kando across the dirt and back into the dry, golden grass. At first, the blades were quite short, but before long they were in a field with patches of golden grass that towered high above them, soft patches of soil, and a few trees which bloomed bright red flowers.

"If we're lucky," Kando said, "we'll find some berries or even a few nuts that have been scattered by the wind."

"I thought the entire point of purchasing rations from the inn was so that we didn't have to forage," remarked Del.

"Hm," Kando looked back at him. "You're very quick to question my leadership. Do you perhaps think yourself more adept at outdoor survival than a mouse who has taken down a deer with only his two paws?"

"No, I..." started Del. The thought of Kando killing a dear sent a shiver down his spine. But then he remembered Roderick and Denya's bravery, and it caused him to pause, puff out his chest and speak honestly. "It just seems a waste of time to bring me on such a simple task, rather than send me on my own to complete it or leave me to set up camp. You never had any problem barking orders at me before. What changed? Have I really screwed up so much that I can't even be trusted to pick berries?"

"Are you calling me bossy?" asked Kando, slightly exasperated.

Del did his best impression of Batman, lowering his voice so that it was gruff and gravelly. *"Gather the honey jars and the beetles, Rook. Take the cart back to Crom's house, Rook. Don't get eaten by a snake, and when you DO get eaten, don't bleed on me. Got it, Rook? I'm Batman!"*

He knew Kando wouldn't understand the last part, but it just felt like the right note to end on.

Kando stared at Del with a raised brow, clearly unamused. "Fine. You're right. You could have done this by yourself, but I didn't actually bring you out here only to find berries."

"Oh . . ." Del was suddenly reminded of Arthur's suspicion of Kando being secretive and wondered if it involved some nefarious subplot for him which involved the two of them being alone. *And what better place than a field in the middle of nowhere where no one can hear me scream!?*

Kando reached a paw up to his katana, unsheathed it and then pointed it at Del in a single fluid motion.

"Woah!" cried Del. "Okay, I'm sorry about the whole Batman thing. I just thought—"

Kando charged at him, swinging the blade at lightning speed, cutting down the tall grass. Del dodged the blade, rolling to his left. He just barely stood before the blade came down once more, nearly missing him as he fell backwards.

"Please!" Del cried. The tall grass obstructing his view was very stressful. "Can't we just talk about this?!" Groveling on the ground between patches of grass, Del grabbed a fistful of dirt and flung it at Kando, who deflected it with a swing of his katana. With an overhead thrust, the blade came down on Del as he pushed backwards, falling on his back and flattening the grass around him. The tip sunk into the dirt between Del's legs, just barely missing him. Kando pulled the blade out of the ground and continued to press the attack.

He would have cut Del in half, but a sudden gust of wind burst from Del's paws, launching him upwards. He spun in the air, doing an acrobatic flip, but came up short. The wind abruptly stopped, and Del crashed back down into an untouched section of tall grass which mercifully cushioned his fall.

Kando sheathed his blade. "You're a Trelock alright. A fairly inept one, at that."

Del sat himself up and looked at Kando from the ground. "That was . . . some sort of test?!"

"Yes."

"Did I pass?!" Del was breathless, and his voice reeked of panic. He could barely even process the fact that he had just managed to summon wind for the first time.

"*Pass* is a strong word."

"I thought you were going to kill me!" Del dusted off his face as he stood up.

"I considered it." Kando gave a wry smile, and Del realized it was meant to be his attempt at a joke. Maybe. "When I first went to Handies Peak to learn the way of the Demons, my instructor forbade me from using a sword." Kando began to walk, and Del, not knowing what else to do, followed. "Every day, all I did was chores. Sweeping the monastery. Mopping. Polishing the golden statues.

Climbing to the tops of the pillars to dust the ceiling. For months, it went on like that. Then, one day, he gave me a sword and asked me to fight him. To my great surprise, I was able to wield the heavy thing and, to some extent, defend myself. Without ever once having trained with it."

"I'm really happy for you," Del replied sarcastically. He thought of Son Goku, who had been trained in just this way by Master Roshi in the original *Dragon Ball* manga series: forced to do chores every day until, one day, he was simply stronger than his opponents. Somehow, Del did not think that sweeping floors was going to make him any better at summoning the elements.

"The point of this story," Kando bit back, "is that sometimes we learn to do something by doing other things instead. Before we left Verden, I did my best to study what little writing there was about Trelocks. I'll admit, the reference material on the subject is limited. In fact, only one Trelock ever seems to exist at a time. A new one is never awoken until the last has died, and often times, many generations seem to pass in between them. Which makes the prospect of training you a bit of a predicament."

Del thought back to his dream from the night before. *There is only ever one.*

"It seems that Trelocks typically start to awaken their powers through dreams," continued Kando. "As a Trelock, you are directly connected to the life force of the earth itself, but as a mouse who can barely connect with other mice . . ."

"Hey!" interrupted Del indignantly.

"Do you deny this fact? It is my understanding that you were a shut-in before all of this. Content to read books all day and all night. Rarely did you ever have any real connections to the outside world *or* its citizens."

"How do you—"

"I do my research before taking on a job."

Kando pulled his sword from its sheath, waving it around as if it were as light as paper in his paws. "Imagine that this sword is your power."

He turned the sword so that the hilt was facing Del and offered it to him. "Go on," he said.

Del reached out and took the sword, but no sooner had Kando let go of it did it drop directly to the ground. Del tried desperately to lift it, but it was no use. It was too heavy.

"You cannot wield the sword because your muscles are too weak to lift it. You cannot summon your powers because your mind is too weak to connect to them. In order to lift any weapon, you must train, building your muscles to support the weight. In order to use your Trelock-given gifts, you must do the same for your mind. Nothing is learned overnight. Everything worth doing takes practice and honing."

"Reading enhances the mind," Del retorted.

"Yes, but elemental control is all about balance, a trait which you are sorely lacking." Kando retrieved his sword and sheathed it. He then looked up. "See the dew on that flower way up there?"

Del peered up, shading his eyes with his paw. There were indeed several droplets of dew sitting on a red-petaled flower, which waved gently in the passing breeze.

"Yeah. So?"

"Trelocks have the ability to control the elements: water, wind, fire and earth. According to my reading, water is the easiest of these. Especially if you are controlling it in a direction it *wants* to flow. I can only imagine that pushing it against its natural inclination would be much harder. Water, as an element, is intangible, but flows naturally. It is not as solid as the earth, not as erratic as fire, and not as imperceptible as air. So, for your first lesson, I want you to reach out and summon one of those droplets to you."

Del abruptly turned to Kando with dismay, surprised by this request. "I would love to do that," he said bitterly. "But here's a question: how?"

Kando's raised his shoulders. "I don't know."

"Is that like an old Demon proverb?"

"No," Kando dissented. *"Cutteth the tongue from ye who cannot hold it.* That is an old Demon proverb."

Del gulped. "So, you were saying something about summoning that water droplet?"

"My understanding is that Trelocks do not force nature to obey, they ask it to. My sword is a weapon which I have full control over. But the elements are alive and have motivations all their own. Thus, your job is to be something of a diplomat as well as a conduit of balance between yourself and the elements. Your power lies in the subtle art of communication and connection."

"Oh, why didn't you say so before?" asked Del, forgetting that he was dangerously close to having his tongue *cuttethed*. "Now it all makes perfect sense! Are you saying I should just ask the water to come down here? Maybe invite it over for some tea and cookies?"

"Wouldn't hurt to try, would it?" asked Kando, who seemed to be taking this ridiculous idea very seriously.

Del sighed, and for a moment he considered having nothing to do with this foolish activity. But then he decided that if Kando was going to ask him to consider something so absurd, then Del was going to match it with an equally silly show. He held his paws up to the sky and called to the heavens.

"Oh, great water droplet," he chanted. "Heed my call and *falleth* atop the head of Kando, for he is joyless in all things."

Kando rolled his eyes and crossed his arms. "Has anyone ever told you you're funny?"

"Not lately," Del jeered, lowering his paws.

"That's because you aren't," snapped Kando. "Now try again. This time, do it as though you are actually taking this lesson seriously."

"Are you kidding?" Del exploded. He was clearly fed up. Weeks of frustration and self-loathing had been building up and had now finally reached a tipping point. "This is insane! You have no idea how to use my powers. *I* have no idea how to use them. I'm completely useless until every once in a while when my power decides, *Oh, hey! Just for fun, I better help Del out, so he doesn't die!* This whole thing is so stupid! I shouldn't even be here. The elements are either playing some sick joke or they just chose wrong! I was perfectly happy to stay at home, playing *Mario Kart* and reading *Green Lantern*! I AM NOT SPECIAL! I WAS NEVER MEANT TO *BE* SPECIAL!"

Kando waited patiently for Del to end his rant. "Are you done shouting?" he asked, calmly.

Del took a few deep breaths and then closed his eyes. "Yeah," he whispered.

"Good. Then try again."

There is no try. He shook his head, trying to stop Yoda from interfering. Del was not, after all, a Jedi. The same rules didn't apply.

He took a deep breath, then opened his eyes and looked up at the water droplet. He raised one paw up towards the flower and held it there. In his mind, he imagined the water droplet coming to him, floating down and gently plopping into his paw. He tried to envision what that would look like, what it would feel like when it finally touched him.

The droplet remained where it was, not moving.

Use the force, Del. He closed his eyes again and tried to focus. He remembered how he had felt when using his powers to attack Barrel-Fist. Despite his rage at the time, giving himself to the power had been almost calming. It was like a strange zen had washed over him. He remembered a gentle tingling sensation which had started at his toes and worked its way to the crown of his head, ending in the tips of his ears. He searched for that feeling inside himself, trying to recreate it.

Please. Maybe water droplets *did* like to be asked to tea. And who didn't like cookies? *Please come to me.*

In the distance, far far away, he thought he heard Kando calling to him. But it was like sound heard underwater. It was muffled, as if he were deep in a dream. He gently pushed it from his mind.

He focused harder. He visualized water—really saw it in his mind. He saw the way it shimmered and refracted light. He saw the red of the flower petal beneath it, tinting the droplet with a pale pink hue. The droplet was so pure and perfect, like a bubble that could burst at any moment. *What if I can't move the water droplet? What if I never can?* He let the doubts slip past him, never letting them sink their teeth in. His thoughts plunged inside the droplet, and he became a part of it. It was all around him, and he was all around it. There was no telling where Del ended and the droplet began. This made him feel comforted—safe, even.

So, when next he spoke to the water, he did not beg or plead, he simply invited it to join him. *Come along now, old friend.*

"DEL!" His eyes burst open as the drop of dew splashed down on him, wetting the fur atop his head, cloak and scarf.

"I did it!" he exclaimed. "I really did it!" He was, perhaps for the first time in his life, truly proud of something he'd accomplished.

But Kando, who raced towards him, did not look pleased. "Yes, you certainly did." He motioned towards the sky. Del's gaze followed Kando's paw. The clouds had turned pitch black and were swirling menacingly above them.

Another drop of water fell to the soil near them. Then another. And another. Large raindrops careened towards the earth like liquid bombs, exploding in the soil and turning it instantly to mud.

"HELP!" A crying voice echoed on the wind. A voice they knew. Arthur's voice. Del's blood ran cold.

"Come on," ordered Kando, grabbing Del's arm and heading back towards Arthur. As they ran, rain pelted the ground and a terrible wind rushed all around them, displacing the golden blades of grass so that it was hard to make out a path.

"Did I do this?" asked Del, trying desperately to keep up as the two of them dodged left and right, pushing through the violently thrashing grass which relentlessly blocked their path, like an army of snakes.

"If you did, I'd appreciate if you would undo it!" Kando shouted back to him, wrenching Del to the left just in time to avoid a huge drop of water.

Puddles were quickly forming, sucking up the soil and turning it into mud. These watery obstacles were becoming increasingly difficult to avoid.

A droplet landed directly onto Del, further drenching his clothes and shoving him down into the muck. Kando stopped and ran back to pull Del out of the grimy trap. He yanked Del out and pushed him along the path ahead of him.

The grass became shorter and then ebbed away, revealing the cliff which was now covered in gooey mud running in all directions. Up ahead, they saw the beginnings of a small unfinished campfire, built from stone and sticks. The air was thick with precipitation, and the ground was becoming slippery. Muck clung to their feet, making it hard to take a single step, let alone run. Del searched frantically, but Arthur was nowhere in sight.

"Arthur?!" he called, taking a step forward, but no sooner had he done so, did he hear a sound like thunder, crackling not from the sky, but behind them. The earth gave way and dropped dramatically, angling the plateau into a steep hill. Del felt his stomach lurch into his throat as both he and Kando fell to the ground on all fours. They immediately began to slip and slide down the slope towards the cliff face which hung precariously over the river rapids.

"AHHHH!" they both squeaked.

Del tried to focus his mind; tried to reach out to the water once more, but it was no use. He was far too distracted by thoughts of falling, sliding and drowning. The cliff lurched again, increasing the angle of the incline so that they were sliding even faster towards the river.

Del's whole body abruptly stopped falling. A blue aura surrounded him, suspending him in place. The same could not be said for Kando, despite using his sword as an anchor, which proved useless in the mud.

"I've got you!" yelled a voice from above.

Del looked up to see Arthur, drenched in rain, his white fur made brown by the mud. With his paws outstretched, he strained to keep Del magically in place.

"Get Kando!" yelled Del.

"What?!" called back Arthur.

"Kando!" tried Del once more. But it was no use. The rain and wind were howling and relentless, gobbling up his voice as soon as it left his throat.

With great effort, Arthur pulled Del up from the other side of the chasm created when the plateau had fallen. The chasm uncovered a cross-section of the earth: soil, rocks and slimy worms, some of which fell with Kando into the water below.

Del tried desperately to turn his head, to find Kando in the haze of wind and rain, but it was no use. He was incapacitated. Arthur brought him up over level ground and then unceremoniously released his magical hold, plopping

Del down into the muck. Del wasted no time in clawing his way to the newly-formed cliff and looking over the ledge for Kando. The black mouse was nowhere to be found.

"We have to get Kando!" Del shouted.

"He's gone!" cried Arthur, who looked as though he might weep. "I wasn't strong enough to grab both of you. I tried . . . but he fell . . . before I could . . . and the river just. . . took him!"

"No," whispered Del. All the memories of Roderick's death resurfaced, surging through him. The guilt and pain tore at Del like a monster inside him trying to get out. "NO!" Before Del could clearly process his own thoughts, he took off running and lunged off the cliff, diving for the tumultuous river below.

"Del!!!" cried Arthur, reaching out for him. But he was already gone.

Del crashed into the water, and darkness instantly enveloped him. Every sound was muffled. Torn up chunks of earth and grass swam past him, churning in the water and causing him to spin and topple over himself. He broke the surface, long enough to gasp for air and was pulled back under. Up was down and down was up.

Del was flung into the side of the riverbed before breaching the surface once again. He managed to grab half a breath before he was dragged back under the violent rapids, sinking deeper this time.

The water roared around him like a raging beast. A rock careened into him, knocking him down further. He spun endlessly until he saw the riverbed racing towards him, and everything went black.

CHAPTER THIRTEEN

Captain Artemis Truffel

The first thing Del noticed as his eyes fluttered open was how incredibly weightless he felt. His body was floating gently in place. Darkness surrounded him from all sides, save for a soft blue light casting down on him from somewhere high above.

He tried to remember how he came to be in such a place. His mind slowly replayed the moments before losing consciousness beneath the surface of the river. This memory did little to enlighten him about his current location.

"How cuuuurious," purred a voice in the darkness. The voice was smooth like butter spread across toast. Del thought it sounded like a male voice, but it was high-pitched enough to be somewhat androgynous. "You're quite smaaaaaall, for a Trelock."

"H-hello?" asked Del, his voice weak. At first, he had thought he was floating in air. But as he tried to move, he felt resistance, and he realized that he was actually submerged entirely in water. But then, how was he breathing? How was he speaking? *Am I dead?* he thought. *Am I Aquaman?* No, that was far less likely. This, he decided, must be the afterlife. He never suspected it would be so wet. His fur undulated softly, like it did on a spring day as the breeze rushed through it. "A-am I dead?" he asked out loud, hoping to rip off the proverbial band-aid.

"Deeeeaaaaad?" asked the voice. "Here, there is no *dead*. There is no *alive*. This place exists apart from such things. Here, there is simply *being*."

Del thought about this statement, but it only confused him even more. Was this place the Phantom Zone? Was General Zod going to jump out at him and demand freedom, so that he could be on his way and finally kill Superman? He needed more information.

"Who are you?" Part of him actually hoped it *was* General Zod. Or, at least, Mister Mxyzptlk, a less known comic book character who was capable of bringing him into another dimension but was far less scary than the General. Del had been through a lot these last few weeks. Didn't he deserve to meet a comic book character? *Any* comic book character?

There was a childlike giggle which rippled the water around him. "You should know who I am. After all, you called to me."

"Called to you?" asked Del.

Suddenly, a creature nearly four times his size emerged from the darkness, spinning playfully through the water. In many ways, it resembled an otter. But instead of brown fur, it was blue, with yellow stripes down its sides and two more along either cheek. It had two small horns protruding from the crown of its head, and its tail seemed to stretch out, becoming a bright blue stream of water trailing behind it. There was no telling where the tail stream ended, and the surrounding water began.

The blue otter swam up to Del and came to a stop in front of his floating body. It smiled a big, dopey smile, as if prepared to say "cheese" and to pose for a photograph.

"I am the oooooocean, the rivers, the rains," said the blue otter. "I am the snow of winter and the storms of spring. I am the spirit of water."

"Spirit of *water*?" asked Del, who had never imagined the elements he'd been attempting to speak with as actual beings.

"But I imagine that is an aaaaaawefully big thought for a little mouse. You may call me Urabzu." The otter smiled. "May I ask whyyyyyy you called me?"

Del was baffled. "I . . . I didn't realize I was calling you. I just thought I was . . . I don't know . . . moving water with my mind."

"To move an element is to summon its spirit to your aid," said Urabzu. "That is the way of things. But if you have no neeeeeed of me, then I will be off." Urabzu spun in the water.

"Wait!" called Del.

Urabzu twisted his body, contorting so that he was looking at Del upside down. "Yes?"

"Could I . . . ask a question?"

"I suppooooose. Would you mind if I offered an answer?" Urabzu moved a paw through the water so that he twirled lazily in place.

"That's sort of the point of me asking," said Del.

"Oh! What a fun game!"

Del cleared his throat and pressed on, not wanting to explain that this was simply how one was meant to talk to another and not really a game.

"Could you tell me... why was I chosen? To be a Trelock, that is?"

The otter laughed. "Silly mouse. Every generation, there is one who may commune with us. One whose soul is connected to our world. Some are more receptive than others, but there is always one, and one there shall always be."

"But why me?" Del pressed. "I didn't ask for any of this. And I'm definitely not worthy of any sort of big responsibility."

Urabzu pondered this fact. "Perhaps that is why. Our mother works in mysterious ways. Alas, I cannot answer the question you ask, but perhaps my brothers and sisters can."

"Brothers and sisters?" asked Del.

"Wind, fire and earth," said Urabzu. "Each one will appear to you in their own time. In a way, you are as much a stranger to us as we are to you. I only found you because you decided to dream in my river. But now that we have met, we are connected. Though, our connection to one another is still quite weak. I sense you still do not believe in your abilities."

"That's an understatement," sighed Del.

"Then your ability to summon my aid will continue to be weak until you learn to trust yourself. Spirits are not tangible beings. We exist through belief, the way you survive on food and air. I cannot force you to believe, but I will do my best to aid you in the meantime—albeit, at a limited capacity. Know that I cannot go where there is not water. And I will not assist you should the request be too self-serving. Our goal, and yours, should always be to protect the continuation of life on this world."

Del considered this new information and recalled his dream. "I dreamt of a tree, and it said I would not be ready. That darkness was coming, and I wouldn't be able to stop it."

"Something terrible *is* on the horizon," said Urabzu. "And it is true that you are merely a trickling stream . . . for now. But every stream can flow into a river and every river may flow into a lake or an ocean." The otter twirled in place, the water swirling around him, causing a flurry of bubbles to rise up. "I cannot say if you will be ready. For some things are up to you, and only you can decide your own fate." The otter suddenly looked up at the light above them. "The storm is ending now. Time to gooooooo back." Then he wrapped his big furry arms around Del and hugged him tightly. "Until next we meet, Del Hatherhorne."

*   *   *

Del gasped and coughed, spewing water from his lungs as light flooded his eyes, blinding him. He was lying on his back and soaked from head to toe. He felt completely disoriented. There was a low humming noise somewhere in the distance, and sunlight washed over him, heating the skin beneath his brown fur.

He tried to cover his eyes with his paws, but his paws couldn't move. He turned his head as much as his body would allow and saw that he actually wasn't lying down at all but standing on a wooden floor, which vibrated ever so gently. His back was up against something hard and cylindrical. He was tied to this cylindrical thing by thick rope which bound his chest, arms and legs. His paws were fastened together behind him.

"Glad to see you're alive," said a familiar voice beside him. It was Arthur. Del craned his neck as much as was possible, so that he could just barely make out the white fur of his compatriot next to him. Arthur, it seemed, was restrained to the hard, round thing as well. "I thought for sure you were jumping to your death."

"Which, I might add, was incredibly stupid," growled Kando, who Del realized was also tied up in the same way on his other side. "Brave, but stupid."

"Where . . . are we?" asked Del. His voice was hoarse, as though he'd spent the past day screaming or, in his case, inhaling river water.

"We've been . . . detained," sighed Kando.

"Detained?" asked Del.

"I tried to tell them we were innocent Longtails on a mission of high importance," offered Arthur. "How was I supposed to know they were *skyrates*?"

"Skyrates?" Del repeated.

"Your blabbering mouth got us all captured!" barked Kando.

"My blabbering mouth?" Arthur scoffed. "Whiskers to the fire! Thanks to me, these fine fellows fished you lot out of the river. So, you might say, I saved you both."

"Which means a lot, considering we'll probably be sold to the highest bidder or thrown overboard to our deaths," said Kando irritably.

"Oh, will you three shut up!?" ordered a fourth, unfamiliar voice. It was deep and scary to Del, despite the fact that he hadn't seen its owner. A creature that was much taller than them and had a big bushy tail stepped into view.

"A squirrel?" Del exclaimed.

"A mouse?!" the squirrel retorted mockingly. He was dark gray with pointy tufts atop his ears, and a large eye patch over his right eye. Del noticed that the squirrel had one normal leg, covered in fur, and another that was made of dull metal and seemed to be powered by steam that was leaking from its nuts and bolts. Around his waist was a large black belt with a golden buckle. A wood-handled revolver, several small pouches, and a sharp scabbard hung from the belt.

"Kando," snapped Arthur. "He's got an eye patch as well. Perhaps you can reason with him."

Kando sighed. "Yes, I'm sure we know each other from the one-eyed rodent conventions."

"Oh!" laughed Arthur. "Perhaps the river has done you some good after all! I don't recall any displays of wit from you before the bath. And look at you now, cracking jokes with the best of us."

"Um . . . Mr. Squirrel?" started Del, feeling extremely intimidated by the squirrel's scowl. "Who are you? And what is this place?"

"We'll be the ones doing the question asking," snarled the squirrel. "Now, we might've pulled you out of that there river, but it don't mean we hafta trust ya. It surely don't. Perhaps you're on your way to meet with them minks, eh? We don't rightly care for this newfound friendship between your kind and the minks, least of all Barrel-Fist's pack: The Copper Clan. Hmph. More like . . ." The squirrel thought very hard about his insult. ". . . the *Garbage* Clan!"

The mice were silent.

"That was a joke!" the squirrel growled.

The mice each gave a weak, forced laugh.

"That's better," said the squirrel.

Del was trying to put together everything this squirrel had just said, but it seemed like an incredible amount of information for such a short statement. "What makes you think the minks and the mice are working together?"

"Oh, ho, ho," chortled the squirrel. "Going to play dumb, are ye?"

"Honestly, old chap, we don't know what you're talking about," chimed in Arthur.

"Did you *see* mice working with minks?" asked Del, whose curiosity now far outweighed his fear.

"Enough," said a silky voice from behind them. Another squirrel stepped into their view. This one was female, and while she may have been the same size as the first squirrel, she stood up so straight that it made her seem much taller. Her fur was a warm auburn color, and the tufts on her ears pointed perfectly upwards, as if standing at attention. She wore a black vest, with shimmering gold buttons beneath a long, velvety blue overcoat with golden tassels. A sheathed rapier and flintlock-style pistol hung from her waist. Atop her head was a triangular hat, which Del thought looked awfully similar to those most pirates wore in some of the books he'd read.

"I will answer two of your questions, and then you will answer *all* of mine. I don't care for time-wasters. And I certainly don't care for jokes." She eyed Arthur with disdain. Del hung onto her every word, taking in the way that she pronounced every letter and syllable to its fullest.

"My name is Captain Artemis Truffel and these squirrels are my crew," she announced haughtily. "That is the answer to your first question.

"Aren't you forgetting something?" sighed Arthur. "You're skyrates, plain and simple."

"Ha," laughed Artemis coldly. "*Skyrate* is such a boorish word. We prefer *profiteers,* or even *free spirits.* To answer your second question: *this place* is my ship—the Black Acorn—the finest squirrel-captained, araucaria-powered cloudship from here to the Grizzly Hills and back."

"And we're . . . your prisoners?" asked Del, who did not care to be restrained, no matter what kind of ship he was on.

"For the time being, yes. But you are alive," said Artemis. "Which is more than you might have been without our help. So show a little gratitude, mouse." Del didn't like the way that she said the word, *mouse*. Her voice was rife with condescension, like they were mere peasants compared to her.

"*Why* are we your prisoners?" asked Del, coming upon the question he should have asked in the first place.

"No no, little mouse. I've already broken the rules and answered a third question," said Artemis, wagging a finger in front of him like a mother warning her pup not to have any more chocolates. "It's my turn. Those were the rules. Now, why are you mice traveling out this far?"

"That's classified," said Kando.

"We're searching for an assassin," Del answered.

"Rook!" growled Kando.

"We won't get anywhere hiding things," said Del. "Besides, maybe they can help us."

"You are quite smart for one so little," said Artemis. "This assassin. Who did they assassinate?"

Del didn't get a chance to answer. Far in the distance, as if it had materialized from another dimension, there was a screech. The cry sounded as if it could have journeyed up from the depths of hell itself. Del was reminded of the Canary Cry, a sonic sound which the Black Canary, a female superhero, could make to disable her enemies. Artemis turned her head and reached out a gloved paw to the first squirrel.

"Scope," she barked.

He obliged, pulling a small brass cylinder from his pocket and handing it to her. She grabbed it and extended all three tiers, then peered through the small end with one eye. For a moment, she stayed perfectly still. Then she abruptly lowered the telescope, exhaling angrily.

"Damn," she muttered. "Shrikes."

"What a lovely coincidence," jeered Arthur. "We were almost killed by some shrikes. But don't worry, we killed them right back, so I'm sure we're all on delightfully pleasant terms. Perhaps they're sending flowers. Or maybe pastries. I would kill for a good raspberry pie right about now."

"Shut your mouth," snarled Kando. "For the love of every mouse and their mother, I beg you to stop talking!"

"To your stations!" shouted Artemis. "Cannons at the ready! Helmsman! Prepare for evasive maneuvers! Do not let those birds knock us out of the sky. Do you hear me!?"

There was a resounding "Aye aye, Captain!" from the crew somewhere behind them.

"Out of the sky?" Del whispered to himself.

"Never been on a cloudship before?" asked Arthur, who had still apparently heard him. "Oh, they're quite fun when they're not being decimated by angry shrikes."

There was a sudden slack in the rope holding them captive, and a second later it fell loose around their feet.

They all pulled away to see that they had been tied with their backs against a tall black wooden pole—the mast of the cloudship.

As they looked around, they saw all sorts of black and brown squirrels in a wide array of colorful attire running around on the deck—fastening ropes, moving cannons and preparing for battle. In the distance, to the portside of the cloudship, Del could see the watch of shrikes, which seemed to blot out the sky like black paint splattered across a blue canvas.

"Time to earn your freedom," snarled Artemis. A beige squirrel approached with a pawful of weapons. He quickly handed Kando his katana and wakizashi blade, and Arthur his rapier. Artemis looked at Del and cocked her head to one side. "You haven't even got a weapon."

"I'm a Trelock," said Del. "I'm supposed to be able to summon the elements to aid me. No weapon required." He laughed nervously.

"*Supposed* to be?" she echoed, with a hint of condescension in her voice. "That doesn't sound too promising." She reached over to a neighboring squirrel and pulled a small single-paw crossbow from his belt, along with a tiny quiver of arrows.

"Hey!" yelped the squirrel.

"Don't *Hey* your captain, Scurge," barked Artemis. "You stole this weapon off a dead rat. It's too small for you anyway."

227

"But it makes me look threatening," whined Scurge.

"It makes you look like your paws are too small to wield a real weapon," she jeered and then turned to hand the crossbow and quiver of bolts to Del. "Take these. I'll not have you running around with no defenses when the shrikes attack. We'll have enough problems without having to save you. We need every squirrel, mouse and otherwise on this ship to fight these things, or they'll knock us out of the sky."

Del had never shot a crossbow before in his life, but he already knew that declining an offer from the captain would not go over well. And besides, he'd seen Batman shoot a grappling hook enough times to know the basic gist. He accepted the gift, slinging the quiver and crossbow over his shoulder so that they rested on his back. "Thank you, ma'am," he said. She nodded approvingly and then strutted off into the crowd of squirrels.

Del turned to walk towards the front of the cloudship, where he could glance overboard, down to the world below. A small squeak escaped his mouth. They were miles and miles up in the sky. He watched as the cloudship glided over the landscape below. A gentle breeze ruffled his fur. He could see everything from this height. The Tower of Toleloo rose in the distance, and further off, he could even make out the thin outline of the sprawling metropolis of Verden.

There were thick forests, yellow plains and the Rocky Mountains, which jutted up in the west. Their peaks were dusted with white snow. Taking it all in, Del realized for the

228

first time in his life just how small he was in comparison to the vast world around him. He wondered if he would ever see all the corners of the land now laid out before him. He wondered if it was even possible for one mouse to do so in his lifetime.

Despite the threat of oncoming shrikes, Del couldn't help but appreciate the sense of serenity that came with realizing his place in the world. He couldn't fully embrace the feeling in the moment—circumstances being what they were—but it was something that he knew would stay with him from this day forward.

"Del," snapped Kando. "The shrikes are nearly upon us. Are you ready?"

Del turned to face his Alpha, who had his katana drawn. Arthur stood ready beside him, brandishing his rapier in one paw and a ball of blue flame in the other. Del pulled the crossbow from behind his back and nodded. He'd spent his whole life hiding. Now, all he wanted to do was explore the wonders of the world below him. And as far as he was concerned, the only thing standing in his way was a watch of angry shrikes. He would not let that be the thing that stopped him.

"Yes," he nodded. "I'm ready."

CHAPTER FOURTEEN

The Battle for the Black Acorn

Del couldn't help but notice that there were far more shrikes now than there had been on the road to Toleloo. Perhaps the birds had redoubled their efforts in order to take them down once and for all, or perhaps they had decided not to underestimate them this time. Del wondered how the shrikes had managed to track them down. They were far outside the normal boundaries of places mice tended to go. But as the black cloud of feathers, talons, and beaks rounded on the cloudship, he decided that such questions were better left for later.

"Ready at the guns!" ordered Artemis. She pulled a long sword from a sheath at her waist and pointed to a spot at the center of the watch, her chosen target.

Now that Del was able to see the entire ship, he had to admit that he was impressed. The Black Acorn was equipped with six fusion-energy cannons on each side, along with eighteen laser-powered rail guns. It had been built with a combination of black wood and alloyed black steel. Coupled with the two large sails crafted from black solar cloth, all the components came together to give the cloudship the appearance of an ominous shadow as it raced through the sky.

Two masts held the fore and main sails, one to the front and another to the back. The thick expanses of cloth plumed forward as wind filled them from behind. The cloudship was kept aloft by araucaria-repulsor energy which pulsed like a gentle blue light from eight small engines on the underside of the hull. The engines themselves glowed brightly, but what they lacked in visual subtlety, they made up for by being virtually silent. During the daytime, a reflective screen on the ship's underbelly camouflaged the engines, making them bright enough for the cloudship to blend in with the sky. At night, the flashing bulbs of blue energy looked like a small band of fireflies. In this way, the ship was able to soar silently over the land below without alerting every creature to its presence.

Artemis called out to her crew of skyrates. "Ready . . . aim . . ." The captain paused slightly in anticipation, her rapier raised above her head. Then she whipped the sharp weapon downwards swiftly. "*Fire!*"

The fusion canons erupted with red spheres of electrified energy. The three mice watched as shrikes scattered and fell, their lifeless bodies plummeting to the earth below. Angry squawks filled the air as the watch spread themselves further apart to avoid the projectiles flying towards them. Del watched in horror as they then began to circle around the cloudship, eliminating any possibility of escape.

"They're surrounding us!" Del yelled to the captain.

"So it would seem," she replied calmly. It was going to take more than some angry birds to fluster her. "Ready the cannons!" she barked. "Are the rail guns online?"

"Aye, aye, Captain!" called another squirrel.

"Let's give them everything we've got!" shouted Artemis. "Ready!" The shrikes were getting nearer now, closing in on their prey like a pack of winged wolves. "Aim!" Del spun around. He could see the detailed coloring on the birds now, white and gray, with black stripes on their faces and wings. He could see the desire for revenge in their cold black eyes. "*FIRE!!!*"

The cloudship shook as the cannons sent another blast towards the shrikes, taking down a few of the birds but not nearly enough. At the same time, the rail guns engaged, filling the sky with a spectacular light show of red lasers. An explosion of feathers rained down as birds fell around the cloudship.

Captain Truffel turned to face the three mice. She brandished her sword and pulled the long flintlock style pistol from her belt. "Time to show us what you're made of, mice," she demanded. Then, in a single fluid motion she turned, cutting down one of the shrikes in midair as it swept over them. She then raised her pistol and fired at another. Del was surprised to see that the gun shot red laser blasts rather than bullets. The shots were followed by an eruption of feathers as a shrike's body slammed into the deck, crashed into the taffrail at the deck's edge and rolled overboard. A trail of blood streaked across the dark wooden deck in its wake.

Del shook himself, trying to focus, and grabbed a bolt from the quiver on his back. He fumbled as he slid the bolt onto the crossbow, trying desperately to remember if he'd ever actually seen Chewbacca load his crossbow in the *Star Wars* films.

"I really hate these birds," Arthur grumbled. "They don't seem to understand when they are unwanted."

"Sounds like someone else I know," remarked Kando.

"Oh, Kando, you can joke all you want, but you'd miss me if I were gone."

"Let one of these shrikes take you so we can test that theory."

"Roll over and play dead? Where's the fun in that? *Firenze!*" Arthur's paws lit with blue fire, and he shot a stream of flame towards three shrikes which were dive-bombing the cloudship. The trio was instantly set ablaze. Arthur then quickly directed a blast of blue energy towards them so that they fell away rather than into the ship. Their flaming corpses narrowly missed the sails.

Kando simultaneously swung his katana and smaller wakizashi blade, slicing one shrike's head from its shoulders, and then cutting the left wing from another. *Shwing! Shwing!* The blade moved at lightning speed, whistling as it sliced through the air. He twirled the wakizashi in his paw before leaping over an incoming shrike, stabbing the blade into its back and landing on top of it. The bird cried out in anguish but didn't fall. Kando had been careful not to kill the shrike with the blow. Gripping the impaled wakizashi, he rode the bird away from the cloudship and out into the heart of the watch.

"Foolish old mouse," grumbled Arthur. He swung his rapier, clipping the wings of two birds passing on either side of him. Feathers drifted down around him like gently falling winter snow. With his opposite paw, he shot a blast of blue energy into another group of shrikes attacking one of the cannons with their beaks and talons. The birds exploded in flames and toppled out of the sky.

Del hoisted up the crossbow, trying his best to manage the weight while looking down the sights. Even though it was only meant for a single paw, he still found it quite heavy. Combined with the jarring commotion of the besieged cloudship, he found it difficult to maintain his balance and kept teetering, first to the left and then back to the right, narrowly avoiding diving shrikes and leaping squirrels as he did a clumsy dance across the deck.

It was during a near-fall, after tripping over a coiled rope that Del realized one of the shrikes was in his sights. If he could just keep his eye trained on it, he might even be able to hit it. He tried to calm his breathing and keep his eyes fixated on the bird, tracing its path with the arrow head at the front of the crossbow. He placed a claw on the trigger, ready to pull. One last deep breath.

Suddenly, a shrike came out of nowhere and landed on top of Del, knocking him onto his back. It screeched into his face, and in his panic, he pulled the trigger, launching the bolt directly into the shrike's mouth. Its cry became a strangled cough as it stumbled backwards, knocking over several squirrels in the confusion of battle before finally falling overboard. Del's head dropped back to the deck in relief as he wiped blood from his face.

Above them, Kando was riding the shrike through the watch, slicing at any who passed with his katana in one paw. His other paw held tightly to the wakizashi still planted into the back of the mounted shrike, using it to steer the bird.

"Get off me!!" screeched the bird.

Kando ignored the plea. He veered the bird into a turn, twisting the blade so that the bird stretched out its wings in pain. The cloudship came into view once more. It was beginning to list to the side, unable to keep its hull upright through the attack. Worse yet, Kando noticed something that no one aboard even realized. The shrikes were attacking the engines on the underside of the ship, clinging to the wood and steel with their talons and pecking at the engines one by one, attempting to dismantle them. The cloudship wouldn't stay afloat much longer. He yanked sideways on the wakizashi, piloting the bird back towards the Black Acorn.

FWOOM! A blast of fire shot past him. He was too far from the ship to see its origin. Another blast of fire. He yanked left on the wakizashi, launching the bird into a barrel-roll to avoid the blast. He searched desperately for the source of the fire. But before he could attempt to pinpoint it, another came at him. He sliced at the blue flame with his katana, trying to dissipate it. But instead, his blade deflected the flames, sending them back the way they'd come. "No!" Horror rippled through him as he watched the blue ball of fire drift, as if in slow motion, until it collided with the main sail. The black solar cloth burst into flames.

Del sat up on the deck, finally catching his breath. He suddenly felt very warm, as though the sun had just emerged on a cloudy day. But as he looked up, he realized that it was not the sun he felt.

"Fire!" yelled one of the skyrates. "Fire on the main sail!" Chaos ensued as squirrels began running for buckets, filling them with water from a hose which extended from a large steel vat at the back of the ship. Shrikes ferociously pecked at the squirrels as they ran back and forth between the vat and the sail. Del dashed across the deck on all fours until he reached Arthur.

"What did you do?" Del snapped accusingly, pointing at the blue flames.

"I-I was trying to help Kando!" stammered Arthur. "I don't know what happened!"

"Well, undo it!" cried Del.

"I can't!" Arthur yelled. "It doesn't work like that. I can only make fire, not take it away."

Meanwhile, Artemis shouted out to members of her crew, directing them towards the burning sail. "Put that fire out!" she commanded.

"We're trying, Cap'n, but it's spreading too fast!" reported one of the squirrels, who scurried past her hoisting a bucket of water. He flung it at the spreading fire, but only managed to douse out a few of the flames. The billowing sail was quickly being engulfed. "We need more water!"

"We don't have more water!" snapped Artemis. "Find a way to put it out, or I'll use your tails!" She turned and shot her pistol five consecutive times. Five laser blasts hit five separate shrikes, blasting charred holes into the birds. The captain's aim was flawless.

Del hurried to add another bolt to the crossbow, his paws shaking with stress. He aimed without thinking and released the bolt. To his great surprise, it found its mark and took another shrike out of the battle.

Overhead, Kando guided his mount back towards the cloudship. Once he was within range, he pulled the wakizashi free from the bird's back and leapt onto the deck. There was a loud *thunk* as he landed next to Del and Arthur, who cowered before him.

"What was that?!" he growled at Arthur.

"I was j-just trying to help," stammered Arthur. He wasn't used to being the one in the group who messed up, and certainly wasn't used to being yelled at for it. "I never meant to . . . I mean, you're the one who—"

Kando grabbed Arthur by the scruff of his white shirt and pulled him close, glaring threateningly with his one good eye. "Don't lie to me, Scrapper," he said. "What was *really* happening?"

"We don't have time for this!" Del interrupted. "The fire's going to take the sails and then the ship! We need to help the squirrels put it out."

"That's not our only problem," snapped Kando, pulling away from Arthur after one final glare. "The shrikes are taking out the engines beneath us."

Del opened his mouth to respond but stopped as something caught his eye. Several shrikes were flying in close formation. They were moving as a unit. They soared around the ship together and then took aim directly at its side. As one, they dove down towards the ship at full speed. Del only realized what was happening just before it was too late.

"They're going to ram—" But his warning was cut short.

SLAM! The shrikes collided with the side of the ship, knocking everyone aboard off balance. Del careened sideways, grasping at the air with his paws, but it was no use. There was simply nothing to grab a hold of. As he lost his footing, he stumbled and then flipped backwards over the taffrail and into the vast open sky.

He screamed with all the breath in his lungs as the air whipped through his fur, his small body plummeting towards the world he'd been marveling at only minutes before. But as he was falling and watching the earth approach closer and closer, he stopped yelling, and an unexpected sense of peace came over him. The world below him was beautiful: full of lush forests, snowy mountains, golden fields of wheat, deep blue lakes and winding rivers. *Lakes and rivers.*

Del closed his eyes, drawing the fear from his throat down into the pit of his stomach. He did his best to slow down his heart rate, which he felt racing at a mile a minute. He took a long, deep breath and let a cool rush of air fill his lungs.

Urabzu, he thought. *I need your help . . . already.* He felt guilty for disturbing the otter so soon after they had just had their first meeting. *If our mission ends here, the mice back home will be in grave danger. I don't know if this is a self-less request or not, but I'm begging you. Please help us. Please.*

239

He opened his eyes. He was still falling, and now he was much closer to the earth than he had been when he'd first closed his eyes. A lake stretched beneath him, surrounded by oak trees, leafy bushes and thin cattails. If some miracle didn't end his fall, he was going to smack right into it. While water was not nearly as solid as land, he still assumed the collision would be enough to end his life. His short, meaningless life.

He thought of all the superhero comics he'd read. Superheroes seemed to die all the time, but they always came back. Del doubted that would be the case for him. He wasn't needed by the world like Superman, Captain America or Thor. He didn't want to be a hero, but he had always harbored the hope that one day he might at least be needed. But so far it just hadn't happened. He was just a mouse. A mouse who had never really done anything great for anyone. Even Urabzu had decided Del wasn't worth helping. Hopefully the next Trelock after him would do a better job. Surely the spirits would choose better next time.

Del considered that perhaps he had simply been too selfish. He had lived a solitary life. He wasn't a savior to his people. He had barely even made time for them. If asked, he couldn't even offer the names of his neighbors.

Kando was right. Del couldn't connect with the elements because he couldn't even connect with other mice. He was a shut-in. A forgettable, self-indulgent one at that. If someone were to write a story about him, it would have been quite boring, save for these last few weeks. It would be filled with chapters and chapters of blank pages, and a final paragraph of exhilaration before an ultimately disappointing ending. He certainly wouldn't want to read a book like that. Knowing full well that his life, what little there had been of it, had been wasted. Del closed his eyes once more as the glistening lake came speeding towards him. He took a resigned breath and waited for the end.

But it never came. He never crashed into the lake. In fact, the lake rose to meet him. A long funnel of water rushed upwards and cradled his body. Del opened his eyes to see water swirling around him, rising from the lake below.

"Ssssssorry I'm late," came Urabzu's voice in his ear, although the otter was nowhere to be seen.

"Better late than never," cried Del, a smile on his face and tears in his eyes. Never in his life had he been so completely happy to be alive. "Will you help me save my friends?"

"I'll do what I caaaaaan," said Urabzu. "But heed this warning, little Trelock. Your heart is full of doubt and self-hatred. These traits have weakened my connection to you even further. Should nothing change, this will be the last time I will be able to help you. Even now, I only appear to you because of the thin thread of courage which resides within you. If you do not foster it, that thread will snap, and our connection will be severed fooooorever."

Del bit his bottom lip. It was strange to be called out for being a pessimist, especially because he'd always been that way. Throughout his entire life, his mother, father, brother and sister had all told him so many times that he was a disappointment. He'd simply come to accept it as fact.

"This lake is too far beloooooow that cloudship to have any real effect upon it," the water spirit said to himself.

Del thought for a moment. Maybe he wasn't a master of the elements the way everyone expected him to be, but he *was* quite good at solving puzzles. He had an idea, and ideas made him feel energized, fearless even. It felt like the blood in his veins was pumping harder and hotter than ever before. "You're right," he agreed. "The ship is too high to use the lake water. So we'll need another source. Maybe instead of fighting the shrikes from below, we take them on from above?"

"Ohhhh," marveled Urabzu. "Now you're thiiiiinking like water. Even the mightiest oceans begin in the sky."

"Can you get me back to the ship?" asked Del.

"Yeeeeees," the otter replied, excitement in his voice.

"Good. In the meantime, think you could cook me up another storm?"

Though Del couldn't see Urabzu, he had the keen sense that wherever he was, the water spirit was smiling. "I thought youuuuuu'd never ask. Storms are my speeeeecialty!"

The water funnel cradling Del suddenly shot straight up with him at the top of it, so that it looked as though he were rocketing upwards and taking the body of the lake with him. He felt very much like the water version of the Human Torch.

"*Water On!*" he yelled. On second thought . . . no, that didn't sound nearly as cool as he'd hoped it would.

The ship now looked like a flying fireball. It was surrounded by a black cloud of angry birds and was starting to arc downwards. With much of its power gone and its sails ablaze, the Black Acorn was completely crippled.

As Del reached the ship, the water finally released him, giving him just enough momentum to flip in the air before landing back on the deck of the ship. It was the single coolest move he had ever done. It was also, he assumed, the closest he'd ever get to looking like one of the Power Rangers.

"Rook!" shouted Kando, a look of relief spreading across his face.

"But . . . how?" asked Arthur, who looked totally and completely perplexed by what had just transpired.

All around them, squirrels were running, shooting the shrikes, tossing barrels of water at the fire that had now spread to the deck, and doing their best to not be thrown overboard by the lurching cloudship.

"I'll explain later," Del promised. "Right now, we all need to hang onto something!"

KRACKABOOM! Thunder ripped through the heavens. As if a giant pause button had just been pressed, everything abruptly froze. All the mice, squirrels and shrikes stopped to look up at the dark black clouds which had suddenly formed in the previously clear sky. Lightning rippled across the clouds. Without another moment wasted, bulbous raindrops began to pour, sizzling as they hit the blue flames overtaking the Black Acorn. The fire was snuffed out in a matter of moments.

But once they were over their initial surprise, the shrikes resumed their unrelenting assault. For them, the fire had been a happy accident, but had never been a part of their plan to down the ship.

Arthur and Kando ran for the mast, securing themselves with a length of rope which they tied around their waists and then to the mast. They grabbed onto the wood tightly with their paws as the water soaked the deck, making it slippery and wet, like running on a frozen lake. A shrike caught sight of them and dove, flying straight for Kando who it had recognized as the murderer of a large portion of the watch. The shrike screeched and stretched out its talons, bearing down like a small hawk.

"No!" yelled Del. Hail crashed into the shrike as if shot from an ice-cannon somewhere above, knocking it off course. It slammed into the deck and then skidded overboard, taking some of the black taffrail along with it.

"Del?" said Arthur. "Are you . . . how are you doing this?"

"I'll try to explain later," said Del, worried that if he thought too hard about what was happening that it might stop all together. "I don't want to jinx it." He reached his paws up to the sky and motioned towards the shrikes all around the ship. Hail fell all around them, bombarding the watch and everything else except for the Black Acorn.

A cacophony of shrieks and cries could be heard from the birds. The shrikes were simply no match against the large chunks of ice, which snapped their tiny bones in half and ripped them from the sky. Their corpses and feathers fell like black and white snow.

The battle, like the sail fire, had ended abruptly. The ship leaned to the side, slowly lowering away from the storm clouds. The sails were thoroughly scorched, and only half of the ship's engines remained glowing. Some flickered weakly, while others had gone completely dark.

The squirrel crew gathered around the mice, eyeing them with a mixture of fear, suspicion and respect. As quickly as they had appeared, the storm clouds dissipated and then vanished, replaced by a warm sun and peaceful blue sky.

Thank you, thought Del to himself, hoping that Urabzu would hear him. He felt like he could actually sense the spirit swimming inside of him. It was a distant hum in his heart, both there and not there at the same time. In a way, it was as if Del were a radio, reaching out to receive the signal of some faraway frequency. And if he could tune in just right, the transmission would be able to come through.

Del thought of Alec Holland, otherwise known as Swamp Thing, and his relationship to the plant-life of the world, *the Green*. He could feel everything that happened to all the plants on Earth, from the blossoming of a flower, to the death of a rose bush. He could do it even if it was happening on the other side of the world. Maybe the Green omitted a frequency to him too.

"That storm..." started Artemis, whose eyes were wide and full of amazement. No longer did she look at the mice with disdain and mockery. Now her expression was one of respect and even gratitude. "That was you?"

"It's sort of complicated," Del replied. "I sort of asked the water spirit to help us." He continued, "The mice of Verden . . . they need us to complete our mission. Otherwise, more danger could come to them. I wouldn't have asked the water spirit to help, but if we had all died here, we would've risked the lives of everyone back home."

"So, then it's true," whispered Artemis. "A Trelock roams the world once again." She knelt down on one knee and bowed her head. "You have saved us, young mouse. You have my—*our* thanks." The other squirrels followed suit, kneeling and bowing to him. This demonstration of adoration made Del uncomfortable, and he wished for the moment to end.

"You . . . know about Trelocks?" he asked nervously.

Artemis looked up at him with concern in her eyes. "Only a little." She rose from her kneeling position and stood before him once more, as did the rest of her crew. "I can tell you what I know, but we ought to go inside." She took a step towards an ornate wooden door at the back of the ship which lead to the innards of the Black Acorn. She turned back to her crew as the mice followed her. "Get the ship docked so we can start repairs," she barked. The squirrels went to work, bustling about the deck as they made the necessary preparations.

Artemis' eyes fell on Arthur and Kando. "You two will stay topside and help my crew clean up your mess."

"I think we'd prefer to stay with the Rook," said Kando.

"The information I offer is for his ears only," said Artemis. "And given that we'd all be dead without him, I think he's earned a little respect and trust from you two. We won't be long." She then turned and entered the cabin, leaving Del staring awkwardly at Kando and Arthur.

"I'll be fine," he said.

"Call for us if there's trouble," said Kando. There was a slight hint of worry in his words. He didn't like the prospect of letting Del out of his sight. Del nodded and turned to follow the captain but stopped when Kando placed a paw on his shoulder. "And, Rook . . ."

Del looked back at his Alpha, expecting another tongue-lashing.

"Good job back there." Kando gave his shoulder a tight squeeze and then backed away.

"Thanks," Del mumbled, uncertain how to respond. He nodded once more to Arthur, who waved him on encouragingly, and then headed down into the bowels of the ship.

Despite Kando's brash demeanor and Arthur's crude sense of humor, he found that he was truly happy to have the two of them with him. And that sense of camaraderie, he realized, was what he'd always imagined it would feel like to be part of a team.

CHAPTER FIFTEEN

The Codex

Artemis led Del down a long set of black steps and ushered him into her cabin. Inside her chambers, there was a long birchwood desk against one wall. Beneath the desk, there was an intricately woven rug, embroidered with emerald and beige designs. A candelabra with five wax candles perched on top of the desk, accompanied by several unfolded maps and several more rolled up parchments. A small stack of thick leather-bound books, which looked as though they had been pried straight out of history, were piled onto the desk as well. Their pages were tattered and yellowed with age. A large globe rested on a pedestal at the far end of the room, underneath four large windows which overlooked the endless sky. Black curtains were drawn over the windows, making the room seem darker than it actually was.

Artemis quickly strode over to the desk, pulling off her blue coat and hanging it over the back of a tall chair. She then dug into the top drawer and pulled out a small swatch of matches. She struck one of the matches and brought the flame to the candles, giving the room some much needed light, while simultaneously casting ominous shadows across the walls and floor.

"Now, Del," the captain began. "Are you aware of the history of the Trelocks?"

Del bit his bottom lip nervously. "I know that they are rare, and that there is only one at a time, ever," he said, repeating what he had learned from Kando, Urabzu and the leafy dream face.

"Very good. And *why* is there only one?" she asked pointedly.

Del thought for a moment, not about the answer to the question, but why he had never thought to ask it. "I . . . don't know," he admitted.

"Yes, well, few do," she said with a heavy sigh. "To be able to speak with the elements is tricky business. Nature has a way of balancing itself. It also doesn't like to be told what to do. We need only look back at the fall of mankind for proof. They bent nature to their will in every possible way, and nature punished them for it by crushing their species into the annals of history. Fools, if you ask me. Still . . ." She trailed off, momentarily lost in thought. Then she brought her focus back to Del. "Nature is not inherently good or evil. It simply *is*. As such, when humanity was dying, nature gave them one final chance to set things right."

Del was enraptured by the story. He'd always found the stories of humans to be far more interesting than stories of any of the animals or mice of his time.

Artemis briefly turned away from him and pulled a small, triangular, metallic object from a shelf adorning the wall. As she did so, she unsettled some dust as well, as though the object hadn't been touched for many seasons.

It was only about the size of a kernel of corn, albeit shinier and flatter, with a thin black line from the center of one edge to one of its points. "This device is called a *codex*. It's how I've come to know so much about Trelocks. Humans used them to store information, communicate with each other, and access the knowledge of the world. It is my understanding that at one point, every human had one, wearing it on their temple so that they were fully integrated with one another at all times. This one, however, is special. It contains a journal written by a young woman who was tasked with setting things right. A human woman." Artemis paused for dramatic effect. "A *Trelock* human woman."

Del recoiled. "A human who had powers like mine? But I thought that the first recorded magic happened when the war ended, after humanity destroyed the world and filled it with radiation. They died off because their bodies couldn't handle it, but ours could."

"You are correct. However, Trelocks are not magical beings," she said curtly. "A Trelock is the result of Mother Nature gifting one being with the ability to bring balance to life itself." She eyed the small device, nestled between the claws of her thumb and forefinger. "The war tainted everything, causing crops to die and disease to spread. Death ravaged the planet."

Artemis continued with her story. "The human Trelock's name was Alyana. She was gifted the power to stop the spread of death and decay. Or as she called it, *the Blight*."

Del's blood ran cold. A shiver ran down his spine all the way to the tip of his tail at the sound of that dreaded word.

Artemis pressed a thumb to the device. The thin black line glowed green, and then one corner of the small triangle began giving off a soft glow as it projected a holograph. It was an image of a young woman with brown skin, raven black hair and a bold smile. But these details paled in comparison to the ball of fire she was holding in the palm of her right hand.

Del reached out, his paw grazing the holograph and then passing through it. "What happened to her?" he asked. "If she had the power to stop the Blight . . . then why didn't she?"

"According to the data on the codex, she tried," said Artemis. "But humans were a species highly motivated by fear; willing to destroy anything they didn't or couldn't

comprehend. All accounts that I can find say that they killed
Alyana before she got the chance to save them. Before she
got the chance to stop the Blight for good. After that, Mother
Nature turned her back on them."

"That's horrible," said Del.

"Quite," Artemis agreed. "Over time, there have been
those who have claimed to wield the powers of the Trelock,
but they've all been tall tales at best, vehement lies at worst.
In truth, until you, I believed animal Trelocks to be a
complete myth. By my estimation, you are the first real
Trelock since Alyana. It seems that the line of Trelock's
followed a human lineage for most of history, ending with
her. Therefore, you are, at the very least, the first *confirmed*
animal Trelock."

Del inhaled deeply. The thought of being so unique
made his chest hurt. It made him want to slap himself until
he woke up from what must have been a terrible nightmare.
Yet he knew that he was far beyond the point where that
might be possible now. "I've got another question."

"I thought you might," she grinned.

"Why *now*?" he asked.

Artemis sat back in her chair and pulled a glass bottle
filled with an amber liquid from the desk's bottom drawer.
She then pulled out a drinking glass and poured a small bit of
the liquid into it. She placed the glass to her lips and drank
the liquid in a single gulp. Del might have been imagining it,

but he could have sworn the hair on her paws and face stood up straight for just an instant and then settled once more.

"You see a lot when you're flying around on a cloudship. You see the cities and the forests and the mountains. And you see other things. Frightening things. Death. Decay. The rotting of the earth itself, which only seems to spread." Her eyes glossed over, as if she were momentarily caught in some other place and time. "Something is on the horizon. Something we aren't prepared for because it defies even our worst nightmares. It stalks the night, just outside our view, desecrating and devouring the very ground it walks on. Purging the world one blade of grass at a time."

"The Blight?" asked Del, feeling goosebumps run up and down his arms, legs and tail.

"We've never seen it up close. Only the destruction it brings," she said. There was genuine fear in her voice now, her words shaking ever so slightly. "As I said, Mother Nature has a way of self-balancing, course correcting. A creature appears, rotting the land it walks on. A new Blight, as it were. And then, as if on cue, a Trelock shows up. Some coincidences are too obvious to be mere happenstance."

"So you think I'm supposed to stop whatever this thing is?" asked Del, hoping she would say 'no.' He didn't like the idea of the fate of the world resting on his very small shoulders.

"Think?" she asked, bemusedly. "No, little mouse. I *know* you must be the one to stop it. Either you do, or we'll all follow in the footsteps of humanity." She took a deep breath to calm herself.

Then she tossed the small codex to Del, who just barely caught it. (Like the 'geeks' he so affectionately adopted the ways of, sports had never been his forte.) It was cold to the touch, the metal smooth in his paws.

"Take it with you," she said. "Perhaps her journey will help you on yours. Learn from her mistakes. Avoid her failures. That sort of thing."

"Thank you," said Del, bowing his head to her. He placed the codex just beneath his right ear, and to his surprise, it stayed there, nestling into his fur as if magnetized. Several windows appeared in front of him suddenly.

Calibrating . . . Loading . . . Initiating . . .

More windows flashed until finally only one remained. *Welcome.* He was now gazing at a scenic view of a mountain trail overlooking a sunset. He knew this sort of image from his computer back home. It was a background. Several file folders sat off to the left of the screen. *Journal. Index. Net. Contacts.* He eyed each one in turn, not sure where to begin.

The floor suddenly shook for a split second. Del splayed his paws on the wall to maintain his balance. Artemis merely grinned and stood from her chair. "It seems we've landed." She took a step towards the door, but a question from Del stopped her.

"Why didn't you want Kando and Arthur here? Am I meant to keep this all secret?"

"That is entirely up to you," she replied. "But learning the truth about ourselves can often be daunting, and I prefer to do it with as few witnesses as possible."

Del considered this, and then nodded. "Thank you," he said.

"You, young Trelock, are most welcome."

Del placed a single claw to the metal at his right temple and the image disappeared. Investigating the inner workings of the codex would have to wait.

*   *   *

Artemis and Del emerged from the captain's quarters, basking in the sunlight which covered the deck like a warm blanket. The Black Acorn had landed in the gentle waters of the lake which Del had almost fallen into during the fight. Kando and Arthur were helping the squirrels upturn barrels displaced by the battle.

Though very little time had actually passed since the battle with the shrikes, Del couldn't help but feel as though a new day had dawned while he'd been below deck. So many questions still raced through his head, yet somehow, he felt revitalized and full of energy, like he'd awoken from a very long sleep. There was something comforting in knowing when others experienced your struggles. Even if that individual was a human. Even if they failed where you were expected to succeed. It made Del feel just the slightest bit less alone in the world.

"Still alive?" grinned Arthur. "Didn't think the old squirrel would eat you, but stranger things have happened."

"This mouse saved the lives of my crew," snapped Artemis. The list of animals who found Arthur's sense of humor funny was growing slimmer by the day. "I'm not so ruthless as to kill him afterwards. We squirrels have honor."

"Or as much honor as skyrates can have," winked Arthur.

"I dislike this one," grumbled Artemis, just loud enough that only Del could hear her. He laughed to himself. The captain then raised her voice and addressed the trio of mice once more. "Del has informed me that you are journeying to the center of Aurora in search of an assassin."

Del eyed Kando, wondering if the Demon's expression might sour with the news that he had shared their mission. But the Alpha's face betrayed no reaction.

"Though you cheeky rodents are what brought this attack on us, we only survived with your help. Lucky for you, I'm a good sport. Therefore, my crew and I will take you as far as the bend in the Cherry Creek river which goes through the outskirts of Aurora." She shivered at the thought. "We dare not go further than that."

"Any help on this journey is greatly appreciated," said Kando with a slight bow. "You have our gratitude."

257

For the rest of the day, Kando, Arthur and Del helped the squirrels fix up the ship: nailing in loose boards, hanging new sails and servicing the engines. None of the mice were actually much good with electrical handiwork, however squirrels were one of the few races who were good with tech and used it in their day-to-day lives. Del did, however, manage to craft a fine wrench holder for the squirrel engineer who did the actual work.

That night, they dined together with the squirrels, who sang and danced and celebrated their victory over the shrikes. The food was different from what Del was used to, but that wasn't a bad thing. Hashed sweet potatoes and glazed brussels sprouts. Rich pumpkin soup and candied walnuts. Crunchy wheat crackers and perfectly ripened blueberries. Del felt as though it was the first time he'd really eaten in weeks. The food was both sweet and savory, making it easy to eat far too much. Before long, his stomach was protruding more than usual as he rubbed a paw over it, smacking his lips with satisfaction.

"Absolutely divine," exclaimed Arthur. "I feel as though I won't need to eat for the next month." All around them, squirrels were hunched over the extended dining table, sleeping amid the remains of the meal. Crumbs and unfinished last bites lay discarded in bowls, plates and pots which would need washing in the morning.

Del nodded happily in agreement with Arthur. He was just about to doze off into a short food coma when he noticed the absence of Kando. He craned his neck around, not wanting to get up if he didn't have to but saw no sign of the black mouse. Begrudgingly, he hoisted his considerably heavier body off the little wooden seat.

"Where are you off to?" asked Arthur.

"The toilet," he responded gravely, dropping the volume of his voice to give implied meaning that he might be a while. He didn't care what Arthur might think, as long as it meant that he wouldn't be followed.

"Ah," smiled Arthur. "I take it that's code for *going to check on our brave Demon.*"

Del was surprised at his companion's perceptiveness. He didn't deny it.

"I imagine he's off sulking somewhere," Arthur continued breezily. "He nearly got us all killed with that little stunt back there. Flinging one of my perfectly good fireballs back at the ship. And then blaming it on me? Honestly, I think he's got a lot to learn about being a good leader."

"He's doing the best he can," said Del, surprising himself at how quickly he came to his Alpha's defense.

"Says the Rook who's criticized him the whole mission," chuckled Arthur. "Well, I'm not convinced. Roderick would have told us everything before asking us to risk our lives like this. Trust is a two-way path."

Del hadn't thought about Kando keeping secrets for a while now. But the feeling was certainly still there. Even so,

Del also recognized that Arthur was the type of mouse who lived for debauchery and scandal. He was probably more prone to looking for trouble where there was none. Del didn't want to make accusations unless it became absolutely necessary.

"Perhaps . . ." started Arthur. "But—no."

"What?" Del prodded.

"Well, just consider if you and I were to go it alone for a while."

"We can't!" exclaimed Del. A nearby squirrel gave a disgruntled snore and nearly awoke from his food-induced slumber.

"I figured you'd say as much." He shook his head, placing his feathered hat over his eyes to block the candlelight of the ship's dining hall. "Still, it was worth a shot."

Del didn't respond any further. Instead, he turned and left the dining area. He ascended a short staircase and emerged onto one of the upper floors, into the cool evening air. He could see out over the deck below and all the way up to the stern where Kando stood, looking out over the water. The lake's surface glistened, reflecting the light of the moon above.

"Can't sleep?" Del turned around to see Artemis lurking in the shadows. She approached him and smiled. "Your friend can't either."

"I don't know if *friend* is the right word," he said.

"Alpha then, or Captain, if you prefer," she said. "At least that's a word I'm more familiar with. Of course, a good captain shouldn't be friends with their crew. It muddies things. Makes them more prone to weakness and emotional decision-making."

"Sure," Del nodded, looking out at Kando who, if he heard them at all, didn't react. "Do you think your crew ever questions your motives?"

Artemis answered without hesitation. "Yes," she said. "We *are* skyrates after all. I'd think them fools to blindly follow me. I'd think them fools to follow *anyone* without a little hesitation, or at the very least, a couple of well-timed sideways glances." She demonstrated a sideways glance as an example, which made Del laugh. She smiled as well. "But they do respect me. And they trust that, even when my methods are questionable, I only ever do things in our best interest. Or, maybe they're just too afraid to ask questions. Fear can be quite valuable in this line of work."

Del quietly pulled the small bronze emblem with the bear paw and snake-eye from his pocket and stared down at it pensively.

"Did you and your crew really see a mouse working with the minks?" he asked. When he had questioned the captain before, he was denied an answer. He had to try at least one more time.

"Yes," she said. "From afar. The mink was one they call Barrel-Fist. Devil of a beast, that one. The mouse . . . I couldn't tell you. We steered clear. Best not to get involved. We're better pillagers than politicians."

"Is there a difference?" Del asked, a cheeky grin on his face.

Artemis laughed. "Touché, Del. Touché."

What did it all mean? he wondered. Were mice and minks really working together, killing in the dead of night, all to appease the Blight? It truly seemed like the sort of plot that would be cooked up by Penguin and the Riddler within the pages of *Batman*. It was outlandish—foolish, even. Full of more questions than answers. He simply couldn't grasp the end game of it all. It was as if he'd been slowly piecing the outside edges of a puzzle together but was now missing the middle pieces which made up the subject of the image.

"Your Captain has many scars," said Artemis, changing the subject. Del re-pocketed the emblem. "Some you can see and some you can't, I suspect. Sometimes, even the best of us make a choice not because it's the right one, but because for that moment in our lives, it is the only one.

"I've never had to trust anyone," said Del. "Having a leader and trusting that they'll make the right choice . . . it's all new to me."

"As your Alpha, he deserves your respect," she said. "But before you can trust anyone, you must learn to trust yourself. I trust my crew to steer this ship and aim the guns, but I began with trusting myself to lead them." She eyed him carefully. "Don't forget, you were given this gift for a reason,

Del. Trust in that! I look out on the world, and all I see are choppy currents ahead. But we each have a choice. We can either be a light in the darkness, or we can do nothing, and become another dark cloud in the sky."

Del let this sink in before speaking. "I want to thank you, Captain," he said. "For everything."

"You are very welcome. Perhaps we will meet again someday." She grinned slyly. "Let's hope it's not with me pillaging you. That would be severely awkward."

"Let's hope," he agreed, smiling back at her. She was the first squirrel that Del had ever really spoken with. More importantly, she was the first one he considered to be an ally. Perhaps skyrates weren't as bad as all the stories made them out to be.

*　　　*　　　*

The following morning, the mice awoke and ate a hearty breakfast with the squirrels. Del watched Arthur help himself to another bowl of grains. *So much for Arthur's claim that he wouldn't need to eat for a month,* Del thought to himself.

The ship had taken off from the lake in the early hours and was now flying over golden fields of wheat and barley. In the sky, swirling bands of purple, pink and blue undulated over and under each other, creating a symphony of dancing lights.

The squirrels docked the ship beside a rushing river, the same one that Del had fallen into several miles back. The terrain up ahead was open and flat. There were very few areas to hide, which made Del feel quite nervous.

Del, Kando and Arthur disembarked down a long wooden ramp and waved their farewells. Artemis shook Kando and Arthur's paws, but when she got to Del, he grabbed her in a fierce hug, not caring what sort of message it would send to the others in his team or her crew. To his surprise, she hugged him back.

"Be well, Del Hatherhorne, young Trelock and savior of the Black Acorn," she said.

"And you, Captain Artemis Truffel, sharpest shot in all the skies," he replied, smiling at her as he pulled away. He gave her a salute—placing his paw in a face down fist out in front of his chest and bowing his head—and she saluted him back in response.

"Oh, I almost forgot." Del pulled the single-paw crossbow and bolts from his back, ready to return them to her.

Artemis waved a paw, declining the offer. "Keep them. You'll need them more than Scurge. Besides, if I ever need them back, we'll just loot your band and take them." Del grinned and swung them back over his shoulder. And with that, they waved their final farewells once more and set off into the wilds of Aurora.

The trio of mice were far outside the Mouselands now. The map that Denya had given them showed that they were less than a day's journey from the last known location of the stolen gigabee. Whatever questions they had, they would surely have answers to before the next sunrise.

They fastened their satchels and packs, secured their weapons and set off into the unknown.

CHAPTER SIXTEEN

A Normal Life

"Hullo, miss. Didn't see ya there," said the tubby mouse to Denya. He turned to greet her in his merchant's stall. He had a thick gray mustache beneath his pointed nose and a checkered blue apron around his large waist.

Denya was nearly unrecognizable in comparison to the mouse she had been before her decision to stay in Toleloo. She now wore a pale blue dress and a wide-brimmed white hat, both of which her mother had gifted her. In a matter of days, she had become the proper lady and beekeeper that her mother and father had always hoped for. But perhaps even more surprising than the change in her appearance itself, was the fact that she didn't mind it.

There was something to be said for not running headfirst into danger every day. She appreciated not feeling like every choice had life-or-death consequences for herself or some other mouse.

This newfound peace did not stop her from occasionally looking off into the distance from the apiary at the top of the tower, across the forests and fields, and wondering what her band was up to at that precise moment. Was Arthur driving Kando mad with another sarcastic retort? Was Del surviving their reckless journey? Had they found the missing gigabee? She snuck her way into her father's lab once to check the tracking signal, only to find that it hadn't moved. She immediately scolded herself, remembering that her life was in the tower now, not off on some gallant quest into the most dangerous lands known to mouse-kind.

"What can I do ya for?" asked the mustached mouse from behind the counter of the small stall. She snapped back to reality. Denya was on the bottom-most floor of the tower, purchasing groceries for her parents and herself from the market stalls which did business there. She had stopped at this particular stall to admire the various nuts displayed in partitioned rows on the seller's counter. Walnuts, almonds, cashews, peanuts and macadamia nuts lay in small troughs, assorted by size and type.

"I'll take some almonds, please," she said.

"Perfect," exclaimed the mouse. "They're delectable this time of year. I've added a bit of salt to them to give them a savory note. I recommend seeing Mr. Falsparder down the way and picking up some grapes. Salted almonds go with grapes like cinnamon goes with apples. A match made in paradise. Stuff both of 'em in your mouth at the same time for a flavor so delicious, it can't be described."

Denya laughed. "I'll have to give it a try."

"That you must, ma'am," he said. "That'll be five chez."

She produced five bronze coins from her purse—a small yellow bag with several silver buckles and zippers, which had replaced her leather satchel—and placed them on the wooden counter. The mouse handed her a burlap bag full of almonds. She politely waved him farewell and headed off down the aisle to find this Mr. Falsparder.

She stopped abruptly when she noticed one of the stands was completely empty. This was only her second time coming to the market, and the first had been so hurried and overwhelming that she had completely missed this stand. The counter was bare and covered in a thick layer of dust, as though it hadn't been used in some time. Above the counter hung a wooden sign which read 'Cromwell's Honey.'

Denya felt a twinge of heartache in her chest as she remembered the charismatic old proprietor who the stall had once belonged to. What had lead this honey-peddling mouse to become a part of something so nefarious?

She was surprised that his wife Delilah hadn't taken up the mantle of running the honey stand in his stead. Then again, losing a husband and finding out he was a traitor all at once was a hard thing to bear. Denya imagined that if it had been her, she would probably need to take several seasons, if not years, in order to grieve. Guilt overtook her, and she silently chastised herself for judging Delilah's absence.

To the left of the former honey stall was a narrow cart. A hunchbacked old ladymouse sat in a rocking chair behind the cart, wearing a plaid dress, a bonnet and large spectacles. The cart was filled with lovely bouquets of flowers: marigolds, daisies and bluebells mostly. Denya selected one with bluebells and daisies and paid the woman seven chez. Then she set off towards Delilah's home. Perhaps a little kindness would go a long way to mending a broken heart.

She took a single lift up to the third level of the tower, where several smaller cottages had been built into a portion of the tree trunk that was nestled against the steel tower wall. Each cottage had a hay roof and was constructed from small grey pebbles held together by dried mud. She found the one she was searching for quickly, recalling it from her quick visit with Del to deliver the beetle cart. The cottage had a small mailbox out front which looked like a birdhouse with the name *'Cromwell'* written on it in slanted, golden letters. The beetles were nowhere to be seen. She stepped up to the door and knocked. No answer. She knocked again.

"Don't think she'll be coming to the door, deary," said a female voice to her right. Denya turned to see the neighbor, a middle-aged ladymouse in a crocheted apron, looking upon Denya with sorrow in her eyes. "Been sick ever since her husband died. Won't even come outside, let alone allow any visitors."

"What's she sick with?" asked Denya.

"I suspect she's lovesick."

"No such thing," said Denya. "Must be rat-bite fever. Or badger pox."

"Mice have died from far less than a broken heart."

"Mice have survived far worse," Denya replied mildly.

The ladymouse, clearly not impressed with Denya's wit, scoffed and went back inside her house. She shut the door loudly behind her, grumbling something about young mice today not having any respect.

Denya turned back towards the Cromwell's closed front door and placed a single paw on it, feeling the grain of the wood beneath her fingers.

"Delilah," she called out, hoping to be heard through the door. "I know right now it feels as though you've lost everything, but I promise you that the world is going to keep spinning. Summer will come, and then autumn and winter, and then spring again. You are going to survive this. Sometimes, we get dealt a bad hand. But eventually, we all remember what it feels like to win." Denya smiled, thinking of her own life as of late. "Chin up, love. The world will be waiting for you when you're ready. And if you ever need to talk to someone . . . I may be younger, and we might not know each other, but I've got a great pair of ears on me. You can find me at the apiary at the top of the tower. That's my home . . . now . . ."

She laid the bouquet of blue and white flowers at the foot of the door, inhaling their fragrance one last time before walking away from the silent cottage.

*   *   *

Denya helped her mother prepare a dinner of carrot soup, which they would have with a side of crackers and blackberry jam. They also cooked some mushrooms stuffed with tomatoes and garlic. The savory dish's aroma filled every room of the house as it slowly baked in the oven. Her father came home as they were making the meal, rubbing his stomach and licking his lips.

"It smells delicious in here," he said, hanging up his beekeeper's apron. He sat down at the dinner table, where forks, knives, spoons and napkins had already been laid out for the three of them.

"Mother's teaching me to cook all her recipes," said Denya proudly.

"Oh, please," retorted Raisha. "Denny's a natural."

"Well, I should be. I was a Concoctor for long enough. Mixing things goes with the territory." An awkward silence fell over the table. Eventually, she hoped they would be able to talk about her past without it putting an end to all conversation. But that day was not today. Denya quickly changed the subject. "I picked up some grapes and salted almonds in the market. I thought we could start our meal by

271

trying them together." She brought out a cutting board of chopped grapes and finely sliced almonds, separated into two small piles.

"Together?" asked Gillean, who clearly thought the idea mad.

"I know, I know," Denya cooed. "But the man at the nut stall told me that they're delicious together."

"Pshaw," scoffed her father. "He must have some sort of under-the-table deal with Mr. Falsparder at the grape stand."

"At least try it before you go accusing anyone," said Denya.

"Mr. Falsparder's one to keep your eye on though," he scolded.

"I'll remember that," laughed Denya.

They tried eating the grapes and almonds combined, which to their great surprise were absolutely delightful. "What'll they think up next?" exclaimed her father, as though he were experiencing electricity for the first time.

As the family enjoyed their dinner together, her father and mother talked about the business of the day and what orders needed to go where and by when. Sounds of chewing, slurping, sipping and stirring filled any silence between the three. The noisy enjoyment of food provided a comfortable soundtrack to their meal, as the family learned once more how to interact with each other.

After dinner, they enjoyed a blueberry cobbler which Denya's mother had made. It melted in Denya's mouth, spilling warm juices and cream filling across her tongue. She had forgotten that food could taste so good.

Removing the napkin he had tucked under his chin to wipe away the crumbs, and with a kiss on the forehead for his wife and daughter, Gillean retreated to bed. Raisha busied herself with cleaning the kitchen: washing the dishes, scrubbing the counters and returning pots to their proper storage spots. Denya offered to help, but her mother insisted on doing it herself so that everything would be put back exactly where she liked it. Denya, after being shooed away, left the house for some fresh air.

She strolled along the narrow walkways under the honeycombs. Only a few gigabees still buzzed about as they finished their rounds for the day. When she reached the edge of a long platform, she peered through a crack at the top of the tower's wall.

At this height, the walls of the tower had begun to deteriorate, giving way to the branches of the great tree. It was through one of these small spaces where the wall had cracked apart that Denya was able to peek through. She looked out over the world to the east, towards where Del, Arthur and Kando were at that very moment. *What were they up to?* She wondered. *What new things had they seen?* A familiar taste of regret struck her.

Denya was happy for this second chance with her family. Truly, she was. But she already felt as though she was trying too hard. She found herself thinking that, one day, at any moment, she would be down in the market shopping, and someone would point her out for the fraud that she was. This mouse she'd become—this mouse who wore dresses, bought almonds and grapes, took flowers to old widows, cooked carrot soup, and ate cobbler before bed, only to sleep and repeat it all over again the next day—wasn't her. She wanted it to be, but it just wasn't. A bee wasn't a butterfly just because it wished it. And Denya wasn't a stay-at-home ladymouse.

But she hoped one day she would be. She imagined that, eventually, the line would blur, and she would no longer see where Denya the adventurer ended, and Denya the domestic mouse began. Perhaps she would realize a new version of herself, one which didn't conform to the life she'd known or the life she'd chosen to lead in the tower. She hoped that day would come sooner rather than later, if only to put her out of her misery.

After a long while of thoughtfully gazing out over the fields and forests beyond the tower, she finally returned home and retreated to her room. She crawled into bed and burrowed under the quilted blankets. They were just as warm and cozy as they had been when she'd been a young pup.

As she drifted off to sleep, she couldn't help but feel that she'd forgotten something. Or perhaps that something had escaped her attention, some vital thing that she should have noticed, but just managed to miss. Alas, nothing in her new life mattered so much that it couldn't wait till morning. If she'd left the grapes out or forgotten to return a knife into the wooden knife block, she'd surely be able to rectify the mistake when she awoke the next morning. She let the thought get lost in a wandering herd of random thoughts until her dreams finally overtook her.

CHAPTER SEVENTEEN

The Robot Graveyard

The day's journey was grueling. Kando marched out front, slicing at overgrown grass and weeds to carve them a path through the thick undergrowth. Arthur followed close behind, trailed by Del, who was kept busy with the codex. While he was interested in every aspect of it, he'd decided to start with the folder marked *Journal,* which was, unsurprisingly, a detailed account of Alyana's journey to becoming a full-fledged Trelock, written in her own words.

This was the first chance Del had gotten to read in some time. He felt like someone who had been starved and was now being allowed their first bite of bread. As such, he devoured the files ravenously and without any regard to aiding in the journey.

Having finished an entry, he closed it with a press of his paw on the holosensory construct in front of his face. He then swiped to the next entry and opened it.

"Honestly," said Arthur, "how do you not run into something with that mess in front of your face the whole time?"

Del didn't respond. He didn't even hear Arthur as he dove into the journal entry.

April 24, 2079

I conjured fire today. I didn't think I'd be able to, but Mr. Allucard at the temple assured me I could. He helped me to meditate and to speak with the Fire Spirit, who was a little scary at first, but soon agreed to help me. I could only create little embers in my hands, and the heat kept making me think I was going to burn myself, but I pressed on. It's strange, holding fire. It's like hovering your hand a safe distance over a stovetop. You can feel the heat, but it's never quite close enough to burn your skin.

That's two elements down and two to go!

Mr. Allucard says I'm doing well and making good time, but I can see the worry in his face when he says it. Sometimes, I think the monks intentionally try to seem more positive around me. Perhaps they think that if I really knew the state of things, I'd buckle under the pressure.

Russia fell yesterday.

The word *Russia* was in red text. Del pointed a finger at it, which opened an image. In the image, he saw a massive human city made up of several towering buildings. All of them were on fire, as well as many smaller ones below them. They plumed enormous clouds of black smoke up into the blood-red sky. He closed the image, not finding it to be very comforting.

The news is reporting it as a new form of the flu. But I know what it really is: The Blight. The monks say that the Blight is simply an old story, a fairy tale. But I don't buy it. I swear, when I meditate and listen for the four elements, there's a fifth there, calling out from some dark place. I think that's the Blight. Apparently, all that's left in Russia are a few groups of militarized survivors. It's mostly mutants, zombies and burning corpses now. I fear for the day that happens here.

No. I can't let it. I have to train hard to make sure that my family, especially my little sister Raquia, never sees those things. The stuff they show on the news is bad enough. All the bodies look charred and half-human. Mom turned off the computer when she caught us watching, and even though I wanted to continue to watch, I didn't blame her. It was almost too much to bear.

It's time for bed. I'm waking up early tomorrow to climb to the peak of a nearby mountain. Hopefully it will bring me closer to the Wind Spirit. I'm just worried about getting worn out before I get to the top. I'll fill you in on the results!

As Del read, he couldn't help but notice that she seemed so hopeful, so determined, so positive. It made his heart break to know that she hadn't succeeded. Though he knew how it all ended, he soldiered through the files, reading some entries over and over again in the hopes of finding some clue to awakening his powers. The journal read like a fantasy novel, and Del was often unnerved knowing it had all been real.

At midday, they stopped in a small clearing next to a pond. Normally, they would have taken the opportunity to refill their water skins but decided against that when they saw that the pond water was a bright purple color. They ate bread and blueberries from their packs and said very little to each other. Del was too absorbed in his holosensory book to talk anyway.

The day continued to grow later as they trudged along their course. Del barely noticed that the deeper they walked into Aurora, the fewer sounds he heard. Birds no longer sang. Crickets no longer chirped. Any gurgle of rushing water had faded away until it was non-existent. None of this caused Del any alarm though. In fact, it wasn't until he ran right into Kando's backside that he looked up from the augmented image in front of his nose.

Kando and Arthur were both staring ahead, frozen in a mixture of shock and terror. Del followed their eyes, and then he too felt his blood run cold.

They were on a hill overlooking a seemingly endless field of golden wheat. Enormous, hulking mechanisms made of black steel lay interspersed across the field. Their torsos were wide steel chambers, with glass panels at their centers making Del think that this might have been something a human would ride in. Three curved exhaust pipes protruded from the back of each torso. Additionally, two long segmented arms extended out to either side of each chamber. Each mechs 'hands' were different. Some were fierce metal claws. Others were energy rifles or terrifying neo chainsaws, their sharp teeth glistening even after so many years of disuse. Two gigantic steel legs, covered in smoothly curved plating made up the bottom half of each mech. Many of the massive figures had fallen onto their sides or backs, their bodies sinking into the soil under their weight.

As Del took in the sight of these giants, he realized that what they were looking at was not an immediate threat, but remains of what now amounted to a distant memory. It was a vision out of a science fiction book, possibly written by Asimov or Wells.

"It's like a graveyard," he said under his breath, but the dead silence made his voice so much louder than it actually was.

"Mechs left over from the human war," added Kando.

"All that power, and they still couldn't manage to survive," said Arthur. "Makes you wonder what hope we've got?"

"Yeah," Del murmured, thinking of the codex. He placed a claw to the device under his ear, clicking it off for the time being.

"We should keep moving," said Kando.

Carefully, so as not to wake the long dead beasts, they ambled down the hill and through the wheat field, taking care to keep as much distance between themselves and the machines as possible. They tried to ignore the mechs entirely, but it was no use. Each of the mice, even Kando, found themselves looking up at the monstrosities as they passed one and then another.

Del was reminded of the Gates of Argonath in *The Lord of the Rings*, a monument comprised of two gigantic statues, carved to look like the kings Isildur and Anarion. In that fantasy novel, those statues had greeted the fellowship as they had traveled down the River Anduin. The sheer size of their outstretched hands warning travelers to halt had seemed a terrible omen. Del couldn't help but wonder if these robots that stood before them now bore a similar message, warning them to turn back.

One of the dead robots groaned and then sputtered smoke out of one of its pipes. They all froze, waiting for it to rise from its slumber and attack them, but it remained still.

"Stay here," said Kando. He moved stealthily between the stalks of wheat, staying low to the ground. As he reached the mech, he unsheathed his wakizashi and then, to Del's great surprise, he knocked the hilt three times on the steel hull of the mech.

Nothing happened. Kando made his way back to them. "Looks like we're in the clear," he said.

"Yes, now that you've knocked and established that no one's home," said Arthur, sarcastically.

"You have a better idea?" asked Kando. Arthur didn't respond.

Kando waved them onward and the band continued to push through the field, until at last, all the fallen mechs lay behind them.

"What is that smell?" asked Del, sniffing at the air. It was pungent, stale and had an almost sweet aroma of rot and decay. It burned his nostrils and made his eyes water.

"Death," said Kando, with resolute certainty. As they came around a bend, they caught sight of the source of the foul odor.

A spacious clearing created by a circle of flattened wheat lay before them. At the center of the clearing was a huge boulder, with a symbol painted on it in blood-red ink. Del's stomach turned at the sight of the symbol: a bear paw holding an open eye. But the symbol, daunting as it was, paled in comparison to what lay in front of the boulder.

Rotting animal corpses of all shapes, sizes and species were piled on top of each other in a massive heap. The pile was mostly made up of rats, but raccoons, mink, skunks, badgers, a fox and several birds were interspersed throughout. Their decaying corpses oozed green puss, maggots and black tar. The mass grave, sat in the shadow of a tall oak tree and played host to a swarm of flies, which buzzed feverishly around it.

"What in rodent's name?" Kando swore under his breath.

"Well, that's unpleasant," remarked Arthur, who seemed more irritated than scared by the gruesome sight.

"Look," said Del, pointing to the top of the mound of bodies. The crowning piece of the corpse pile was the body of a gigabee, the freshest corpse in sight. *The* gigabee. The one they'd been tracking. All this time, it had been waiting for them. Del felt a prickle on the back of his neck, a feeling that they were not alone. A feeling that they were being watched. *My Spidey-senses are tingling!* he thought.

"I was beginning to think you'd gotten lost," taunted a voice from behind the pile of dead bodies. Del gasped as someone stepped out and grinned at them. There were many things he had thought he might see in Aurora when they'd first set their course for the region. Tribes of barbaric beasts. Radioactive double-headed lizards. Giants who could crush them with a single step. Whatever myths and fantasies he'd dreamed up, *she* had not been one of them.

*   *   *

Denya ran as fast as her feet would take her. Down the four lifts. Through the residential area. And back to the home of Inneous and Delilah Cromwell. She knocked on the door, but this time her knocks were devoid of any pleasantry. She pounded on the door as if it were the entrance to a prison cell she'd just been locked in. At her feet lay the flowers she'd left the day before, their edges wilted and turning brown.

"Delilah!" she called through the door. "I need you to come to the door this instant."

There was no answer.

"If you do not come to the door, then I'm coming in!" she shouted. Still nothing.

"Very well, I'm coming in!"

Denya took a step back and then kicked the door open, splintering the lock and sending the door itself toppling to the floor. She dashed through the doorway into the home. It was dark and reeked of mold and stale bread.

"Delilah!" she called out, moving cautiously. Her guard was up as she peeked around each corner. At first glance, the house seemed unremarkably normal. There was a quaint little kitchen and a living room with two rocking chairs facing a fireplace full of soot. Denya continued to weave through each room, down the hallways, and soon she reached what should have been the bedroom.

However, there was no bed. There wasn't any furniture at all. The walls were covered from all sides with pages from old books, newspaper articles, and scraps from scrolls which had yellowed over time. Words like *prophecy*, *plague*, and *Blight* were circled in bright red ink on almost every piece of parchment. Thin black twine connected one page to another, pinning them to the wall. Some of the twine linked multiple pages on opposite sides of the room together, creating a giant spider web.

Most terrifying of all, a large symbol had been painted in bright red in the center of the back wall. It reached from floor to ceiling and across many of the pinned-up pages, forming one distinctive image: a bear claw with a snake-eye in the center of it.

"Oh, Delilah," said Denya under her breath. "What have you done?" She turned and ran from the house, forcing herself not to look back.

*   *   *

"Mrs. Cromwell?" Del blurted out in surprise, staring into the face of Delilah Cromwell as she appeared from behind the pile of corpses. Her smile was a far cry from the weeping, desperate Delilah he had met back in Toleloo. This smile belonged to a mouse with hatred and malice burning in her eyes. She wore a black cloak and a green tunic over her gray fur. Two daggers hung from her belt, glinting in the setting sun's light.

"But . . . your husband . . . you were so sad when he almost died!" started Del, trying to find some shred of understanding in what he was seeing.

"I was. I really was. But then I heard him getting ready to betray me and everything we stood for, just so you wouldn't arrest him," she scoffed. At this, she pulled out a bronze emblem just like the one Del had found in Crom's pack. "I should have known that old fool would misplace his communicator. He was always so weak."

"No," said Del, pulling his own emblem from his pocket. He eyed it, realizing the awful truth. If the emblem could communicate two ways, then Delilah had known everything from the start.

"And yet, the Copper Clan chose him to join their ranks," she continued. "Messages to him. Missions for him. Warnings made to him that my safety would be in jeopardy. Crom never had the stomach for any of this. Yet from our first mission for the Blight, all he could do was stand back while I did the all work, and then he'd take credit in the end. He couldn't even properly steal grain from defenseless merchants. I had to do everything from mapping out their path to killing *and* branding them. Then he wheeled the grain back to the minks like he was some hero. Honestly, I think he only joined the Blight with me because he wanted to impress me. But this isn't some game. This is the future. I have dedicated my life to the Blight, and I certainly wasn't going to allow Crom's loose tongue to destroy everything we've accomplished."

"But . . . why? You loved him, didn't you?"

"Love?" she spat, as if the word disgusted her. "Love pales in comparison to the rewards of bringing about the new world order. Crom vowed to serve the Blight. And he broke his promise. So, I ended his life. The Blight rewards those who follow it and punishes those who betray it."

"Delilah Cromwell," Kando addressed the zealous ladymouse. Del turned to look at him. Kando reached for his katana, unsheathing it slowly. "For your crimes against the Mouselands, you are hereby under arrest." He pointed the tip of the katana at her.

"Was it really too much to ask that you take care of *him* before you got this far?" asked Delilah, annoyed.

"Well, it's not as though I didn't try," Arthur responded, nonchalantly.

Del felt as though the ground beneath him had just disappeared, dropping him into nothingness. He turned away from Kando and slowly looked over at Arthur, who was shrugging his shoulders apologetically at Delilah.

"Y-you . . ." started Del, not even sure what he was accusing Arthur of.

"I suppose the jig is up," Arthur confessed, taking a step towards Delilah.

Kando pulled the wakizashi blade from his belt and held it so that it pointed at Arthur.

"You're . . . working with her? With *them*?" Del gasped. "Then . . . *you* helped the minks get into the city?" He held the emblem out to Arthur, pleading with his eyes for him to deny the accusation. "You're the one who told them about me? Who told them where I lived? It was you, this whole time?"

"Oh, Del," tsked Arthur. "That disappointed look on your face is almost too much to bear." He looked back towards Delilah sheepishly. "In my defense, I did get the Trelock this far."

"Arthur DeGandia," said Kando. "You are also under arrest for treason to the Mouselands and all of mouse-kind." He sighed. "For what it's worth, I really did want the Council to be wrong about you. You're truly unbearable, but I had hopes that you weren't all bad."

"You knew?" exclaimed Del, even further shell-shocked.

"Our mission to transport Crom was a front," Kando answered. "I was brought to the Longtails because I was an outsider. The Council had hoped I could withhold any personal biases in weeding out potential traitors from within the bands. They suspected someone from Roderick's team of informing the minks, and it didn't take a genius to figure out it wasn't Denya."

Arthur eyed Kando angrily. "So that's it then? You've just been toying with me this whole time? And to think, I tried so very hard to get rid of you without raising suspicion."

In his frustration, Del could barely sputter out his words. "Please, Arthur," he begged. "Please tell me this is all just one of your weird jokes."

"Afraid not," sighed Arthur. "To be fair, I was merely an informant. I'd meet with the minks once or twice a season to share what I'd learned in Verden. They didn't ask much of me, so as to not blow my cover. A Longtails Scrapper is a valuable resource. Eventually, they had me let a mink into the city now and then.

"Roderick had been the latest on their list. I was so happy to finally be rid of the old sod. Got the feeling he was onto me anyway. But then you showed up, and suddenly they wanted answers. The next time I opened the gate, a whole mess of minks wandered in. Then you went and did your thing and toppled a city street, and I thought that perhaps it was time to step back and see where the dice would fall. I never like to be on the losing side of a fight, you know.

"When you told me about the message to Crom back in Toleloo, I realized just how valuable you were to them. It was my chance to finally gain a high-ranking position with the Blight. If I could deliver you to *him*, I'd have succeeded where even Barrel-Fist had failed!

"I had no intention of doing anything to compromise the mission. Sabotage was never in my job description, but there was one problem. Kando was never going to let me take you without a fight, and I thought you might pulverize me to dust with your Trelock powers.

"I've never been one for mouse-on-mouse violence anyway. Too messy. So, I started trying to separate the two of you through . . . happy accidents."

"Happy accidents?" Del echoed in confusion.

"The cliff breaking, Kando falling into the river. I had hoped to get those squirrels to help me fish you out, but then they went and found Kando as well, and then, if you please, they tied all three of us up. And then the shrikes. The shrikes! Who'd have known they'd be quite so...savage? Certainly not me when I sent a message with our route before we left Toleloo. I really thought they'd just take Kando away and that would be that. That was my mistake, really. That and trying to take out Kando with that fireball. But our Demon friend just kept managing to survive, so I tried a different tactic. I thought I could make you suspicious of the old chap so you'd leave with me. But you just wouldn't turn on your precious Alpha.

"I made every effort to separate him from all of this, but *you* had to keep interfering. You even jumped into a roaring river to save him. You stupid little Rook. Now he's going to have to die, and his blood won't be on my paws. No, his death will be on you."

Kando's eyes bore into Arthur, and it seemed to take every ounce of his restraint to not strangle the white mouse where he stood. Delilah simply stood back with her arms crossed, enjoying the show.

"I'd like to thank you for that dramatic admission of your guilt," Kando growled. "I've known all along you were a traitor. But what can I say, the possibility of coming out here and catching *two* traitors at once was just too good to pass up. My one and only mission was to prove your treason. Now all that's left is to bring you back to Verden to stand trial." His gaze shifted to Delilah. "*Both* of you."

"I-I don't believe this," said Del, still trying to comprehend what had happened. *How did this mouse I trusted all along turn out to be a traitor?*

"We won't be going anywhere," Arthur retorted, pulling his sword from its sheath. "*Our* 'one and only mission' was to deliver the Trelock to our master. And we intend to complete our mission, don't we, love?" Delilah whipped her daggers out from her belt.

Kando afforded himself a slight grin as he readied his katana and wakizashi. "You really think the two of you are a match for us?" That word. *Us.* Del couldn't even think, let alone fight, and yet, Kando was relying on him.

Arthur laughed. "The followers of the Blight are many."

As if on cue, a single mink, then another, then a third, and then many more emerged from behind the corpse pile and the nearby tree. They all held daggers and curved blades. Clay had been freshly applied onto their faces, arms and chests. All of them glared down hungrily at Kando and Del. At the center of the small army was a mink who made Del's blood run cold. Barrel-Fist smiled, showing his sharp teeth as the large minigun where his arm should have been began to spin.

"Hello again, little mouse," Barrel Fist cooed. "I believe you and I have some unfinished business."

Kando stepped forward, his katana in front of him. "I need your help Rook. I need you to stand and fight."

"I...can't," Del protested.

"You will obey your Alpha!" Kando barked. His eyes gleamed, and for the first time, Del saw through the cold exterior to something deeper. "I believe in you, Rook." Kando was not commanding. He was pleading.

The gun on Barrel-Fist's arm spun wildly as he hoisted it up, aiming for the mice in front of him. Aiming for Del, the only mouse who had ever bested him. But the little mouse would not thwart him this time. This time, the leader of the Copper Clan would have his revenge.

"FIGHT!" shouted Kando.

But Del didn't fight. He dropped to the ground and rolled to the side, diving behind a large rock just as the bullets exploded from the gun, spraying the ground around them. As fear engulfed him, he covered his ears and closed his eyes, waiting for the inevitability of death to take him.

CHAPTER EIGHTEEN

The Blight

Del Hatherhorne had never, ever felt like less of a hero than he did at this moment. He was a frightened little pup of a mouse. He had joined an adventure, left the comfort of his home and crossed the Mouselands, all to realize something he'd already known: He was powerless in the face of evil. Crippled by fear when confronted by certain death.

Dirt and gravel exploded around him, displaced by the spray of bullets. He pulled his body as close to the rock as he could, hoping perhaps that one of his unknown powers might be to hide *inside* it. This was not the case.

Carefully, he peeked around the side of the rock, expecting to see Kando lying dead, pulverized by the gunfire. To his surprise and relief, Kando was still standing. The Demon moved the katana at lightning speed, repelling bullets before they could even touch him. Not only was he standing his ground, but he was actually pushing forward.

Del had to do something. He had to help in some way. He couldn't sit by and watch another mouse sacrifice himself for Del's sake. Especially when he felt that he still was not worthy of being saved. He couldn't just sit back and wait for Kando to perish.

He focused all his energy and called out to Urabzu. But there was no answer. *And why would there be?* There were no rivers, lakes or streams nearby, and there wasn't a single cloud in the sky.

Beyond these logistical obstacles, self-doubt and loathing still swam through Del. For all he knew, his precarious connection to Urabzu had already been broken. The spirit had warned him that he would need to believe in himself if he wanted to call for help again. But Del couldn't imagine being less sure of himself than he was right then. He'd already used up his last lifeline at the battle for the Black Acorn, which meant he needed a *plan b:* one devoid of elemental powers.

The crossbow, he thought. He pulled the weapon off his shoulder and loaded a bolt into it in a single, frenzied movement. He then turned the corner and took aim at Barrel-Fist. None of the other minks had moved from their perches. Del figured they must have assumed that two mice did not merit the mobilization of an entire army. To them this was merely an entertaining show before dinnertime, not an actual battle worthy of any concern or effort. Still, they were starting to get anxious, and it wouldn't be long before they'd join the fight. Kando would be no match for all of them.

Del pulled the trigger and let the bolt fly, and to his great surprise, it slammed into the minigun, knocking it sideways. Barrel-Fist cursed as he stumbled with the weight of the weapon.

The break in the gunfire gave Kando the opening he needed. He dashed forward, but before he could get to the mink, both Delilah and Arthur lunged in front of him, intercepting him with sword and daggers at the ready.

"Not so fast, old chap," chided Arthur, who was even more obnoxious now that his loyalties had been proven false. Kando swung the katana hard into Arthur's rapier, parrying his first strike, then swung his sword sideways to block Delilah as she thrust both daggers at his side. He pivoted as he blocked another swing from Arthur with the wakizashi in his other paw. He took a step forward, pivoted a half-circle and brought their blades crashing together with his sword, freeing it for a counter-attack.

The swordplay and close-quarters combat left Barrel-Fist free to turn his attention on Del. The mink bounded down the corpse mound. He strode across the clearing, past the three fighting mice, towards the rock which currently served as Del's cover. Barrel-Fist moved determinedly forward. The other minks took his lead as a call to action, and they followed close behind, weapons drawn and ready.

Del had no choice. He turned and ran, using his front paws to scurry across the ground on all fours from rock to rock. Bullets tore apart the ground around him, obscuring his path with dirt as they careened through the air. Luckily, the dirt provided a smokescreen, slowing down Del's pursuers as he continued to weave in and out, barely avoiding bullets by a whisker's length. He moved past the clearing, finding cover within the tall forest of golden wheat. But while it provided some safety, it also meant that he could barely see anything in front of him. Every leap or scurry came with the caveat that a mink or a cliff could be awaiting his very next step.

The ground beneath his paws shook with the footsteps of the oncoming minks, which were still hot on his tail. "Get back here and fight, mouse!" Barrel-Fist growled behind him.

Del was overwhelmed with fear, guilt and panic. He'd left Kando behind. Arthur had betrayed them. He'd come all this way, conquering so many fears, only to die at the paws of the mink who could have just as easily killed him that first night outside his apartment when Roderick had died. These thoughts flooded his mind. He recalled the old cliché about how, right before you die, your life flashes before your eyes. Now, all he saw in those memories were regrets, missed chances and misplaced loyalties.

The wheat field gave way to a slight hill, sloping downwards into green blades of grass, thick foliage and brambles. Del scurried around a large blackberry bush, revealing a picket fence that had fallen into disrepair. He quickly squeezed under one of the rotting wooden pickets and found himself standing on what appeared to be the front lawn of a human house. While the grass here was still wildly overgrown, it was uninterrupted by bushes, trees, or anything else. It seemed almost well-maintained in its perfection, as if it had been recently landscaped.

In front of him was a two-story house which, unlike the lawn, had been decimated by time and the elements. Thick, thorny vines had grown their way up and over the home, as if they were slowly working to swallow it whole. The shingled roof was collapsing inwards, and the building looked as though it would eventually fold down the middle like a closing book and sink into the ground, disappearing entirely. The oddest thing about all of it—the lawn, as well as the many vines, roots and branches devouring the house—was that they were all dead. Everything before him was a portrait painted in rusty oranges, decaying browns and moldy blacks. It was a harsh contrast to the lush greenery which lay only a few feet away, behind the fence line.

Footsteps pounded on the ground outside the fence, closing in on him. The Copper Clan minks would find him soon. Del weighed his options. He could hide in the house and hope it wouldn't fall in on him or wait for the minks to capture him.

He took off across the dead lawn, not particularly caring for his odds in either scenario. But between the two choices, he decided the house seemed like the better option, considering that he was quite adept at using human structures to his advantage. He reckoned he probably knew the ins and outs of human dwellings far better than any *slender* did.

Del dashed up a set of cement steps, cracked by beige clusters of crabgrass. He raced through the doorway, a simple enough task, given that the red wooden door lay fractured into three pieces within the threshold.

Behind him, the minks had crawled under the picket fence and followed him onto the lawn, but then abruptly stopped dead in their tracks. Their fur stood on end as they gawked at the house, frozen by terror. They dared not go any further. Del, already inside, did not see this collective reaction of fear.

"Mission accomplished, boys," Barrel Fist chuckled. He held his minigun arm aimed upwards so that smoke could roll lazily off its barrels, as a cruel grin slid across his muzzle.

It was incredibly dark in the house. Del guessed that he might be in a living room, as he could just make out large shapes that must have once been sitting chairs and a sofa. A foul stench assaulted his nostrils. The smell was like that of mold or a rotting piece of meat . . . or possibly both. He breathed through his mouth to stop himself from gagging. With one paw held tightly over his nose, he turned slowly in circles, attempting to get his bearings. An archway to his left led to what he assumed was the kitchen. Slim shafts of light in the room beyond provided silhouetted hints of a stove and a refrigerator which was missing its door.

Turning from the archway, something caught his attention that made him freeze in place. Two enormous red eyes were staring back at him from the darkness, glowing as if lit from a fire within.

Del slowly edged away backwards, arms outstretched behind himself, feeling for the foot of a furniture piece that he could hopefully hide behind. The horrible eyes stepped forward into the slightest shaft of sunlight peeking in from a crack in the water-damaged roof. The sparse lighting provided glimpses of what Del now realized was a massive creature. He found himself rooted in place, paralyzed by fear.

An enormous grizzly bear, standing on all fours, towered above him, but it wasn't like the pictures of any bear he'd ever seen before in books. Its fur was a putrid green with splotches of ashen gray, and its flesh was rotting away, revealing bone and muscle beneath patches of skin and fur. Its face was heavily scarred, and a chunk of its lip had been torn off, revealing a sharp set of yellow teeth within its mouth. A black substance, like hot melting tar, dripped from the bear's jaws, sizzling and burning the hardwood floor where it landed. Faint tendrils of smoke wafted up from the tar drops into the air between them.

"At last," the bear growled. Its voice was just as horrific as its appearance. The sound was a mixture between a snake's hiss and the gurgling, croaking noise someone might make as they drowned in the thick depths of a swamp. The red eyes burned into Del's soul. "Welcome to my home, Trelock. Or, if we could do away with formalities—Del Hatherhorne."

*   *   *

"Firenze!" Arthur raised his free paw and ignited a flame in his palm, then thrust a fireball at Kando. Kando dodged left, then rolled across the ground, narrowly avoiding a wide slash from Delilah's daggers. Kando was a better fighter than both of them, but combined, they were beginning to overpower him. His muscles burned, and each dodge, roll and parry was gradually leaving him more tired than the last.

He needed to even the odds somehow. As Arthur reeled back to prepare another spell, Kando took the opportunity to duck beneath the Scarlet's rapier. He dashed away, heading for the nearby oak tree. Arthur and Delilah were taken by surprise by his unexpected retreat. Their swords clashed with one another where Kando had stood only seconds before. But they quickly recovered, turning to chase after the Demon.

Kando reached the base of the oak tree and began climbing, scampering up the jagged bark with his claws. He had not lied to Del when he told the Rook that he had taken down a deer all on his own. He'd climbed the beast as it ran. This tree wasn't even moving, which meant he made short work of its trunk.

He swung up onto the first branch and made it halfway towards the leaves at its ends before Delilah caught up to him. She somersaulted over him, daggers twirling between her paws. He swept the katana up over his head, meeting her blades which pushed her off of him. She twirled like a gymnast in midair, then landed further out on the branch. The entire branch jolted under the weight of her landing, forcing a momentary break in their combat as they each steadied themselves.

Arthur had been trailing closely behind Delilah but lost some distance while scampering up the tree trunk. He pulled himself up to the first branch with difficulty, gasping for air. Climbing was not his specialty.

He had sheathed his sword in order to climb more freely, so now he had the use of both paws. *"Firenze,"* he muttered under his breath, igniting a flame in each paw. He hurled the fireballs at Kando, one after another. Kando deflected one to his right with an upper swing of his katana, then dodged the second, digging his claws into the branch's bark as he rolled off. He swung himself like a monkey beneath the branch they were standing on and emerged once more beside Delilah, catching her by surprise as he kicked her in the side.

He was tired. But up here, he could use their elevated location to his advantage. He didn't have to defeat them both. He merely needed to separate them. The first mouse to fall would lose the fight for their side.

Delilah screamed in rage from the impact of Kando's kick. She fell to her knee, looked up, and pivoted to sweep at Kando's feet with her own leg. As he fell backwards, she cut upwards with one of her blades. The Demon felt a sharp flash of pain as her dagger caught his right shoulder. "Gah!" Kando, grabbed the wound.

"Give up, Demon!" she shouted.

Meanwhile, Arthur had managed to catch up with the pair once more. He deftly swung his rapier and caught Kando's ear, slicing off a small chunk of it. "What a relief," he laughed. "Here I was beginning to think that Demons didn't bleed like the rest of us."

Kando groaned as he lay where he fell. He pushed aside the pain, trying to stay focused. Delilah and Arthur quickly converged on him. *That's right,* he thought. *Come in close.*

As the two acolytes of the Blight came within range, Kando swung his katana and the blade caught them by surprise. With impeccable timing, the Demon expertly spun the weapon in his paw so that the hilt clubbed Delilah across the jaw. She crumpled backwards, blood spurting from her mouth. One of her teeth was dislodged by the blow and bounced off the tree branch, then continued to fall to the ground far below.

Arthur stabbed at Kando's chest. Kando parried at the very last second, pitting them face to face. Their blades met, steel on steel grinding and sparking between them. Arthur applied pressure with both his paws on his rapier. They were locked in a stand-still.

"You shtoopid mouse!" Delilah shrieked, as she grabbed her mouth in agony. Overcome with anger, she leapt up and lunged at Kando, wielding her daggers over her head to deal a killing blow.

Kando knew he wouldn't be able to fight Delilah off in his current position. In a desperate play for his life, he took one paw off his katana, grabbed for his wakizashi, and thrust it into Arthur's left shoulder. Arthur reeled back, blood soaking his red coat. Kando quickly turned, bringing up the katana as Delilah descended on him, in hopes that he could block at least one of her deadly daggers.

There was a sudden whirl of yellow and black as a gigabee reached out with all six of its fuzzy legs and plucked Delilah out of midair, a mere breath away from impaling Kando with her daggers. The gigabee did a back flip in the air, swinging her upside down, then tossed her away like a piece of discarded waste. She screamed as she fell, her paws and feet flailing madly.

Kando swiftly bolted up to his feet and looked up in surprise to see that the bee was carrying a rider. Even more surprising was that he recognized that rider. "Denya?" he exclaimed in disbelief.

"Watch out!" Denya cried out.

"*Firenze!*" yelled Arthur from behind the Alpha.

Kando spun around, slicing with both blades to deflect the blue fireball that had been aimed at him. He lunged forward, using the blunt edge of his katana to strike Arthur's wrist and send his rapier sailing out of his paw. The Scarlet squeaked in pain as his rapier flew out of the tree, leaving him weaponless.

Unfazed, Arthur charged at Kando with his paws outstretched, ready to strangle him. But the wounded mouse was too slow. The gigabee caught him, flipped in midair, and flung him to the back of the branch where it met the trunk of the tree. Arthur's back hit the trunk, knocking the wind from his lungs. He slid down and came to a slumped sitting position on the branch. Dazed, he leaned back against the trunk for support.

"You okay?" Denya called out, landing on the branch next to Kando and dismounting the bee. She had switched out her dress and purse for her traveling cloak, tunic and satchel. Her Concoctor's book was fastened firmly to her back, and she intended to never let it stray far from her ever again. The gigabee buzzed loudly as it lazily floated away.

"You have impeccable timing," Kando remarked.

"All these days living with city mice has taught me the value of being fashionably late," she joked.

"Laugh now, but you two are only delaying the inevitable," spat Arthur as he collected himself. His right paw gripped his wounded left shoulder and was soaked with blood. "Okuma will rule this world, and the only animals he'll spare will be those who join him. Don't you see? I chose the winning side."

"Okuma?" asked Denya.

"The vessel of the Blight," Arthur continued. "It has returned to this world and manifested itself within him." He smiled. "He's been getting stronger. I feel it. All his followers do." At this, Arthur yanked at his coat sleeve, which had been ripped by Kando's attack. The sleeve ripped away, revealing the bear claw and snake-eye which was branded into his shoulder. The brand glowed a phosphorescent green. "To think, you two practically escorted that little mouse into his stomach. You will be remembered as the mice who handed a Trelock over to the Blight and brought about the end of the world as we know it."

"Del," Kando realized angrily.

"Yes, Del," snarled Arthur. "I still can't believe that little mouse turned out to be the real deal. *He* was so sure the Trelock would appear in the form of a rat. Do you know how many rats Barrel-Fist and his clan killed to satiate Okuma's hunger? Chalk it up to a misinterpreted vision, I suppose.

"One by one, the minks killed the rats and fed them to Okuma, hoping to catch the Trelock before he or she could awaken to their powers. Then, when the rats were almost no more, he realized that it was actually a mouse he was after. That was when Crom and I were brought on-board. Crom would put the guards to sleep, and I'd inform the minks of strong mice and let them into the city gates. They'd only taken a few. It didn't seem like much of a loss at all, really. But Roderick—stupid, know-it-all, good-for-nothing Roderick—just had to get involved. He just *had* to beg the Council to investigate the disappearances. And then he started asking . . . questions." Arthur shook his head. "So, I told the minks where he'd be, and when he'd be there. And just like that, they had a new target."

"You're the reason Roderick is dead," Denya hissed through gritted teeth. "You're the reason that first assassin was after us the night we discovered Del."

"Sure, my intentions were questionable at best, but just think. That series of backstabbing actions helped us find a Trelock. I thought I was going to be rewarded handsomely for that. But it wasn't enough. I had to deliver him myself. Because of your help, I will no longer be just some Scrapper, relegated to map duty. I'll be one of the Blight's most trusted allies. I'll be at his right paw when the mice of Verden bow before him. When they bow before *me.*"

"I've heard enough of this nonsense," growled Kando. "Quick, grab him and let's go find the Rook."

"It'd be easier to kill him," Denya argued coldly. "It'd be quieter, too."

"He must stand trial," said Kando. "That is the law, Denya. It's what makes us better than them. I recall you claiming that we aren't murderers."

Denya's cheeks flushed, then she nodded in agreement. As much as she wanted Arthur to pay for his crimes then and there, Kando was right.

"I'm not going anywhere with you," sneered Arthur. He aimed his paw at the branch beneath him. *"Crescere Firenze!"* A huge wave of blue energy exploded towards it. There was a sharp crunch as the wood splintered and the branch broke.

Kando and Denya briefly stared at each other and then at the spot where the branch began to split. They were on the falling side of the split, leaving Arthur was on the other side.

"Run!" yelled Denya. She and Kando turned and raced down the branch towards its leafy ends, all while the branch continued to fall, angling until they were almost running straight down towards the earth below. "Jump!" she yelled. Kando and Denya bounded off the branch, and for a moment the two of them sailed through the air, the ground rushing up to meet them.

Just as they were about to crash to the ground below, two gigabees appeared beneath them and cushioned their falls. Denya and Kando each landed on a bee, grabbing hold for dear life. The branch landed with a thunderous crunch as it hit the ground, sending leaves and dust flying into the air around them.

With a buzzing flurry of wings, the bees sped forward. Kando gripped his gigabee tightly as he turned to Denya, who demonstrated the expert handling of her own.

"We need to find Del!" he yelled over the buzzing wings. "He's got a clan of minks *and* this Okuma after him. We might already be too late!"

"We'll find him," she stated firmly. "I brought an army of my own." Kando turned to see a huge swarm of gigabees trailing behind them, darkening the sky with their numbers.

Leading the gigabees, Denya and Kando angled their mounts downward to fly low to the ground. As they flew, they kept their eyes peeled for any sign of minks. For any sign of the Blight, whatever *that* looked like. For any sign of the young mouse who might just be the world's only hope.

*   *   *

The bear took a step forward, its rotting front paws digging into the floorboards. Del was frozen in place. Terror surged through his veins, causing him to shake uncontrollably.

"I always knew that the elements would send someone to stop me. I even had a vision. I saw a tiny, insignificant creature attempting to destroy everything I had built. I was sure it was a rat. So sure. But . . . a mouse?" The bear laughed to itself, causing more black tar to spill from its sharp teeth. "Have you heard of me?" it asked curiously. "Do you know the legend of Okuma?"

Del remained silent, unable to process the question, let alone respond.

"ANSWER ME!!!" shouted Okuma. His roar shook the whole house, which was in danger of toppling in on itself without the added help.

Del gulped. "I have h-heard of the B-blight, but I d-don't know any Okuma."

"No?!" Okuma did not seem pleased by this. "That is unfortunate. But no matter. Soon, the whole world will know of me. Soon, the whole world will *bow* to me. What's one little mouse when compared to the whole world?" He took another giant step forward and then swung his front paw almost lazily, slamming it down atop Del. The massive yellow claws of his paw rested mere centimeters from either side of Del's face. Black tar dripped thickly from his teeth as he stared down at Del. "I am going to eat you, little mouse. The power inside you will make me unstoppable. My only regret is that you aren't even big enough to count as a proper meal."

Okuma opened his mouth, but Del, even in his mortified state, was not ready to go down without a fight. He quickly pulled the crossbow up. As the great maw of the beast came down on him, he freed his arms just enough to load a bolt and fire it down the monster's throat.

"GRAAAAWWWWGHGH!!!" howled the bear, arching back his head in pain. Del smiled at the small victory, but the moment was short-lived. With a flick of his wrist, Okuma hurled Del's small body through the air. Del flew under the archway, through the kitchen and crashed through the boarded-up kitchen window. He careened over the backyard and finally slammed midway up the trunk of a large, dead tree. He slid down the tree, landing at its base. Every muscle in his body cried out in pain. His head throbbed, and he was fairly certain his tail was broken.

Beneath him, the earth was black, eaten away by some sort of disease. He looked around to find that he was now in the backyard of the house. Much like the front, everything was dead and rotting.

The backdoor of the house exploded off its hinges as Okuma stepped into the yard. In the evening light, the bear was even more imposing. Almost as tall as the doorway while still on all fours, he was gargantuan by bear standards. Green wisps of smoke trailed off his body. The massive creature looked like a half-eaten, rotting corpse that somehow managed to stand up and keep going. In some of the melted away patches of skin, Del even thought he saw worms and maggots writhing around inside.

"I don't blame you for wanting to live," said Okuma in a low growl. "When I was a cub many, many years ago, I wanted to live too. I had a family. Oh, yes. I had hopes and dreams. But then, one of the human creations exploded near us and killed everything and everyone I ever knew." Okuma approached the tree slowly, his footfalls causing the very ground to shake.

"My mother had told me that the humans' mistake was that they destroyed the world, making it impossible for them to survive. That they spoiled it and took from it until it had nothing left to give. But she was wrong. Dead wrong, you might say. Their mistake was that when the world started to die and rot, they ran from it, rather than *becoming* one with it. I waited in the darkness for so long. Because that's what happens when we die, young Trelock. We don't cease to exist. We don't go to some floating world in the sky. We just . . . wait. And just when I thought I would wait forever, the Blight came to me. It *found* me. It offered me its gifts. It offered me *my destiny*."

Del's breathing was strained and desperate. He laid on the ground listening to the bear speak as it slowly moved across the lawn towards him, not because he wanted to, but because he wasn't sure he had the strength to move. He thought about Urabzu. He pictured the otter in his mind and called out to him once more, hoping against all odds that there was still a sliver of the thread which connected them left unbroken.

"When I awoke," continued Okuma, "I realized something important about this world. Death is not the cause of pain. No, no, not really. *Life* is the cause of pain. To live and to know those who live is to ultimately feel loss and despair. Death *ends* pain. Doesn't that sound wonderful, little Trelock? Don't you want to live in a world where there is no more pain? In consuming you, I can bring about the existence of that world."

Del stared at the great bear and the darkness that seemed to emanate around it. *What do I do when the darkness comes?* That was the question he had asked the great tree. *Rise or fall, win or lose, the choice will be yours.* He still had no answer. Once more he was faced with impossible odds, and once more he had no idea what to do.

That's not giiiiiving yourself enough creeeedit, said a voice in his head.

Urabzu? he thought, looking all around for a sign of the water spirit.

Once more you are faced with impossible odds, that much is truuuuuue, said Urabzu. Del didn't think the bear could hear the water spirit's voice, because he was still prattling on about the end of the world and rot and the bowing down of his legions of followers. *But you've always known what to do. You've always made the right choice. Perhaps you haven't always been able to control the elements or even summon them to your aid, but not all superheroes require powers. Wouldn't you agree?*

Del considered this. When faced with the first mink assassin who had been stalking Roderick, Denya and Arthur, he'd *accidentally* saved them. When faced with the shrikes, he'd only managed to save Crom, who had turned out to be a traitor anyway. And when it came to the squirrels, he'd gotten Urabzu to save the day. That didn't mean that Del was a hero. It just meant he was lucky.

But in all those cases, you did something truly incredible, Del. Don't you see?

Del did not see.

Must I spell it out? teased Urabzu's disembodied voice. *You acted. You leaped into danger where others would not. You ran to the rescue, knowing full well you weren't nearly strong enough to do it on your own. When you fell to your death from the airship, you didn't beg to be saved, you begged for me to spare your friends' lives and the lives of the squirrels who you barely knew. For once in your life, Del, can't you see yourself for what you truly are?*

Del played back through every impossible moment in the past several weeks. But this time, he saw it as if through Urabzu's ever watchful eyes. The otter had been with him from the start. Del *had* jumped headfirst into danger. Without even thinking about it. He'd run to the aid of others. He'd run out of his window to stop the assassin and save total strangers. He'd held onto Crom and used his wits to protect the old mouse from the shrike's attack. With Urabzu's help, he'd fought back the shrikes again, this time on the Black Acorn. *He'd* been the one to think of a storm to fight them off. And when Kando had fallen into the river,

Del had jumped in after him without a second thought. He'd put his life on the line so many times, just to make sure that his band and those around him would be safe.

Now you see it, Del. Now you see what others have seen for so long. Now you see what Roderick saw before passing into our realm. Throughout your journey, so many others have believed in you, relied on you and been protected by you. Now, all that's left is for youuuuuu to believe in yourself.

"Are you even listening, mouse?!" growled Okuma, impatiently.

Del glared at the great bear now with conviction in his eyes. Weeks ago, he had left his home as a mouse whose value wasn't even worth a single chez, and certainly not worth Roderick or Kando giving their lives for him. But now, he finally understood that he didn't have to do some amazing thing to be worthy of Roderick's sacrifice or Kando's protection. He had been worth it all along.

"I had thought we might have some light conversation before dinner, but I seem to have bored you," said Okuma, creeping nearer. "Perhaps it is, at last, time for the main course. Any last words, Trelock?"

Del coughed, standing up straight, even though his body begged for him to just lie down and give up. "My name . . . is Del Hatherhorne," he said. His voice was raspy and weak. "And I . . . am . . . a hero!"

Okuma's head turned sideways in confusion. This was apparently not what he had expected to hear. Truth be told, even Del was surprised by it.

"The world you speak of might be pain-free, but that is because there would be nothing left worth losing. Nothing left worth fighting for." Del's voice softened. "Nothing left worth living for." Del glared into the bear's eyes, no longer afraid. "I am a hero. Just like Superman. Just like Harry Potter. Just like Luke Skywalker . . . before he got old and milked weird aliens on an island." He caught himself rambling, which was good because he knew a lot of heroes and the list could go on for quite a while. "I will protect this world until my dying breath. Not for myself, or even my family, but for anyone who still loves, trusts and believes in this world."

Okuma snarled angrily, his teeth showing beneath his rotting jowls. "So be it." The bear launched into a run, charging the tree.

Del held his palms up in front of him and continued to reassure himself under his breath. "I am a hero."

The ground shook and Del watched the vicious maw and dagger-like claws coming for him.

"I am worthy."

The bear pounced, its claws outstretched, ready to eviscerate Del.

"I believe in myself!" An orb of water appeared in Del's paw, turned into a long spike of ice, and shot at Okuma. The spike impaled Okuma's nose, causing him to stop in his tracks and cry out in pain.

"GRAAAWWWW!" Okuma, scraped at his nose with his paw. Smoke billowed off of Okuma's nose as the water melted. The water was *burning* him.

"Ha!" Del let out a laugh of surprise. Urabzu had come to him at last. No. That wasn't right at all. Because he suddenly realized that Urabzu had nothing to do with it. Del had summoned the water all on his own. *He* had turned it to ice. All on his own.

"You hateful little mouse!" cried Okuma, lunging for Del once more with his paws outstretched.

This time, Del summoned two orbs of water. He turned them to ice, then shot them to either side of the bear. He spun them in midair as he controlled them with his mind, aimed them, and then let them fly, so that they stabbed into Okuma's rotting ears.

"GRAAWWWWWW!!!" the bear yowled even louder. He grabbed at his ears with his paws as more smoke rose up from his melting skin.

Within himself, Del felt something click. With no way to possibly explain the new sensation, he could have sworn that it felt as though a key had just unlocked a door within his mind.

"That's it, Del," came Urabzu's voice. *"You are one with the water now. This gift is yours to use freely. Now show this bear what you're made of!"*

Del smiled. He knew that this was a horrible situation, and that this bear was absolutely stronger than he was. He knew that he would probably be eaten, and it was probably inappropriate for him to be smiling right now, but he couldn't help it. All his life, he had read about humans who could wield amazing superpowers, knowing full well that he could never actually be one. And now, he could literally shoot water out of his paws. And no matter how bad his odds were, he had to admit that it was pretty cool.

Okuma charged once more. "Die already!" the bear shouted.

Del ran to the left, shooting several more ice spikes at the bear's front legs. Okuma overestimated his own heft and momentum and slammed into the tree. The ground shook, knocking Del off balance. But before he toppled to the ground, he shot out a path of bubbling water in front of himself and rode it like a surfer riding the top of a wave. All the while, he continued to shoot ice spikes at Okuma, who spun in a furious circle, slashing and grabbing for Del, only narrowly missing the mouse as he continued to rise higher into the air.

Del was surprised at how easily the movements came to him. Then again, he'd spent his whole life studying superheroes, unknowingly preparing for this very moment.

"That's it, Del!" sang Urabzu. *"Feel the water within you! Feel the rush of the river and the waves of the ocean."*

Del rounded on Okuma's backside, spraying jets of water so that the bear's skin fumed and melted away into a puddle of tar on the ground. All the while, the bear shrieked in pain. Suddenly, Urabzu was beside him, swimming through the sky next to him playfully. He spun and twirled next to Del, egging him on.

"Be the ripple of the pond and the trickle of the stream."

"I HATE YOU!" shouted Okuma. "I HATE YOU, LITTLE MOUSE!!!"

But Del could not hear the bear as he danced on the jet of water which propelled him through the air. He continued to bombard Okuma with streams of water and ice spikes from above, blasting them into the bear's side. Above them, dark clouds were swirling, converging on the backyard of the house.

"Be the snow on the tallest peak of the mountain. Be the rains which give life to the driest desert."

Del came back to the ground, landing just in front of the tree, directly in front of Okuma. Urabzu disappeared in a puff of mist. The bear took a gasping breath as his skin continued to melt into tar at his feet. But still he lumbered forward, shaking the earth with his weight.

"You are the flurries of winter and the showers of summer," echoed Urabzu's disembodied voice.

As Okuma limped towards him with hatred raging in his red eyes, Del reached up to the dark clouds gathering above him in the sky.

"You are the frost of autumn..." Del clenched his paws and, with a downward motion, brought rain pouring down on Okuma as though the ocean itself had opened up above them. *"...and the storms of spring!"*

"NOOOOOOO!" cried Okuma. "Make it stop! MAKE IT STOP!!!" The water would not stop though. The ground shook under the weight of the rain, and with a massive groan, the earth opened up in a sinkhole which spanned the better part of the lawn. Del stepped back as the ground broke apart. Pieces of dead grass and dirt tumbled away into the dark pit. Okuma dug his claws into the earth at the edge of the abyss to no avail.

As the rain finally subsided, Del could see that the bear, what was left of him, was melting into black nothingness. The bottom half of his body was already gone, having fallen into the depths of the gaping hole. Only his top half still hung from the side.

"I will find you, little Trelock," Okuma wheezed. "I will find you, and I will end you. And then I will kill everything you've ever known! I WILL DESTROY THIS WORLD! I WILL—" But Okuma did not get to finish, for at that moment, his face and front paws melted and slid into the sinkhole, disappearing from sight.

Del dropped to his knees, suddenly feeling extremely exhausted.

"I . . . did it," he said, his breathing labored.

"That you did," said Urabzu, who now appeared before him. "And I am very proud of you."

Del smiled, tears rolling down his face. "You know what?" he asked the blue otter. "I'm proud of me too."

Urabzu placed a paw on Del's shoulder, letting him cry. When Del was done, he took a deep breath and tried to stand, but found it very difficult.

"Careful now," said Urabzu. "These powers are still new to you. Using them like that may take a great toll on your body. You will need rest before doing it again. But one day, even a show of force like this one will become easier to you. All in due time." Urabzu patted Del on the head, then vanished, as if swept away by the wind.

Del focused on breathing. He had survived. Somehow, against all odds, he was alive. He had won. He was going to be okay.

Ting. Ting. Ting. The sound of the minigun was unmistakable. Del whirled around to see Barrel-Fist standing mere paws away from him with his gun pointed directly at Del's face.

"You've got some nerve," said Barrel-Fist. "You traipsed all the way here with your little friends, and for what? So you could undo everything we've worked so hard for? So you could destroy everything we've built?" The mink shook his head, overcome with emotions. "You think we chose this life? This life chose us. The Blight chose *us*. And I am not about to watch my clan's efforts go to waste because of some little, flea-ridden *rodent*. He'll be back, you know? The Blight will rise again, and I vow that when he does, nothing will stand in his way." The gun revved up. "So long, Trelock."

What happened next, Del would not actually remember. With no strength left, his body took over much like it had done the night that Roderick had died. The pupils of his eyes turned white, rather than black this time, and he held out his paws as the minigun unloaded a spray of bullets. In less than a second, Del summoned a gust of wind, so powerful that it pushed against the oncoming bullets, stopping them in their tracks. They hovered in the air briefly before dropping down to the dead earth.

But the wind didn't stop. It grew stronger, and although Barrel-Fist fought to hold his ground, a simple slip of his footing was all it took for the wind to carry him away as if he were as light as a leaf.

Del did not see where the mink landed. Nor did he see the swarm of gigabees led by Denya and Kando, which chased off the rest of the mink army, harassing them until they retreated far into the hills of Aurora. He did not see any of this, because as the wind finally subsided, he fell to his knees and collapsed.

CHAPTER NINETEEN

The Call of the Longtails

"So that's it then?"

Denya half-turned to look at her mother. Raisha stood behind her in the doorway to Denya's childhood room with a sad look in her eyes.

"You're going to run off to save the world again?" she asked, her voice shaking with worry or grief or anger, or possibly a mixture of all three.

"The world is much more dangerous today than it was last week," said Denya. "I can't just sit by and watch while monsters destroy it, Mom." She shook her head, overwhelmed by everything that had happened since her band had left Verden.

"You don't owe the world anything," Raisha protested.

"Maybe not," admitted Denya. "But Aurora's not all that far from here. The minks could attack at any moment.

And now that we know about them, they don't have any more reasons to be cautious. Things are going to get worse before they get better. Maybe I don't owe the world anything. But I do owe you and Papa. We may not see eye to eye, but you raised me, and your blood runs through my veins. If something were to happen to the two of you, and I didn't at least try to stop it . . . I'd never forgive myself."

Denya shuddered, pushing back the tears that wanted to escape her eyes. But then she changed her mind and let them fall down her cheeks. She was the kind of mouse who cried. She needed to accept that about herself. She was the kind of mouse who enjoyed almonds with grapes and time spent with her family. But she was also the kind of mouse who stood up for what she believed to be right. And the beautiful thing, she realized as she wept before her mother, was that she didn't have to be just one thing.

"I never wanted to be a disappointment to you," said Denya. "But if it's a choice between saving you or upsetting you, I will always, *always,* choose saving you. That's just who I am. You and Papa taught me to be the best mouse I could be. Every day. No matter what. This is my way of doing that."

Raisha stepped towards her. Denya stood her ground. Raisha put her paws on her daughter's shoulders and gave her the smallest of smiles. "Oh, Denya, I fear I've been quite a fool all these long years."

"Don't say that."

"But it's true. Because only a fool would be disappointed in a daughter as brave as you."

Denya looked her mother in the eyes and smiled warmly. Raisha pulled her into a hug, and it was the warmest, tightest hug that Denya had ever received.

Her father suddenly appeared in the doorway behind her mother. She fully expected him to fall back on his old habits: to chastise her and tell her that she was failing the family all over again. But to her great surprise, he joined in the hug, wrapping his long arms around her and her mother. They stayed like that for a long time.

When the hug ended, they all agreed there was only one option left before them: Denya would rejoin the Longtails, but only *after* she helped round up all the gigabees and put them back to work. The gigabees had been far too excitable since their trip to Aurora. After all, it wasn't every day they got to go on a grand adventure.

* * *

Del's eyes flitted open. The first thing he saw was Kando's bristly face. The gruff mouse sat on a little wooden stool beside the bed where Del lay. He was far worse for wear than Del remembered. His right arm and shoulder were bandaged up, tied into a sling made of cream-colored cloth. One of his ears, too, was bandaged, making his head look lopsided.

Though his muscles ached, and his head pounded, Del was quite comfortable beneath a pile of white woolen blankets. He tried to sit up, but Kando shook his head and told him to lay back down. Del peered around the room, quickly realizing that he was in the Canticle Hall back in Toleloo, this time as a patient. "What happened?" he asked weakly.

"I was hoping you could share that with me," said Kando. "What do you remember?"

Del told him everything he could recall, everything he honestly could remember with no mention of Barrel-Fist. He told him about the bear called Okuma. He told him about the blackness and the decay and how Okuma wanted to destroy the world so that everything would die, and there would no longer be pain.

Then he told Kando how he'd finally believed in himself enough to summon water. To demonstrate, and also to prove to himself that it had not all been a dream, he held up a paw. Just as the thought crossed his mind, a sphere of shimmering water appeared within it. With another thought, the water vanished.

Kando was a captive audience and listened to every word without interruption, asking only a few simple questions here and there. When the story was done, he scratched his chin thoughtfully and took a deep breath.

"You . . . did well, Rook—er—Del. You did well, Del."
Kando patted Del on the shoulder. "I think at the very least
you've earned the right to be called by your name."

Del averted his eyes, embarrassed by the apology he felt
he owed his Alpha. "I'm sorry . . . about all those times I
messed up. And for talking back so much."

"Don't apologize," said Kando. "Learn from your
mistakes. And never stop asking questions. Just, maybe ask
them with less yelling."

Del laughed, but then became quiet. "What happened
to Arthur?"

"Got away," said Kando. "By the time we found you, he
was gone. Delilah too. I suspect it won't be the last we've
heard of that yappy mouse." They eyed each other then and
suddenly, unexpectedly, broke out laughing. Del stopped
himself quickly though because the laughing made his lungs
hurt.

"So, what now?" asked Del.

"Once you are well enough, we will journey back to
Verden and tell the Council all we have seen. After that, it's
up to them what steps we take next." Kando leaned over,
placing his elbows on his knees. "You've come an awfully
long way since your first day with the band. And if you plan
to continue training as a Trelock, you'll have a long journey
ahead of you. If you don't think you're up to the task, our
return to Verden might be your last chance to get out of this
mess."

It was like some sort of test. Had Del been asked earlier, he probably would have failed, but he'd taken on an undead bear and somehow, he'd survived. He had questions. He wanted to know why Arthur would betray the mice. He wanted to know why Barrel-Fist was so hell-bent on serving Okuma. And he couldn't possibly allow the bear to return and enact his plan for world domination. What sort of superhero would allow such a thing? For the first time in Del's short life, he knew exactly what he wanted to do with himself.

"Whatever comes next," he said with a smile. "I'll face it as one of the Longtails."

*   *   *

Several days later, Del was finally feeling well enough to walk. He had a concussion, a broken tail, and several sprained muscles. His final battle with the bear and Barrel-Fist had also sapped much of his energy, not to mention the bruises that had resulted from being thrown through a boarded-up window and into a tree. Now, he was finally starting to breathe easily once more. With bandages over his wounds, and a white cloth wrapped around the break in his tail as well as his head, he packed his things and left the Canticle Hall room. He stopped to say thanks and farewell to Tilly, who had expertly helped nurse him back to health. Del thought that she was also looking more confident than the last time they'd met.

Del boarded a lift and descended the many floors of Toleloo. Walking through the always-crowded ground floor, Del listened to the sound of the merchants as they called out deals and specials. Mice bickered back and forth, haggling and bartering with one another. It was like nothing had changed, and yet, Del knew that everything had changed. The world was going down a new path, one fraught with peril. Still, he took strange comfort in the mundane clinking of chez on counter tops and the smell of warm bread, lavish fruit and sweet honey which hung over everything in the tower.

As he approached his waiting band, Kando nodded approvingly at him and, to his surprise, Denya wrapped her arms around him in a welcoming hug.

As she pulled away, she removed a small rolled up scroll from her bag and handed it to him.

"What's this?" he asked.

"Roderick wanted you to have it," she said. "When you were ready." Her mouth twisted into a grin. "So . . . now."

Del took the scroll and unrolled it. His eyes darted eagerly across the curling cursive writing:

Del,

If you are reading this, then my journey has come to an end. But never fear. To a member of the Longtails, journey's end is but a chance to rest our tired bodies and fill our stomachs. By now you may know why I believed so fully in you from the start. A Trelock is a rare and powerful thing. You hold the key to protecting the entire world in your paws.

What you may not know is that your coming and my death were foretold to me by a blue jay named Kektuk. He prophesized that the dawning of a dark age would be precipitated by the revelation of a new Trelock, and while I would be fortunate to meet him, I would not get to see him grow into his full potential.

I am sure the task before you seems daunting, so I leave this message with you in the hopes that it will make your days less uncertain. Everything you need, every skill you require, is already inside you. You will train hard to awaken these powers but know that you are all you will ever need.

Make allies on your journey. Find friends. Companionship and connection is important but trust yourself above all else. Your instincts will keep you alive. If you happen to journey to the great tree, Nesavary, find Kektuk. He can tell you more, and he has always been a friend to the mice.

Finally, remember that those things that make you different and make you feel as though you are weaker than your comrades, are precisely the reason they need you. You are exactly who you were meant to be. Your so-called differences are actually your greatest strengths. Never forget that.

I leave you now with the Longtails Oath. I'm sure those old codgers at the Longtails Training Grounds drilled it into you by now, but it bears repeating. Remember it when the odds seem stacked against you, and it will raise your spirits just as it always did mine.

When adventure calls, and danger is near,
The Longtails rise, so have no fear.
Swords and shields and magics abound,
Ready to do any task to be found.
Ears up, dear mice! For night will fall,
yet still you'll hear their mighty call.
For Longtails keep the darkness at bay,
and morning will rise again this day.
So when you hear the Longtails call,
be bold and true and brave.
Answer the call. Whiskers and all.
The longest tails forever wave.

Sincerely Yours,
Sir Roderick Kegglefite
Longtails First Brigade

Del wiped a tear from his eye and read the letter once more. He then rolled up the parchment and placed it in his bag, nodding to Denya. "Thank you."

She nodded back to him. Without any more words, the three of them turned and headed towards the tower's entrance, ready for the long journey home.

"Wait!" called a voice behind them. They all turned to see a young mouse running through the crowd. Kando recognized her instantly by the way her coloring was split down the middle of her face: one side black, the other white. Though she was now dressed differently. She wore a black tunic underneath a violet cloak, and a midnight blue bandana was wrapped around her head, tied behind her ears.

"Narissa?" Kando asked. He hadn't been back to the little pub since they'd returned to the tower, and he had never expected to see the barmaid again. But here she was with a satchel over her shoulder and two cheaply-made daggers hanging from her belt. "What are you doing here?"

"I'm here to take you up on your offer," she said. Though she acted boldly, a slight quiver in her voice betrayed her.

"My offer?" asked Kando. The past week had not been kind to his memory.

"Unless . . ." she hesitated. "You don't have room for one more?"

Kando did something then that took both Del and Denya by surprise. He smiled a big toothy grin. "Narissa . . . er . . ."

"Havenwell," she said, making up a last name on the spot. There would be a time to tell Kando who she really was, but that moment was not now. Not yet.

"Narissa Havenwell," continued Kando. "Meet Denya Woodhollow and Del Hatherhorne, my two scrappers." Del looked up, excitement in his chest. Had he just been promoted? "Del. Denya. Meet the Longtails' newest Rook, Narissa Havenwell."

They all shook paws. Del let his paw linger in Narissa's for a moment too long. The strangest thing happened when he held her paw in his. His whole body felt warm, and he suddenly felt as though his tail might catch on fire. He also noticed that Narissa was quite possibly the most beautiful mouse he had ever laid eyes on. He hoped that these two feelings were not related, but he also had the creeping suspicion that they were.

The four of them left the city and journeyed out into a world lit by a golden morning sun, bound for Verden and whatever came next. Del checked to make sure his crossbow was affixed to his back and his scarf was still wrapped tightly around his neck. He wasn't about to start the next leg of the journey with forgetting something in the tower.

"Glad to see you're alive," whispered Urabzu into his ear.

"I'm better than alive," responded Del quietly, so that only Urabzu could hear. He did all of this while taking fleeting glances at Narissa. Once, he even thought she looked back at him.

The weather was already starting to turn hot and humid. Spring was coming to an end, and summer was just around the corner, along with its sweltering heat and brush fires. Del took a deep breath, taking in the fresh air, flowers and life around him. This was what he was fighting for. This was why he had survived. This was his very own destiny. He was nervous as to what the next part of the journey would hold, but he knew that together they could accomplish anything.

He hummed the last words of the oath to himself—it just happened to fit perfectly to the tune of Superman's theme song—as they passed the electrified gate and journeyed down the path towards home.

Answer the call. Whiskers and all. The longest tails forever wave.

*   *   *

Far away, in the heart of Aurora, the mound of lifeless corpses lay still. The soft buzzing of flies was the only sound in the night as they hummed sluggishly around the heap, drawn by the putrid smell of decaying flesh. A few flies would occasionally land on the pile, taste the flesh, and then take off once more.

Without warning, one particular fly sped off into the night. Flies were not prone to fear. They had natural instincts which told them of danger, hunger or thirst, but rarely fear. Yet this one felt a sudden jolt of sheer terror. Before long, more flies followed. And then all the flies were buzzing away, leaving the pile of meat behind as though it suddenly were very unappetizing. With the flies gone, there was only silence. In the night sky above, rays of purple, green and blue light undulated around each other in a peaceful dance.

And then, as if commanded by some unseen force, the corpses—many dead for months, seasons or, in some cases, even longer—did something very peculiar and unexpected. Their eyes all opened at once, revealing glowing green irises.

That was the night that the dead awoke.

End Longtails Book One

ACKNOWLEDGEMENTS

A lot can change in a very short amount of time. If *The Storms of Spring* has taught me anything, it's that what you expect and what actually happens are very often completely different. When I released my last novel, *A Home for Wizards*, over two years ago, in one of the worst snow storms to ever hit New York City, I had no idea I was about to embark on one of the most challenging years of my life, followed by one of the most incredible. Not two days after the release of that book, I signed a contract to write *Apollo's Landing*, an idea which I knew was a sure winner. In fact, I even said that it would be one of the easiest things I'd ever written. Oh, how wrong I was.

After five drafts, each of varying levels of awfulness, I finally gave up on the idea. In the meantime, my husband, Carl, and our dog, Izzy, were relocating from NYC to sunny Orlando. We picked up our lives and headed south. It was one of the best decisions of my life. The year between *A Home for Wizards* and our eventual move was incredibly tough for many different reasons. And at more than one point, I questioned whether or not my writing career had hit a dead end. After ditching *Apollo's Landing*, and trying (and failing) to write a handful of other ideas, I was beginning to get desperate. So, one day, I sat down to write something just for fun. I wanted to live out an adventure and escape the stress and challenges of my day to day life. It was at this point that I began work on *Longtails*.

Writing a novel is a lonely process, for the most part. We, as writers, sit and stew over plot lines and dialogue and witty sentence structure. But I would be lying if I said that this book only happened because I willed it into existence. There are some incredible people who made this book a reality, and they deserve all the praise and thanks in the world.

First up is the fantastic Amy Chang. This is Amy's third time editing a book for me. Her notes and opinions have become invaluable. I often don't feel like a book I am working on reaches the best it can be until she's given it her time and attention. Amy has always been timely, positive and a joy to work with. But beyond that, Amy is the kind of friend who comes to your aid, even when you are bad at asking for it. And for that, I thank her with all my heart.

I need to thank Dexter Allagahrei. Dexter joined my team on *A Home for Wizards*, beautifully rendering a cover at very late notice. With *Longtails*, he has stepped up the game, creating sketches of the characters, images for short stories on my blog and even the front and back covers of this very book. Dexter, who I am proud to say is my real-life cousin, has been nothing but supportive and excited in regard to creating this new series and his sketches of the mice and other members of the cast allowed me to fully realize them as actual living, breathing characters. Thank you for everything you do, whether it be creating art, or just sending me photos of mice eating mini pancakes.

While my mother is not directly connected to the creative process, she inspires me every single day. Those that follow me on social media and on my blog will know that my mom went through some tough health issues this past year, which encouraged us both to get healthy and take care of ourselves. More than 100 lbs. lighter, Mom is shining brighter than she ever has before. Mom, you are an inspiration to me, and your ability to celebrate life, taking the good with the bad, has helped me be a healthier, happier person this year, and Longtails would not have happened if not for that positivity in my life. So, thank you!

I want to give a shout out to my Grandma. We don't talk as often as we should. I know that. But Grandma is always one of the most supportive people in my life. Right before my wedding to my, now, husband, I came out to my Grandma. I expected this to go horribly, but to my great surprise, Grandma has been one of the most supportive people in the entire family. She always checks in to make sure Carl is doing well, and she always reads the ridiculous things I write, remarking "You've got quite the imagination." Thanks for always being a pillar of love and support in my life, Grandma.

Of course, none of this is possible without my husband, Carl. Carl is the ever-radiant light in my life no matter how dark and brooding I feel. Carl sees the best in everyone, even if I sometimes see the worst. But more importantly, he sees the best in me. It is a rare person who can believe in you fully, yet still challenge you constantly. Carl raises me up and pushes me even higher than I thought possible. Since the release of my last novel, Carl and I got married, and it was, and always will be, one of the best days of my entire life. Carl was an editor on this book, but more importantly, he is an on-going editor on my life, always working with me to ensure that every day is better than the last, correcting any typos that life might throw at us.

Last, but certainly not least, I want to thank you! Yes, you! Whether you're someone I know personally, or not, books are written in the hopes of being read. So, the fact that you've read this one deserves my undying gratitude. Writing *The Storms of Spring* has been an amazing experience, but knowing that you read it, really is a dream come true. Thank you for your support, and your time. I literally could not do this without you.

ABOUT THE AUTHOR

Jaysen Headley was born and raised in Lakewood, Colorado. Eventually, he packed up and headed to New York City where he met his husband, and editor of the Longtails Saga, Carl Li. They now live in Orlando, Florida, with their dog Izzy, where they go to theme parks, eat delicious treats and have tons of fun every day.

Jaysen loves to read books, play board games and blast away at monsters in a good video game. He is also an avid healthy eater unless it comes to cookies. He will forego any diet in the name of a good cookie!

Jaysen is also the author of *A Love Story for Witches* and *A Home for Wizards*, both of which can be found in store and on Amazon and Kindle.

COMING
SUMMER 2019

Longtails

Book Two

The Wildfires
Of Summer

Learn more about the Longtails and their
upcoming adventures at:
LongtailsSaga.com

Printed in Great Britain
by Amazon